Seeking the Brown Mountain Lights

Brown Mountain Lights Book 2

CC Tillery

Spring Creek Press

First Edition

ISBN 10 0-9894641-6-4
ISBN-13 **978-0-9894641-6-1**

Published by **Spring Creek Press**

Cover Design 2017 by Kimberly Maxwell

Dedication

With love to our mother Margie Clark, who instilled in us a love of reading at an early age by taking us to the library every two weeks, even when she had to walk there with five energetic kids tagging along. We are so blessed to have her in our lives.

Chapter One

Fall 1859

You Can't Always Get What You Want

My fingertips barely grazed the light when something slammed into me from the side, knocking me to the ground. I heard a man scream then a heavy weight landed on top of me. I lay there stunned, my body tingling from the slight shock I received when my fingers skimmed that light. Muffled voices were all around me, a blur of hands moving in and out of view as they pulled at that awful weight while I struggled for breath. The world turned to a misty haze and I blinked hard, trying to get my eyes to focus. When the weight shifted slightly, I gasped, only then recognizing Abbie's and Josh's frantic tones. And when it hit me that I was still here on Brown Mountain, in this brutal, primitive world, I began to shriek.

Finally that weight was gone and I was lifted to my feet. My vision came into focus, I was able to draw full breaths as Josh and Abbie anxiously looked me over for injuries, talking in what I perceived as gibberish. I ignored them, my gaze darting around, searching for that light, but it had vanished. And with it all hope.

I turned to Abbie and clutched her arms. "Where'd it go, Abbie? It was just here. I almost had it!" Frustration had the last coming out in a scream.

"It's gone, Lizzie," she said, in a sad voice.

I could feel something hard against my foot and glanced down to see Constable Jackson, unconscious on the ground. "You hateful bastard," I screeched, and began to kick his inert body. "Why did you stop me? Why didn't you let me go?"

Josh and Abbie pulled at me but I fought them off. I wanted to kill him, claw his eyes out, hurt him for keeping me in a time and place where I did not belong. I fell to my knees beside him and began to pummel at his body until Josh and Abbie managed to pull me away. I curled into a fetal position, crying into my hands, ignoring their concerned looks and comforting words. After a bit, they seemed to understand there was nothing they could do for me so both stepped away until I cried myself out.

I finally sat up, wiping my eyes and nose with my apron. I looked over at Jackson and said, my voice raw, "I should have killed him."

Kneeling down beside me, Josh touched my arm. "No, no, Lizzie, you don't mean that."

"Oh, but I do, Josh. He's a mean, contemptible man and he had no right to keep me here."

Josh turned to Abbie, whispering in a concerned voice loud enough that I could hear. "She's talking nonsense. Do you think that light might have hurt her mind in some way?"

Abbie ignored him, leaning down and looking into my eyes. I caught the warning in them and tried to glance away but her stare was too intense. She held my gaze until I nodded.

I struggled to get to my feet, then to stand on legs that felt unsteady and weak. "I'm not feeling well. I think I need to lie down." I started walking away, back down the mountain.

Abbie caught up with me and gripped my elbow, urging me to turn around. "Lizzie, home's this way."

"No, it's not. My home can't be found around here."

"At least wait a minute, Lizzie. First, we got to decide what to do about Constable Jackson."

"Shoot him and bury him in a shallow grave. Better yet, leave his body to the animals, if they'll have the worthless bastard." I yanked my arm out of her grasp and continued walking, ignoring Josh imploring me to wait.

I made my way back to the barn where we had hidden Zebediah, the runaway slave, before trying to help him escape. After I climbed the ladder to the loft, I searched the corners, hoping to find the flask of whiskey, but Zebediah had taken everything with him. I slid down the wall in one corner, folding my arms around my abdomen, drawing my knees up and resting my forehead on them, giving into my grief.

I had calmed down by the time I heard the door below squeak open followed by Abbie's and Josh's whispers. The light tread of footsteps on the ladder told me Abbie was coming. I blinked my swollen eyes, trying to clear them, and waited. She hesitated at the top, searching the dark platform.

"I'm over here," I said.

"Is it all right if I join you, Lizzie?" she asked in a low voice.

"Only you."

Her head disappeared and once more I listened to muffled voices below. Finally, the door opened and shut and light footsteps returned to the ladder. Abbie stepped into the loft and made her way over to me. She sat close but didn't touch me. There was enough moonlight shining through the large window in the barn loft that I could see her distress at my state of mind. I closed my eyes against that look. I didn't want her pity, it only made things worse.

"I'm awful sorry about the constable, Lizzie. If I'd a-seen what he was gonna do, I'd a-stopped him some way."

"I doubt you could have, Abbie. You're a tiny thing and he's big and stout and a brute at that."

"We'll find the light again, Lizzie. We just gotta keep searchin."

I sighed in despair. "It was my only way back, and I was right there, a fraction of a second away from touching it. If he

3

hadn't interfered, I'd be back in 1969, where I belong, not stuck here in this horrible place."

Abbie didn't respond, only reached out and squeezed my hand.

We sat in silence for a long time until she said, in a small voice, "Was it your husband Ben you were tryin to get back to, Lizzie? Did you choose him?"

I shook my head. "No. And he's not my husband. I just told Sarie that to appease her." I reached over and took her hand. "I knew I couldn't decide to go back just on which man I preferred to be with. It had to be more than that." I pulled my hand out of her grasp and glanced away from her, twisting my fingers in my apron. "If things here were easier, I'd have stayed." I returned my gaze to her. "I love you like a sister and I have feelings for Josh, but I hate it here. It's either hot and miserable or cold and dreary, and there's no electricity, no indoor plumbing, nothing attractive about this place at all, nothing comfortable about this time. Most men are hateful things who don't have much respect for women. And it seems all we do is work at something or other from sunup to sundown with no rest or time for just relaxing and having fun."

She shook her head. "I reckon it is that to you, Lizzie. But not me. I guess I'm accustomed to it, don't know no other way, so it's of no bother to me."

"I know I can help y'all, with what I've learned in med school. But if I'd returned, I could have finished, become a doctor, done even more good there, much more than I ever could here. I'm just too limited in this godawful time."

"Oh, Lizzie, I don't reckon you see the good you do here."

"It doesn't matter anyway. Looks like I'm stuck here."

"Like I said, we found that light once, we'll find it again."

I grabbed her hands in mine and leaned my face close to hers. "You said once before I'd have the chance. Can you see if I'll get another one, Abbie?"

She hesitated before saying, "I can't see it, Lizzie."

I stiffened.

"It ain't because it ain't gonna happen. It's just, well, I love you now, and like I told you, I can't see what happens to those I love."

I nodded, fighting feelings of despair, disappointment.

"So you reckon you love Mr. Josh?" she said, lightly.

"I reckon so."

I could hear the smile in her voice. "Well, I reckon he loves you too, Lizzie. He's awful taken with you and is a-feared you don't feel the same for him."

"Where'd he go?"

"I told him you needed some time alone so he's gone on up the mountain to see about Constable Jackson."

"What'd y'all do about that bastard?"

"Left him where he was. We're hopin he'll wake up and not remember what happened. If'n he does, I reckon all we'll know to tell him is he got hit by that light and it knocked him plumb out."

"Which is true."

"We just got to hope he don't remember he was chasin us while we was helpin a slave escape."

"I didn't see anyone else with him so he'll have no proof, Abbie."

"I suspect they was others looking for Zebediah 'cause we heard dogs barkin, but I don't reckon they was close enough to see us. But this is the constable we're speakin of, Lizzie. You know him, he don't need proof once he gets an idea set in his head."

"Too bad that light didn't take him."

We looked at each other and I began to laugh at the absurdity of Constable Jackson waking up in my time, confused, unaware that he had time-traveled to a place where he had no authority, no clue as to his whereabouts or even what century it was. Abbie soon joined in, until I began crying once more.

"Oh, Lizzie, I wish I could help you," she said in a sad voice. "You got to hold on to the fact that that light is still on this mountain and I don't reckon it's goin anywhere. I promise we'll get you back home if'n that's what you want."

I nodded. "Like I told you, there's a great war coming, Abbie. Hundreds of thousands of men will die, well over half a million, more in this war than in any other before or since. It's going to be bloody and brutal and thousands of the innocent will die right along with the soldiers. You don't want to be here for that. Neither do I."

She sighed. "I reckon I ain't got no choice but I'll try my best to see to it that you do." She stood up, holding out her hand. "Let's go home." She gave me a slight smile. "For now."

I tried to smile back but couldn't. Instead, I let her take my hand and help me to my feet.

I spent the next week in a self-pitying haze. Each morning, I wanted to stay curled up in bed with the quilt over my head and wallow in grief at my lost life. But I knew the sisters needed my help so eventually forced myself to get up. I ate very little and rarely spoke. Sarie soon grew irritated with me and I heard her ask Abbie more than once what was wrong. But Abbie only told her I wasn't feeling well and it was best just to let me be. Maggie gave me sympathetic glances. I suspect she thought I was mooning over Josh. If only it were that simple.

Abbie encouraged me to take the St. John's wort but I refused, holding stubbornly to my depression. I had asked her to tell Josh I didn't want to see him and was thankful he stayed away. I didn't know how to explain to him what I was feeling and wasn't in the mood to lie.

I hoped Constable Jackson would pay us a visit—I had a few words I wanted to say to him—but for some odd reason he stayed in town. I surmised the shock from the light might have done some sort of physical damage and hoped with all my might it gave him a stroke and he was nothing more than a drooling vegetable. Abbie confided in me that Josh had gone back for the constable but he wasn't where we'd left him so concluded he had gone off on his own. I hoped a bear or bobcat had come across his inert body and decided to have a midnight snack. When I asked her about Zebediah, she said after Josh searched for Constable Jackson, he went looking for the runaway slave, who hadn't gotten far due to his injured leg. I surmised the pepper she gave Zebediah to sprinkle behind him had, indeed, confused the dogs we heard and they hadn't been able to track him. She told me Josh managed to get Zebediah to the next station safely although had no idea how he fared the rest of the trip up north.

Sunday morning, I refused to go to church with the sisters. Instead, I stayed behind, sitting beside the chest where I had hidden the items I had on me when I came through the light, fingering what had become my treasures: my Seiko watch, lip gloss, pack of gum and empty cigarette pack. Would I ever be back in my time where these items were not a novelty but simply things to be purchased and used, I wondered, wiping tears away and praying hard for a way back to where I belonged. I put the cigarette package up to my nose and inhaled. This reminded me of Pokni who shared her homemade cigarettes with me since I traded her my lighter for the privilege. I hadn't seen her since that night and didn't know if she was aware of what had happened, so decided to pay her a visit. Maybe sharing a smoke with her or listening to one of her stories would help ease my depression.

I found Pokni outside her hut, waving a burning branch at a bee's nest hanging from a nearby tree. I watched as the smoke seemed to calm the darting bees until they were lethargically moving around, as if drugged. Pokni reached up, removed the nest from the tree and walked into the forest, the bees lazily following. When she returned, her hands were empty. She smiled when she noticed me.

"Where'd you take it?"

"To another tree far enough away that they do not grow alarmed when I come near." She made a face. "I do not like the sting of bees or hornets. It is painful."

"It is that."

She studied me for a moment. "Do you know why a bee's sting is so painful?"

I nodded. "Bee sting venom contains proteins that affect skin cells and the immune system which causes pain and

7

swelling. It can be lethal if someone is allergic and has an anaphylactic reaction." Her furrowed brow told me she didn't understand that word. "It's an allergic reaction to the venom. They might start itching or break out in hives, they may start to swell, have trouble breathing, might possibly faint. Some die from it."

"Yes, I have seen this when I was young. My father was unable to save a young warrior who was swarmed by hornets and could not breathe."

"In my time, we have medicine that helps with that."

"I am glad. It was a horrible way to die." She sat on a rock and gestured for me to join her. Once I had, she reached into her apron pocket, pulled out two handmade cigarettes, and handed me one. She had some trouble lighting our cigarettes with the neon-yellow lighter, flicking it several times without success.

"Try shaking it." I watched as she did so with no result. "It's probably getting low on lighter fluid."

"What is lighter fluid?"

"Butane gas. That's what's inside the lighter that feeds the flame. And I have no idea how to find it here or even refuel the lighter if I could." I sighed. "Once it runs out, Pokni, we'll have to go back to using the fire to light our cigarettes."

She stared affectionately at the slim lighter. "I will miss using it, Daughter, but will keep it still as a reminder of you." After she coaxed a flame out of the lighter and lit our cigarettes, she said, "I will tell you of Abohli, who gave the venom to the bees and snakes." She took a puff before beginning.

"Abohli is goddess of the swamps and undergrowth. She carries a pipe and floats through the swamps and is seen as a human-sized swirling tornado of light. Her children are the Na Losa Falaya, the will-of-the-wisps, which your people call lighted swamp gas." She glanced at me. "Some on the mountain claim the lights are nothing more than swamp gas but you and I know that is not so. The Na Losa Falaya also glide through the marshes, surprising and at times frightening the humans who see them. But unlike their mother Abohli, they have to remove all of their intestines and internal organs and set them aside before they are light enough to float. In the before, sharp vines, thornbushes, brambles and reeds were poisonous and would kill those who came into contact with them. This disturbed Abohli, who did not like to see her people harmed, and because it caused them to stay away from her territory. So she gave the venom of the plants to the snakes, hornets and bees so that forever after the spines and thorns of the undergrowth that scrape the flesh of humans would no longer cause death."

I found myself smiling for the first time since the light. "It's a lovely story, Pokni."

She patted my knee. "Abbie told me of the light and what the constable did to prevent you from going. I am sorry, Daughter."

I swiped at my eyes, determined not to cry again. "I desperately wanted to go back, Pokni. I don't think I'm meant for this time and place."

"Perhaps not but perhaps so."

I stared at her, waiting for an explanation.

"The decision was taken from you, but there may have been a reason. If so, you will know eventually. If not, perhaps the chance will come once more and you can return to your time."

"I don't want to stay here. I don't belong here. Besides, like I've told you, there's a great war coming over the issue of slavery, and it's a brutal, bloody one. I don't want to be here when it happens."

She shook her head. "But if you are, you will be of great help to those who fight and are injured, is that not so?"

I shrugged. "I don't want to even think about that."

"Then let us have another smoke and talk about something else. I will tell you how Abohli transformed the remains of the stone-skinned demon Nunyunuwi into the gravel that lines the bottoms of rivers."

I squeezed her hand. "Yes, tell me, Pokni, keep me from feeling sorry for myself."

She squeezed back, and as she relayed the tale, I concentrated hard on her words, telling myself at some point in the future I might look back on this time in my life in an affectionate, winsome way. But I doubted it.

When I returned to the sisters' cabin, I found Abbie pacing the porch, waiting on me. She ran to greet me, saying, "We got to go to town, Lizzie. Constable Jackson's arrested Mr. Josh."

Alarm skittered up my spine. Although I strongly suspected the reason, I still asked, "What for?"

"Ever'body was talking about it at church. The preacher asked the whole congregation to pray for the Hamptons 'cause the constable showed up at their place, claimin Josh was helpin that slave escape, and took him into town and throwed him in jail."

"We have to help him."

She nodded. "We'll take ol' Buck, he can get us there quicker than walking."

As the horse picked his way delicately down the mountain, I said, "Abbie, we need to agree on what we're going to say."

"I was waitin for you to tell me."

I thought a moment. "I'll say Josh and I are courting and that you were chaperoning us on a late-night walk. You think that will work?"

"What if the constable says we was helpin the slave escape too, Lizzie? He can throw us both in jail."

I hadn't thought of that. "Why don't you let me go into town? I'll tell the constable Josh and I had a late-night date."

She turned to look at me, her forehead furrowed. "What in tarnation's a date?"

I sighed, reminding myself I needed to watch my words, especially around the constable. "In my time, when two people are courting, a date is when they get together and do something, like go out to eat, to a movie—"

"Movie?"

"Remember I told you about the television shows? Well, this is kind of like that only on a bigger screen." I shook my head. We didn't have time to get into this now. "I'll explain it later. But for now, it's best if I go by myself. You know how he is about you and your sisters. Maybe he'll be more likely to believe me if I'm alone."

She shook her head. "In case it ain't occurred to you, he's just as suspicious of you, Lizzie." She sighed. "I reckon it's best if we both go into town to support one another's story."

When we arrived in Morganton, Abbie guided Buck to a two-story, wooden structure not far from the courthouse which reminded me more of a house than jail. After we climbed down, she tied Buck's reins to a nearby post and we stepped inside the building, relieved to get out of the chilly wind that had its grip on the town. I closed the door behind us and joined Abbie in the small foyer leading to a staircase on the right and narrow hallway on the left. We waited silently as a man came forward to greet us, nodding hello.

"Are you the jailer?" Abbie asked.

"Yes, ma'am, I reckon I am."

"Well, we come to talk to Constable Jackson," she said without preamble. "You any idea where he is?"

The man scratched his head before replying. "I reckon I ain't seen him today. He's probably up on the mountain."

"Then we'd like to see Mr. Joshua Hampton to make sure he's faring well and then the sheriff so we can talk to him about Mr. Hampton, please," she said with a haughty air.

When the man made no response, she continued, "Constable Jackson has arrested Mr. Hampton for no reason, you see, because he was with us the night Mr. Jackson claims he helped that slave escape."

The man studied her for a moment longer. "Well, you're out of luck there. Mr. Hampton's pa done talked to the sheriff and got him released. If'n you want to speak to the sheriff, he's here, at the end of the hall there," tilting his head toward the rear of the house, "seeing to some paperwork."

"All right, then, we'll go see him." Abbie stepped around the man and proceeded down the narrow hallway. I nodded at the jailer before following her.

She led me to a small room in the very back of the building, just wide enough to fit a scarred wooden desk with three wooden chairs scattered around it. A man sat in one of those chairs on the far side of the desk, studying a piece of paper. When he heard us, he pulled the paper down far enough to peer over the top edge. Apparently recognizing Abbie, he smiled as he put it on the desk. "Miss Abbie, it sure is good to see you," he said, rising and nodding at her. "How are you and your sisters?"

"We're mighty fine, Sheriff. And how's Catherine farin? Did that salve we give her help her rheumatiz any?"

His smile widened. "Why, I reckon it did. She's running around like a chicken with its head cut off most of the time, doing this or that."

"Well, that's good to hear." Abbie waved a hand in my direction. "This here's my cousin Lizzie Baker from over Knoxville way. Lizzie, this here's Sheriff Joseph Brittain."

I smiled at the sheriff, who bowed his head in acknowledgement of our introduction before saying, "I reckon you're from Abbie's ma's side of the family. I've never known a Collins that wasn't fair-haired and blue-eyed."

I didn't know what to say to that so simply smiled my agreement.

He pulled the other two chairs close together across from the desk and gestured for us a take a seat. Once we were settled, he sat in the chair he had previously occupied with an air of expectation. "I reckon you come here to the jailhouse for a reason, Miss Abbie. Is there anything I can do for you?"

Abbie leaned toward him. "We've come to talk to you about Constable Jackson arresting Josh Hampton for helping that slave escape. You see, Sheriff, that ain't possible because Mr. Josh was with us that evenin, out for a stroll with Lizzie here." She leaned toward him and lowered her voice. "They're a-courtin and I was acting as chaperone."

Sheriff Brittain nodded as he leaned back in his chair. "Josh's pa's been in here already raising a ruckus about his son being arrested. I released him pending further investigation, seeing as how Jackson didn't have any proof to back up what he claims he saw." He shook his head. "I reckon the constable got a little bit ahead of hisself. He tends to do that," he added as if relaying a secret. He studied us a long moment. "Although Jackson says you two," his eyes traveled from Abbie to me and back again, "were helping that slave too. Fact is, he was headed up the mountain after y'all but I put a stop to that right quick." He raised his eyebrows. "Seeing as you're here, I reckon I'll ask if either one of you've got anything to say about what he's alleging."

"Pshaw," Abbie said, making a face. "I ask you, Sheriff, what is wrong with that man? We complained about him to you before, the way he's always harassin us, blamin us for ever'thin that goes on up on that mountain."

"Well, now, as you well know, I don't like to get involved in petty little squabbles going on up there. I've found things usually work themselves out if you leave them alone. But this time, I stepped in and told him he couldn't arrest y'all without any kind of proof, and until he had proof, to leave you alone. He claims, though, he was chasing that slave and saw you two and Mr. Josh talking to him right before y'all split up and took off running."

Abbie shook her head. "Did he also tell you he touched one of them lights and it knocked him to the ground, unconscious? I reckon maybe he's disremembering things, 'cause we didn't see Jackson till we heard him scream and saw him thrown to the ground." She looked at me. "What do you think, Lizzie, could that light have scrambled his mind, made him remember somethin that didn't actually happen?"

I nodded. "It would seem so if that's what he's saying because we never saw anyone on the mountain that night until Mr. Jackson screamed."

The sheriff's eyes lingered on me long enough that I grew uncomfortable. "I have some medical knowledge," I said, "and, well, to my way of thinking, that could only be why he's saying that about us. We were simply walking and talking, enjoying the evening."

His gaze turned to Abbie. She stared back, an innocent expression on her face. Finally, the sheriff stirred. "Well, I reckon it makes sense to me too. Don't you worry none about this, Miss Abbie, Miss Lizzie, it'll all get straightened out."

"Do you think Josh, uh, Mr. Josh, will have to stand trial, Sheriff?" I asked. "If so, we want to testify on his behalf."

He shook his head. "Nah, I don't reckon that'll happen. Jackson don't have anyone to corroborate what he's alleging. He had two other men with him hunting that slave that night but they were too far away to hear or see anything, or so they say. Without proof, there's no case, so I reckon it'll all go away before too long." He stood. "You two best go on home now. You don't want to be on the mountain after dark this time of year."

Abbie and I left after thanking him and saying goodbye. We didn't talk until we were on Buck and heading back home.

"You think he believed us?" I asked Abbie.

She shrugged. "I didn't get the feelin that he didn't, Lizzie. The sheriff's an honest man, just and fair, and he won't just take the constable's word for it. He'll want proof, like he said. Besides, if Josh's pa's involved, things will go well for Josh. Ol' Mr. Hampton has a lot of power in this town, he'll see to it his son don't go to trial."

As we rode out of town, she pointed to a nearby hill. "That there's Damon's Hill where they hung our ancestor Frankie Silver. Some call it Demon's Hill."

I studied the nearby prominence with a flat meadow at its summit, topped by an enormous oak tree still fully leafed, glowing copper in the sun.

Abbie, following my gaze said, "That's there's the hanging tree. It's an awful purty tree to serve such a devilish deed."

I inwardly shivered, wondering how many had ended their life at that tree and what poor Frankie must have felt when they put that rope around her neck. "I agree. I can't help but feel sorry for Frankie, Abbie. How old was she when they hung her?"

"Why she weren't but 19, not much older than I am now." She tugged on the reins and Buck turned in the direction of the hill. "You want to see it? Won't take but a minute or two to get up there."

I shrugged, not sure I wanted to visit that place, but Abbie seemed to want to. When we reached the top, we both slid off Buck and looked at the town of Morganton below, reminding me of a miniature village in a Christmas decoration sans snow-covered roofs.

Abbie's eyes went back to the tree. "Pa was there, said he seen the whole thing, although I reckon he was right young then as well, probably near your age, Lizzie. He said people come from all around to watch her hang. Said it was more like a festival than a hangin, at least till it happened. A-course, some thought the governor would pardon her, right up to the minute they pulled the cart out from under her. They hadn't hung a woman before and they was a lot of petitions presented to him on her behalf with more'n half the town of the mind that she shouldn't hang. Pa said she probably wouldn't have exceptin she cut ol' Charlie up and tried to burn parts of his body in the fireplace."

I tried to imagine what circumstances would bring a woman, teenager, really, to do such a horrible thing. "Did she say why she did it?"

"Pa said that afore they hanged her, she give some letters to her attorney claiming that all through their marriage, Charlie would get drunk and beat her. The night she killed him, he come home drunk and was loading his gun, sayin he was gonna kill her, so she picked up an axe to defend herself and ended up killin him first. Now, Charlie's folks, the Silvers, was a wealthy family with lots of land, and Frankie's folks, the Stewarts, was real poor. The Silvers claimed Frankie's family was in on his murder, that they schemed to kill Charlie so they could get the land his pa give him for a weddin present."

I knew from cadavers we had experimented on in medical school that cutting up a body was no easy deed, especially for a young woman. "Would she have had the strength to cut him up like that, Abbie?"

She shrugged. "Pa claimed she was a tiny thing and he was of the opinion that they was no way a person that little could chop up and dispose of a man close to twice her size. He reckoned she probably had help from her ma and little brother. They was arrested with her but let go for some reason." She glanced at me. "I recall Sarie telling you Dan'l Boone's great-nephew John Boone was the one what hung her. Pa swore Sheriff Boone cried while he stood there, making the noose."

I gasped. "She had to wait while he made the hanging noose?"

Abbie nodded. "According to Pa. But don't hold that against him. He was a good man, Pa said, and popular with the townfolk. He died of a heart attack a few years later while he was still sheriff."

He must have been a caring man, I thought, to shed tears in public during that day and age.

"Frankie's pa and oldest brother was here, watchin," Abbie continued, "and when Sheriff Boone asked her if she had any last words, she started to speak but her pa yelled out, 'Die with it in you, Frankie,' or somethin like that."

"Why on earth would he say that to her?" I wondered, more to myself than Abbie.

She shook her head. "I'd say Pa was right, that she did have help and her pa was makin sure nobody else paid for it. Anyway, for whatever reason, she listened to her pa and said no more, just nodded to the sheriff she was ready. Pa said Frankie was dressed in a right pretty white dress and she looked like an angel with her blond hair and pretty face and tiny body. They put a white cloth hood over her head, I guess so people couldn't see her while they strangled her. They made her stand while they tugged on the rope till it was good and taut and tied it to the tree, then one of the deputies led the horse and cart away from the tree, right out from under her. Pa said her little feet tried to hold onto the cart as long as they could then ever'body present just stood there and watched her struggle till she died. Pa said it made him sick to see it."

I looked at that tree, so beautifully limbed and huge, and saw only death. "Do they still hang people here?"

She nodded. "Ever once in awhile. And like with Frankie, people come from all around to watch." She made a face. "You'd think it was a big ol party the way some act." She shook her head. "I wonder at times what God thinks of us, Lizzie, the way we are, the things we do. I reckon he's right ashamed of himself sometimes for creating people so hateful and cruel."

I couldn't help but nod in agreement.

We stood there for several moments, each thinking our own thoughts. After a bit, I turned to Abbie to ask if she was ready to leave and noticed her staring at a spot beyond the tree. "What is it?"

She startled, blinking her eyes. "Oh, ever once in awhile I see a person ain't crossed over yet, stayin behind for some reason or t'other."

"Do you see one now?"

She nodded. "I can't help him, though," she said in a low, sad voice. "He's got to find the way on his own."

"Have you ever seen Frankie?"

She shook her head. "I hope that poor girl found peace. Pa said she had a baby girl and it about killed her that she couldn't see her child afore they took her life."

"What happened to her daughter?"

"Charlie's people had her for awhile then Pa heared the Stewarts got her. He never heared no more."

"What'd they do with Frankie's body? Is she buried nearby?"

She shook her head. "Her pa and brother took the body, wrapped it in a blanket and put it in the back of a wagon. Said they was headin home to bury her with her own people. But that was 40 miles away up the mountain and they hung her in July. I don't reckon a body would hold up well in that situation, what with the heat and all. It's rumored she's buried near a tavern somewhere nearby where her pa and brother stopped. Didn't even put up a tombstone or nothin to mark her grave." She went to Buck and began rubbing beneath his mane. "Now, Charlie, he's got three tombstones." She turned to look at me. "Different body parts in different graves." Without another word, she mounted Buck, motioning for me to join her.

Once we were on our way, I said, "Where are Charlie's body parts buried?"

"Over in Kona, right beside the Toe River."

"Toe River. That's a strange name for a river."

"Oh, they's a reason it's called that. Pokni told me the story 'cause it's named after a Catawba princess."

"Catawba? Isn't Pokni Choctaw?"

"Shore is, but the Catawba been on this mountain for hundreds of years, just like the Cherokee, and Pokni's known quite a few. I reckon she heared it from one of them."

"Can you tell it to me?"

"I reckon I can, though I won't do as good a job as Pokni." She was quiet for a moment then said, "This took place during what Pokni calls the before." She glanced at me over her shoulder. "Meaning before the white men came to these parts. They was two Indian tribes that lived in these parts back then. The Catawba was to the east, in what she calls the Blue Ridge, and the Cherokee was in the foothills of the Unaka Mountains. The land in between was a right good spot to fish or hunt and she said they used mica they found there for trading or to make jewelry. But it was also the fightin ground for the Cherokee and Catawba.

"It's said she was a beautiful princess, the daughter of the Catawba's chief, and her name was Estatoe. Pokni said she was skilled at making jewelry and one day went to a nearby creek to admire in the clear water a necklace she had made. She was a-lookin at the reflection of the pretty necklace in the water when she was startled by a sound nearby. She turned and close by saw a young Cherokee warrior. He told her he got separated from his huntin party and was on his way to meet them. Well, the two of em commenced to talkin and found they had much to talk about so spent a good bit of time beside that creek gettin to know one another. Finally they realized they had to return to their people but they wanted to see each other some more so decided their signal to meet would be late in the afternoon when the whippoorwill called.

"Late one evenin when Estatoe returned to their camp after meetin her Cherokee lover, she seen a council was in progress in her father's lodge so she stopped outside to listen. She heard the warriors giving warnin of a Cherokee warrior seen lurking near the village. The warriors decided they'd go seek him out and kill him. Estatoe knew they was talkin about her lover so she rushed away to warn him. She begged him to escape but he refused to leave without her. So they took off together. But she didn't know that a sentry had followed her and overheard their plans. He went back to her pa, the chief, and told him what he heard so the tribe chased Estatoe and her lover until they was surrounded on a high bluff overlookin the river. They didn't have no way to escape so the Cherokee warrior tried to push Estatoe back to her tribesmen but she refused to go. Instead, she placed her hand in his and stood by his side right there at the edge of the cliff. They faced the sunset, said a silent prayer to the Great Spirit, then jumped together off that cliff, holdin hands, away far down into the foaming waters. The Catawba chief and his braves went to the edge of the cliff and searched the river below, and I reckon he either seen his daughter drowned or knew she wouldn't have lived, 'cause he raised his eyes to the heavens and stretched out his arms and committed his daughter to the keepin of the Great Spirit. The chief declared that the river whose waters took his daughter in death should forever be called by her name, Estatoe." She shrugged. "And a-course as they always do, it weren't good enough for the white man so one of em shortened it to the Toe River."

"What a sad story." I put my arms around her waist and hugged her. "Thanks for telling me, though."

We rode home in silence, each of us, I'm sure, thinking about Frankie and Estatoe and how unjust this world can be.

Chapter Two

Fall 1859

Heart of Stone

As we drew nearer to the sisters' cabin, Abbie broke the silence with a chuckle, drawing me out of my somewhat morbid thoughts. "Do you hear that, Lizzie?"

"Hear what? All I can hear are a few birds and … crickets? Are those crickets?"

"Sure are. Crickets during the day, fall's here to stay." She looked up at the sky. "Won't be long now afore we see some snow. I love snow. Don't you?"

I shuddered at the thought. I'd just barely made it through the stifling heat of the summer. It was way too early to think about snow and the cold weather that would come with winter. "How bad are the winters up here on the mountain?"

"They can get pretty cold. Most of the time, though, they're not too terrible bad. January and February are the coldest months. That's when we get most of our snow but they's been a few years when we were snowed in by Christmas and didn't see the ground again till late March or early April."

I moaned, thinking of blizzards and ice storms and everything that came with them, and worse, in my mind, snow so deep and temperatures so cold you couldn't go outside without danger of frostbite or full-blown hypothermia. Knoxville had its share of bad winters but the city was equipped to handle it. I wondered if they even had sand or plow trucks in the small town of Morganton. If they did, I doubted they would venture up here on the mountain, even as close as the sisters lived to the bottom. And then I remembered I wasn't in the 20th century anymore and even in Knoxville they wouldn't have trucks of any kind or any of the modern conveniences that helped to make winter bearable. An involuntary shudder ran through me at the thought.

Abbie must have felt the shaking of my body because she glanced back with a quizzical look on her face. "Don't you like snow, Lizzie?"

"No, not really. I loved it when I was a kid and we got days off from school but I grew out of that. Mostly it's just an inconvenience."

"Okay. Did I use that word right?"

I smiled, grateful for this friend with whom I could speak freely and who believed that I belonged in this time but was willing to help me find my way back to 1969 because I wanted it so much. I really don't know if I could have survived a day, much less three months, if I hadn't found her. To me, she was a blessing, a miracle that got me through the days. "Thank you, Abbie."

"Why, what for?"

"For being you." I banded my arms around her waist and gave her a squeeze then let go when she stiffened and pulled on Buck's reins to make him stop.

"What's wrong?" I whispered.

"Did you hear that?"

I opened my mouth to answer, but before I could get any words out, she said, "Shh! What in tarnation is that? Is it Sarie?"

"What? I don't hear anything."

She didn't answer, just tapped her heels against Buck's side, sending him into a fast trot.

I wrapped my arms around her waist again, this time to

keep from falling off. After a few seconds, once I had my balance, I simply enjoyed the ride through the autumn-tinged forest, marveling at the faded blooms on the tall Joe Pye weed and shorter purple asters that flashed by us, the hints of red, yellow and orange of the quickly turning leaves. I breathed in deeply the pungent smell of dying plants and rotting leaves shutting down and taking to their beds for the long, cold winter that would soon be upon us. Death, I realized could be, in some ways, as beautiful as it was sad.

We didn't have far to go, and when we trotted into the clearing surrounding the sisters' cabin, I heard what Abbie had been talking about.

Her sister Sarie stood in the doorway, hands fisted at her hips, facing my dreaded nemesis, Constable Jackson. He was on the porch, likewise facing her, his right hand resting on the butt of the big gun in the holster at his waist and his other hooked by the thumb in the pocket of his pants. He looked cocky and a little dangerous.

My blood began to boil, remembering it was his fault I had missed my chance to go home and get out of this awful time.

Sarie's eyes flashed toward us as we broke out of the woods. I swear, I could feel the heat of them though Abbie and I were still a good forty or fifty feet away.

I whispered, "Oh, man," seconds before Abbie drew back on the reins and shouted, "Whoa," to stop the horse. As I'd seen her sister Maggie do, she lifted her right leg, swung it over Buck's neck and slipped to the ground before he came to a complete stop.

I moved forward, grabbed onto a handful of Buck's mane and waited for him to stop moving then slid off.

A visibly irate Sarie stomped out of the doorway onto the porch, brusquely shoving Constable Jackson aside when he tried to block her way. His hand flew away from the butt of his gun. My blood ran as cold as the snow Abbie and I had been speaking of only a few minutes before. I fully expected him to strike Sarie in retaliation, maybe even shoot her, but he only brought his hand back to rest on his gun.

Sarie took Abbie's hand and drew her up to stand beside

her as if the two of them could form some kind of barrier against the hulking constable.

"What's goin on, Sarie?" Abbie said.

Sarie's eyes cut to her and she shook her head. "You and Lizzie need to get to your chores," she snapped. "Constable Jackson was just leavin." Her eyes flicked back to Jackson. "Weren't you, Mr. Jackson?"

He smirked, tapping the shiny silver star on his chest. "Well, now, Miss Sarie, I'm here on official business and I'll leave after I get it done."

"Git off my land, you yellow—"

Constable Jackson raised a hand in the air as if to ward off her words. "Miss Sarie, I come all this way to talk to your sister and cousin. I'll go as soon as I do that, not one minute before."

Sarie ignored him. "Abbie, Lizzie, go on inside and git to your chores. I'll handle this."

Abbie surprised me when she put a restraining hand on Sarie's shoulder and said, "No, Sarie, we'll handle this." She looked at Constable Jackson, actually mustering up a sweet smile for him. "What is it you need here, Mr. Jackson?"

"I need to know where you and your cousin vanished to t'other night when we were up on the mountain."

I joined Abbie on the porch. I wasn't sure she could handle this nasty man but I figured my anger gave me some measure of protection from him. "You mean when you touched the light and fell flat on your, um ..." I wanted to say "ass," or even better, "fat ass" but caught myself in time "... backside when the light knocked you out? It scared us so much we just took off. Mr. Hampton caught up to us and told us to go on home, that he would go back to check on you and help you if you needed it. So, Abbie and I came back here. Surely there isn't a law against walking on the mountain at night. Is there?"

He ignored my question, looking at Abbie as if she'd been the one to speak instead of me. "That so, Miss Abbie?"

"Yes, Constable Jackson, that's so," I said as Abbie nodded.

"What were you doing that far up the mountain so late at

night?"

This time Abbie answered before I could. She still had the same sweet smile on her face. "Well now, not that it's any of your concern, but … well, Mr. Josh is courtin our Lizzie." Sarie gasped as she said that. "They went for a walk and I went along to chaperone them, as is right and proper."

Jackson kept his eyes on me as if waiting for me to break down and confess my guilt. "Mighty far piece to walk just to do a little spoonin, ain't it?"

Abbie giggled. "Well, you know how it is with people who are in love, Mr. Jackson. Why they could probably walk from here to Asheville and back and not even notice. Ain't you never been in love afore, Constable?"

He cut his eyes to Sarie but didn't answer Abbie's question. "That ain't neither here nor there. Did you know me and a search party was up there with a couple of dogs chasing a runaway slave?"

"Why no, we didn't. Fact is, we didn't see nobody but you and that was only after we heard you scream." Abbie turned to me. "That must've been what all that barkin was about, Lizzie. Remember what you said?" She laughed. "Lizzie thought for a minute the hounds of hell was comin for us."

I watched her, wondering why in the world I thought she needed my protection. She was as cool as a cucumber, calmer even than me, which, I admit, wasn't saying much since I was sweating like a stuck pig as we faced the constable. I could actually feel the sweat dripping down my back. Still, I smiled at Abbie. "Must've been."

Sarie stepped forward, taking Abbie's hand in hers again. "They've answered your questions, Mr. Jackson. Now, I'd be much obliged if you'd git off my land and leave us to get back to our chores." She looked pointedly up at the sky where the sun rode low on the horizon, lazily dropping its way down to touch the taller mountains in the distance, casting a rose-tinted halo over their tops. "We ain't got that much daylight left and we still have half a day's work waitin for us."

His lips lifted in a sneer but he nodded as he touched his

finger to his hat. "Miss Abbie, Miss Sarie." He turned to me, his eyes blazing hot. "Miss Lizzie."

My mouth fell open when he mounted his horse and rode away, keeping his eyes on Sarie the whole way. His hateful look was enough to make me shiver. It didn't seem to bother Sarie, though. She merely glared at him as if she wanted nothing more than to see him dead in his grave. Which, I guess, she did. It was one of the few things Sarie and I had in common. We would both celebrate that odious man's demise, and as far as I was concerned, that couldn't happen soon enough. But if I couldn't have him dead, I'd settle for him suffering horribly from some terrible sickness or injury that would keep him in town and away from us.

As soon as he was out of sight, Sarie dropped Abbie's hand and turned to face her, tossing a hateful look in my direction. Her face stony, the words came out in a hiss. "What have you two been up to? Ain't we got enough trouble with that mule-headed idiot without you drawing more to us?"

I moved closer to Abbie's side, forming a barrier much like Sarie had done with Abbie against Constable Jackson.

"We ain't done nothin, Sarie." Abbie turned to me. "Have we Lizzie?"

Not giving me the chance to answer, Sarie huffed. "Don't you lie to me, Abbie. Don't you never lie to me, do you hear me? I won't stand for it." She pointed at me. "I expect it from her but not you. She ain't done nothin but lie since she got here."

I gasped and would have responded, but once again, Abbie beat me to the punch. "That ain't fair, Sarie, you know it ain't. She ain't lied about nothin, not that I know of. You should apologize to Lizzie right now." She crossed her arms over her chest and raised her eyebrows.

Sarie stared at her sister for a few seconds then shook her head with irritation. "Fine." She spit the word out as if it was bitter on her tongue then looked at me. "I'm sorry, Lizzie."

I nodded even though I had my doubts about her sincerity.

"Now," she went on, looking at Abbie, "where have you

two been and what have you done?"

Abbie shrugged. "We was down in town checkin to see if Mr. Josh needed help. You heared Jackson throwed him in jail, didn't you? And as far as the other night, we didn't do nothin but what we told the constable. I don't understand why you're so all fired up about this."

"He weren't here to pass the time of day or ask if we need somethin from town. He wanted you two, and I'd stake my life on it he'll come back again. And when he does, it'll be to arrest both of you and throw you in jail."

"So, what if he does? We ain't done nothin wrong, Sarie, I swear it on Ma's grave." Abbie lifted a hand and placed it over her heart. "And I ain't lyin to you. Neither is Lizzie."

I laid a hand over my heart. "Really, Sarie, we haven't done anything. Jackson's just mad because Mr. Hampton talked to the sheriff and got Josh released because the sheriff said Jackson didn't have any proof. I imagine that didn't set very well with Jackson, being the kind of man he is."

We all turned at a rustling sound as Maggie strolled out of the woods to the right of the house. It was obvious, to me anyway, that she'd been on one of her long walks with Randall. Her cheeks were the delicate pink color of the sunset and her eyes had that same dreamy look they always did when she had been with him.

I breathed a sigh of relief when Sarie turned her irritation on her unsuspecting sister. "And just where have you been, Maggie?"

Maggie jumped at Sarie's demanding tone. "For a walk." She held up a bundle of something wrapped in one of Abbie's beautiful embroidered handkerchiefs. "I had a hankerin for some dandelion leaves to add to the soup I'm fixin for supper. I seen Mr. Randall on my way back and we stopped to chat for awhile about Connie's and Martin's babies. I swear, that man's more in love with them babies than their pa and ma are. He says they're just the cutest things he's ever seen. Went on and on about how Martin and Connie are so happy. I think he's a little jealous of his brother, but who wouldn't be? Martin has everything anybody would ever want."

She smiled at me. "We should go by and see em some time, Lizzie, since we birthed em. I reckon we should've checked on em before this, but with the harvest and ever'thin else goin on around here, I just ain't had the time. We could go tomorrow if it's all right with you."

I smiled, remembering how sweet Connie's and Martin's twins were right after we delivered them. Truth be told, I was also a little jealous of them. They were so much in love and so happy with their new babies. At some point in my future, I wanted that as well, but not here, not now. "Of course, Maggie. I'd love to see how those precious babies are doing."

"Good. We'll go tomorrow then." She turned to Sarie. "What's got you so riled up, Sarie? Your face is as red as a ripe tomato. Did somethin happen? Is somebody sick? Do they need our help?"

Once again, Sarie huffed out an annoyed breath. "No, not really. Ever'body's fine as far as I know. Constable Jackson was here. He just left."

"Oh, laws, no wonder you're so het up. What did he want this time?"

"He wanted to talk to Abbie and Lizzie. Apparently, they was up on the mountain t'other night while he and a search party was lookin for a runaway slave. He thinks they had somethin to do with helpin the slave escape."

"Why in the Sam Hill would he think that?"

"Because he saw them up there on the mountain, them and Mr. Josh, and he's convinced they was helpin that runaway."

"I told you, Sarie, Mr. Josh is courtin Lizzie." Abbie smiled. "He's awful sweet on her and I think she feels the same way about him."

Maggie smiled at me. "Oh, how nice. We could use a little romance up here. Haven't had one in a coon's age. Come to think of it, not since Martin and Constance were spoonin. And look where they are now, married nigh on a year and with two new babies. Are you sweet on Mr. Josh, Lizzie?"

I could feel my cheeks heat as they all stared at me. I shrugged. "I might be. He's awful handsome and nice, the epitome of a Southern gentleman."

Sarie jumped on that like a cat on a June bug. "What about your husband? What was his name, Ben? It ain't decent for you to spoon with Mr. Josh if'n you're married to somebody else."

I had forgotten that's what I told Sarie, but Abbie jumped to my defense. "I know you don't believe she come through the lights, but her husband's over a hundred years in the future and ain't even born yet. She might never get back to him, so what's the harm in spendin some time with Mr. Josh? It's not like she's marryin him or nothin."

Sarie ignored her sister, pinning me with a suspicious glare. "It pains me to say it, but I agree with the constable on this one. That's an awful far piece to be walkin just to be spoonin someone. Why couldn't you walk around here?"

"Oh, that was Mr. Josh's idea," Abbie said. He needed to go check on the Scarbrough place for his pa. Mr. Hampton bought it after old Mr. Scarbrough died, you know. Lizzie and me went along and was lookin for Joe Pye weed in that big field back of Scarbrough's barn while Josh did what he needed to do."

"Fine but why is he so suspicious of you two? I was afraid he was goin to cart the both of you off to jail. And he still might."

Abbie shrugged. "He don't have no reason to do that. You of all people know how he is, Sarie. Like a dog with a bone when he gets somethin stuck in his mind. 'Sides, Lizzie and I talked with Sheriff Brittain while we was in Morganton. He told us not to worry about Jackson." She smiled. "Truth be known, I'm startin to think the constable just might be a little sweet on our Lizzie."

I jumped at that. The constable and me? Oh, gag a maggot. That would only happen over my dead body. And even dead, I hoped I could do something to drive him away.

Thankfully, Sarie ignored Abbie's words. "What did you mean when you said Josh went back to check on him?"

"Well, while we was all standing there in the field, we

seen one of the lights. It pert-near ran into us, and for some reason, Mr. Jackson ran straight toward it, knocked Lizzie down then touched the light on an accident. It knocked him clean out. Tell the truth and shame the devil, it scared Lizzie and me so much we took off runnin into the woods. Dropped all the Joe Pye weed we'd collected." She shook her head. "Mr. Josh, being the gentleman he is, come to check on us first to make sure we wasn't harmed in any way. When he found us and seen we wasn't hurt or nothin, he told us to go on home while he went back to see if the constable was all right. That's all there was to it, I promise."

Sarie scoffed as she shook her head. "Well, all I got to say is if Jackson is sweet on you, Lizzie, you better find some way to turn his attention away. Else you'll have him hangin around you all the time, givin you them suspicious looks of his'n and accusing you of ever'thin under the sun."

"I'll do my best," I said. "I don't want any more to do with that man, he's downright awful."

Maggie stepped up onto the porch. "I'm goin to go in and finish supper. Y'all best get to the evening chores afore you lose the light. Come on in when you're done. I'm makin cornbread to go with the soup."

Sarie turned to me. "Lizzie, take Buck down to the barn, brush him down and get him fed. Abbie and I'll tend to the milkin and feedin of Miss Bossie."

Abbie shot me a look from under raised eyebrows and I swear I could all but hear her heartfelt sigh of relief even though she held the gesture inside. I glanced at Sarie, and seeing her eyes were on the barn, winked at my sweet friend.

Buck, who had been standing nearby munching patiently on grass, shook his head and snorted, as if he was in on the secret Abbie and I shared. I smiled as I slipped the reins over his head and walked with him to the barn, remembering the way Abbie had so skillfully stretched the truth in order to calm her older sister down. Tell the truth and shame the devil, indeed.

She'd saved my bacon, that was for sure, and I loved her even more for it. I hoped I would be able to return the

29

favor one day.

As for Sarie, I was afraid I'd lost even the small amount of trust and friendship we'd managed to eke out of the work we'd done to save the slaves at the Hampton plantation during the smallpox outbreak. Barring another outbreak of some deadly disease that I could help the sisters cure, I didn't imagine my relationship with her would ever get any better.

Chapter Three

Fall 1859

19th Nervous Breakdown

I awoke the next morning to the clanging of pots down in the kitchen and bitter cold. My nose and forehead, the only parts of my body exposed to the frigid air, felt as if someone had dumped water on them and it froze into a solid block of ice. I snuggled under the blanket and quilts, dreading the moment when my toasty warm feet would meet the freezing floor. Abbie stirring beside me was enough to have me slitting one eye open, chancing a peek from under the covers. I moaned. It was as dark as the seventh level of hell still and the steady drips of raindrops pinging on the tin roof had me slamming my eyes closed again as I tugged the covers back over my head, hoping my warm breath was enough to make up for the loss of Abbie's body heat.

I heard the rustle of clothes and felt the bed dip as Abbie sat down to put on her shoes. Keeping the covers pulled tight over my head, I mumbled my protestation over the early hour but I doubt Abbie could understand me.

She patted my shoulder. "Go on back to sleep, Lizzie. I hear somebody movin around downstairs and I'm hopin it's Sarie. I want to talk to her and see if I can get her out of her snit."

I shivered at that and told myself it was from the morning's chill and not the prospect of facing Sarie's wrath before the sun was even up. Resisting the urge to say, "Better you than me," I instead whispered a heartfelt, "Good luck."

Abbie chuckled as she patted my shoulder once more. "Don't you worry none about me. I know my way round Sarie and her cantankerous moods. She might even be smilin by the time you get up."

And with that, she doubled her side of the covers over to my side of the bed. I snuggled into my cozy cocoon, tracking her footsteps as she walked over to the ladder, then went down, saying something to whoever was up when she got to the bottom.

After that, all I could hear was the soothing sound of the rain falling on the roof. It, along with the warmth of the bedclothes, soon lulled me back to sleep.

An unknown time later, I was in the middle of a dream where Ben stood on one side of me and Josh on the other, both tugging on my arms, trying to pull me to their side. My father was there as well, with a whistle in his mouth, watching as they pulled. Apparently he was acting as referee. The shriek of the whistle jolted me out of sleep. More than happy to leave that dream behind, I uncovered my head.

The sun was up and the rain had stopped. But that wasn't what cut through the usual morning fuzziness. No, that would be the whispered argument going on downstairs.

My eyes popped open wide when I heard Abbie snap at Sarie. "Stop it, Sarie. Just stop it right now." Her tone angry and more than a little flustered, she said, "We wasn't doin nothin but lookin for some Joe Pye weed plants 'cause we're runnin low and we'll need them with the cold weather comin on. Mr. Josh had gone into the barn to check on somethin for his pa. Lizzie and I stayed out in the field. How was I—or Lizzie, for that matter—supposed to know that Constable Jackson was up there lookin for a runaway slave?"

Sotto voce but loud enough for me to hear, Sarie said, "You said you heard dogs barkin, that should've been enough to warn you that somebody was up there, possibly huntin. You know that's a dangerous place to be when people are traipsing around with guns. And in the dark too. What in heaven's name got into you, Abbie? You coulda been killed."

"Oh, dogs barkin and I oughta know they was a manhunt goin on and we should get out of the way," Abbie scoffed. "You hear dogs bark up on the mountain all the time and it usually ain't because they have a manhunt goin on. Most of the people up there have a whole mess of coon dogs and they'll bark at anything that moves."

Thinking Abbie might need my help, I reluctantly threw the covers back and sat up, still half asleep but determined to come to my friend's support. The coldness of the floor on my bare feet was enough to shock me into full consciousness, sending a shudder through my entire body. I wrenched my nightgown over my head and grabbed my dress off the hook on the wall, jamming it on while I danced from foot to foot in an effort to minimize the cold floor's impact. For once I was grateful the dress was made of heavy cotton and had long sleeves and an ankle-length skirt that covered my legs, but, man, I'd have given my eye teeth for a pair of jeans, warm wool socks, and knee-high boots. Making do with my shoes, an old, leather pair the sisters' mother had worn, I slipped them on over my stockings and wiggled my toes in a futile effort to get the blood circulating to warm my feet.

Turning back to the bed, I pulled the covers haphazardly over the mattress and pillows. It was still lumpy and bumpy but it would have to do. I knew Abbie wouldn't mind but heaven help us if Sarie came up here for any reason.

I walked over to the ladder and climbed down. Looking over my shoulder, I smiled at Maggie, Abbie and Sarie, watching me. "Good morning, everyone." I wrapped my arms around my torso. "It sure did get cold last night. I hope it warms up later when the sun is fully up."

Judging from Sarie's flinty glare, Abbie hadn't been able to charm her out of her snit, at least as far as I was concerned. I squared my shoulders and started to tell her to go jump in a lake or, better yet, off a high cliff, but instead met her angry look with one of my own, vowing to myself I would not be cowed by her.

Abbie must have seen the pending smart-ass remark in my eyes because she stepped forward, placing herself neatly between her sister and me. "Good mornin, Lizzie. It did get cold last night but I think it'll warm up to be right nice later. How did you sleep?"

I sighed. Abbie the peacemaker was in full swing. I was furious with Sarie that she so often put us in this position but decided to let it go and, as Abbie so obviously wanted me to, try to be pleasant. After all, Abbie knew her sister better than I did and maybe this was the way to drain her anger. Worth a try, I thought.

"I slept pretty well, Abbie, how about you?"

"Well enough that I was up with the chickens."

I turned to Maggie, extending my smile to include her. "Are you ready to collect the eggs from those mean old hens?"

She nodded as she moved a cast iron skillet filled with nicely formed circles of biscuit dough over to the center of the fire. "Those should be ready in about fifteen minutes, Sarie. Don't forget to turn em and don't let em burn now, you hear?"

Abbie gave her sister an affectionate smile. "I'll keep an eye on em, Maggie. The porridge should be ready by the time y'all get back."

I took a deep breath, dreading stepping out into the cold. Abbie seemed to read my mind. "There's one of Pa's old jackets hangin on that hook aside the door, if you need it, Lizzie. It ain't much, but it'll keep you warm."

In my peripheral vision, I saw Sarie stiffen and fully expected her to blast me for using her father's things as she had when she had given me two of her mother's old dresses and a pair of shoes to wear. I often wondered if Sarie's bristly temperament was a result of her father's abuse or guilt over the fact that she had killed him when he tried to barter her to Constable Jackson to pay off a debt owed. Although I didn't know that to be entirely true, I strongly suspected it was so and from some things Maggie had said, thought she did as well. I said a hasty thanks to Abbie and grabbed the coat on my way out the door. I think that was the one single morning during my time with the sisters that I actually wanted to gather eggs. The hens and I had disliked each other from the first day I'd entered the chicken coop and it seemed the animosity between us, much like the ill feelings between Sarie and me, only got worse as time went on.

Even with the jacket—which was rather gross as it smelled of stale smoke and body odor—I shivered as I followed Maggie out the door. It surprised me when she grabbed my hand and pulled me quickly toward the chicken coop. I started to say something but she shushed me so I remained silent.

It wasn't unusual for us to spend the entire time gathering eggs in silence. Maggie wasn't much of a talker and kept most of her feelings and opinions to herself. It was her best quality, if you asked me. But this time, as soon as we stepped inside where the chickens sat their nests, she turned to me and spoke in a breathless voice, as if we'd run a long distance to get to the coop.

"Merciful heavens, I don't think I've ever seen Sarie this mad. She loses her temper a lot, usually at Constable Jackson, but hardly ever at Abbie or me, and when she does, she usually gets over it in a couple of hours. And if she doesn't, Abbie can almost always talk her out of it. We got to think of something to get her over it, else she'll make our lives miserable."

"She already is. Abbie got up early today because she wanted to talk to Sarie alone but it's probably been more than an hour now and it doesn't seem to be doing any good where I'm concerned. I think she's totally forgiven Abbie, though, but from the way she glared at me in the kitchen, I think I'm still in the doghouse—I mean, still on her bad side," I hurriedly added before she could question my choice of words. I didn't know if doghouses were a part of the mountain vernacular yet. "I'm sorry, Maggie. This is my fault, and if I knew what to do to make it better, believe me, I would."

She waved that away then picked up the baskets sitting by the door and handed one to me. "I know. I really wish I could help you, Lizzie, but she's already put out with me for going off yesterday and leaving her alone to deal with Jackson by herself."

I started to ask her where she'd gone but figured I already knew, judging from the look on her face when she came back. "But how could you know he would show up?" I waved that aside. "She sure does hate that man."

Maggie slipped her hand under one of the hens and a few seconds later drew it smoothly out, cradling an egg in her palm. How the heck did she do that? I wondered.

Trying to mimic her calm and gentle moves, I reached out my hand only to get it pecked when Abbie's two dogs set up a ruckus outside.

I swore under my breath as Maggie rushed over to the door and looked out to see what had Billy and Bob all stirred up. She set her basket down by the door as she pulled it open. "Come on, Lizzie, Sarie's gonna need us."

"What? Who is it?" But I knew even as the words came out of my mouth. "Constable Jackson? Again? What the devil does he want this time?"

Maggie shook her head with frustration. "I swear, that man likes nothin better than keepin Sarie riled up. He's like a cat playin with a mouse." She looked at me. "I don't know what he wants but let's go. This could be the way for both of us to get back in Sarie's good graces."

"Does she have good graces?" I mumbled to myself as I set my basket down beside hers and went out the door behind her, thinking Maggie had a good point. Sarie might get so mad at her archenemy she'd forget her anger at me.

It was purely selfish of me but I didn't care. If I was going to have to remain in this horrid time and place for however long it took to find my light again, I didn't want to deal with a sister who hated me and might possibly want to do to me what I suspected she'd done to her father.

As if I'd conjured her up just by thinking about her, Sarie stepped out of the front door and stood scowling as

Constable Jackson slowed his horse, pulling cruelly on the reins as they came close to the porch.

Shaking her head, she called the two dogs. "Here, Billy, here, Bob." They obediently ran to her, skidding to a stop and sitting calmly at her feet. She leaned down and ran her hands over their heads, murmuring something as she did. Both of the dogs got up and trotted in the direction of the barn.

My gaze went back to the constable. I didn't like the man but I had to admit he made a pretty picture on his huge horse. His back as straight as a ruler's edge, his body followed the horse's gait as if he were an extension of the animal. Honestly, it looked as if he'd been born to ride that beautiful horse. It was just too bad that he had such a harsh hand with the reins.

"Whoa, boy." he said. Keeping his eyes on Sarie, he tipped his hat. "Miss Sarie. How are you this fine fall morning?"

Sarie didn't bother to mask her irritation. "Seems to me you was just here, Jackson, and I'm wonderin what you're wantin now. Ain't you got nothin better to do than come around here botherin us?"

He smiled, shifted in his saddle and took a quick scan around the yard, tipping his hat to Maggie and me followed by a nod to Abbie as she stepped out of the door to stand at her sister's side.

"Well, now, Miss Sarie, I'm afraid I have some bad news."

Sarie sighed audibly as she placed her hands on her hips and waited for him to go on. But he only sat there, watching her with his lips curved gently. I wondered if he enjoyed their constant bickering or if he was just so confident he'd get what he wanted in the long run that everything about the situation with Sarie amused him.

Sarie wasn't as patient, huffing out a short-tempered breath before she said, "Well, Constable Jackson, I don't have all day. Just spit out whatever it is you come here to say and then get off my property. Two times in as many days is too much when it comes to you."

His lips curved up more, almost in a grin. Then he turned in my direction. "Miss Lizzie, I'm going to need you to come with me."

As I gasped, he turned back to Abbie. "You too, Miss Abbie."

Sarie grabbed Abbie's arm but kept her eyes on Jackson as she went off like a Fourth of July firecracker. "They ain't goin nowhere with you, Jackson, so you just get off our land and leave us alone, you, you yellow-bellied, lily-livered jackass. I'll see them both in hell before I let you take them."

Jackson's grin notched up to a sneer as he nodded. "Ain't no need to be that way, Miss Sarie, but knowing you, I figured that would be your reaction so I brung this with me." He pulled a piece of folded paper out of his jacket pocket.

Sarie shoved Abbie behind her, holding her there as Maggie and I walked up to stand beside her.

"You and Abbie stay right here," Sarie snapped at me. "Maggie, you keep em here. I'll take care of this."

With that, she stepped off the porch, reaching out to snag the paper out of Jackson's hand. His smile grew wider, as if he enjoyed teasing her, as he jerked the paper up, holding it aloft where she couldn't reach it.

Sarie stomped her foot then stepped back and held out her hand. It amazed me her voice came out sugary sweet when she spoke but her eyes still flashed blue fire. "I would like to see the paper, Constable Jackson, if'n you please."

"If'n you don't mind, Miss Sarie, I reckon I'll just read it to you."

Sarie waved a hand in the air. "All right, I reckon that will do. That is, if'n you don't mind, Constable Jackson." I had to admire her coolness. Her voice was still as sweet as honey but her face was the ruddy red color of the apples still hanging on the trees in the orchard and her hands were clenched into tight fists at her sides. I wondered if Constable Jackson was so stupid he couldn't see the danger and step back out of the reach of those fingernails which I suspected were cutting bloody half moons into her palms right then.

Jackson puffed his chest out. "Well, now, this here is a warrant signed by the Circuit Court Judge giving me the authority to take Miss Lizzie and Miss Abbie in for questioning."

"I see." Sarie craned her neck as if to try to see what Jackson was holding then in a flash she jumped and snatched the paper out of his hand. She glanced at it before Jackson could grab it away again. Crumpling the paper up, she threw it at him, hitting him dead center of his puffed-out chest. I would've gone for his face but I had to admire her aim. "That ain't nothin but a letter to the sheriff, you lyin jackass."

Jackson's face flushed redder than Sarie's. He shrugged. "Still need to question them girls and I ain't leavin here until I do."

"Question them about what? They done told ya they wasn't up on the mountain to help that runaway slave. What more do you want?"

"Oh, I won't be talking to them about that. No ma'am, I'll be talking to them about where they was for the last two nights."

He still had that smug grin on his face and I wondered how Sarie could stand there talking to him instead of slapping that smirk off his face.

Then, it finally came to me what he'd said. The last two nights? I didn't think Josh had another runaway up on the mountain—at least he hadn't said anything to me if he did. Of course, I hadn't seen him since the night we helped Zebidiah escape.

Sarie's control finally snapped, her voice turning harsh and sharp as a jagged shard of broken glass when she asked the question that was on the tip of my tongue. "What happened the last two nights?" Unfortunately, she didn't wait for Jackson to answer, waving it away as if it wasn't important and she didn't really want to know, nor did she care. "Don't matter none. I can tell you they both was right here. Maggie and I will swear to it. So they're innocent of whatever it is your nasty little brain has come up with."

"Could be they are but I still need to talk to them and I'm taking them back to town with me where I can question them without any interference from you." He turned to Abbie.

"Where's that horse of your'n?"

Abbie stepped out from behind Sarie despite her sharp hiss. "Buck's in the barn, but if'n you're plannin on havin us ride him to town, I'm afraid we can't."

"Why not?"

"He's hurt, come up lame yestaday. Ridin him will only make his injury worse." Tears sparkled in her eyes as she turned to Sarie. "I won't have it, Sarie. Buck's the only horse we got, and if'n we ride him now, he might end up permanently hobbled." She looked back to Jackson, folding her arms over her chest. "I ain't gonna add to that poor animal's misery. If'n you want to talk to us, you can either do it right here or go back into town and get a wagon then come back and get us."

I saw Sarie's lips twitch. I imagined she was as proud of Abbie as I was. I took her hand in mine, hoping to present a united front. My own voice sweet, I said, "Or, Constable Jackson, you can wait for us to walk into town but that may take a while. Why, it might even be tomorrow sometime before we get there."

Jackson frowned. "I ain't got time to wait. We'll do it here and we'll make it fast. I need to get back up the mountain to the search party as soon as I can."

"Search party?" Maggie asked. "What search party? Oh, dear, don't tell me somebody else has gone missing."

"Mr. Joseph Westcott went up on the mountain a coupla nights ago to do some huntin and he ain't been seen or heard from since. A coupla his slaves went looking for him yesterday and they ain't come back neither. Some people are wondering if they took the opportunity to run away so that's where we're concentrating our search, up on the mountain where we looked for that other runaway."

"You mean to say you ain't searchin for Mr. Westcott?" Sarie asked. "Seems to me that's where your focus should be instead of on those poor slaves who, for all you know, are still lookin for him or maybe they's with Mr. Westcott. They mighta found him hurt, and since I'm sure they don't have a horse, they'll have to carry him out of the woods. And that, as you very well know, Mr. Jackson, could take a while."

Jackson's scowl notched up a bit. "I'm doin my job," he snapped at Sarie.

She crossed her arms over her chest and regarded him with narrowed eyes. "Looks to me like you're sittin on your horse there doin nothin more than pesterin innocent civilians. Why ain't you up there with your search party doin what you're bein paid to do?"

Jackson's lip tightened into a straight line as his face hardened. I couldn't believe Sarie was challenging him like this. The only thing that would accomplish would be to make him more suspicious and more determined to find something that would allow him to put her in his jail—or under it.

Though I expected him to defend himself, he took a deep breath before nodding at Abbie. "There somewhere we can talk, Miss Abbie? I'll take you first and then I'll talk to your cousin."

Abbie looked at Sarie, shushing her when she opened her mouth to lay into Jackson again. Meeting the constable's steely look, she smiled at him. I could see Sarie go as still as a rock, but Abbie flashed her a warning look and she kept her mouth shut. "We can go inside, Constable Jackson, if'n you don't mind me and Sarie finishin up breakfast while we talk. Lizzie can go with Maggie and finish collectin the eggs. By the time me and you are through, I'm sure she will be too. That all right?"

Jackson only nodded as he dismounted and wrapped the reins around the railing. Then he walked up on the porch to the open door, gesturing politely for Abbie to go before him. I bit my lip to hold in the laugh when he closed it behind him, right in Sarie's enraged face.

I worried about Jackson and his questions as Maggie and I went back to collecting the eggs. Was this the way it would always be after this? Whenever something bad happened on the mountain, Jackson would show up to question Sarie or myself. If it was, I considered it something of a miracle Sarie hadn't killed the man by now.

Right as we gathered the last egg, we heard hoofbeats from outside the chicken coop. By the time we opened the door and got back to the house, Jackson was gone.

Setting the basket of eggs on the table, I turned to Abbie. "Where did the constable go?"

She shrugged. "I must've answered his questions to his satisfaction. He said he'd be back if he needed to talk to you."

I smiled at her as I took one of the bowls she was carrying to the table. "How in the world did you do that?" I leaned in and whispered in her ear. "Maybe you could teach Sarie and then he wouldn't hang around here so much."

She laughed. "Mayhap I will. I did tell him we'd join the search for poor Mr. Westcott. I hate to think of him lost up there on the mountain. He's a sweet man even if he does hunt and kill animals. His wife's been gone three or four years now and his only daughter married a man from up north somewheres so she don't come around much. His slaves mean a lot to him and he treats them like they was his children. They would never try to run away, and if Jackson paid attention to the people he's hired to protect around here, he'd know that." She lowered her voice to a whisper. "I figure lookin for him will give us a good excuse to look for your light. We can go back where we were the other night with Mr. Josh when the light appeared. Maybe it'll come back again. But first, we'll eat breakfast and then get our mornin chores done."

"Do you think it would be a good idea to go down the mountain? I mean, we usually go up but maybe we'd have better luck if we go down instead."

"Couldn't hurt. We'll try that tomorrow night." She turned and smiled at Sarie, standing by the fireplace stirring the porridge, and Maggie, carefully transferring the golden brown biscuits from the cast iron skillet to a plate. "We ready to eat? I'm as hungry as a bear just wakin up from his winter nap."

Everyone took their designated spot at the table, bowing their heads and joining hands as soon as we were seated. Abbie said grace, adding in a sweet prayer for Mr. Westcott and his slaves before saying, "Amen."

Sarie had added some maple syrup and diced apples to the porridge, giving it a sweet taste I enjoyed. Usually it was a little bland for me and I sometimes struggled to eat it all but the added ingredients had me scraping my bowl clean.

As we ate, Sarie handed out chores for the day. She and Abbie were to join the search party and help in any way they could. Maggie and I were to pick the rest of the apples and prepare them for drying or storing in the root cellar.

My mouth dropped open in surprise when Maggie said, "I'll go with you, Sarie. You know it scares me senseless to climb up in them trees. Abbie can stay here with Lizzie. She's a much better climber than I am."

Sarie frowned but nodded in agreement. "All right, go get your bag, we'll forage a little while we're lookin." She turned to Abbie. "Anythin else we need to look for 'sides Joe Pye weed?"

"Might be a good time to look for some 'sang. We have some but not enough to last the whole winter, 'specially if it's goin to be a hard one like the farmers are sayin."

I breathed a sigh of relief as I watched Sarie and Maggie cross the porch and head for the woods. "Well, that was a big surprise. I figured one of us, most likely me, would be stuck with her all day. I owe Maggie for that one."

Abbie nodded. "She didn't have no choice. Maggie really is a-feared of climbin trees and Sarie knows it." She sighed. "I know Sarie seems heartless at times, Lizzie, but she loves Maggie and me and she wouldn't put Maggie through that on purpose." She shrugged. "Maybe she figured you and me've already caused enough trouble around here and we can't possibly get into any more."

I mimicked the shrug, not really caring, just happy to be with my friend instead of her irritable older sister. "Dishes first?"

"Yep, then we can start on the apples. You'll probably be wishin by lunch time that Sarie had taken you with her."

"I doubt that. Besides, how hard can it be picking apples, even if some of them will have to be peeled and cored?"

Abbie grinned. "Don't forget washin and sortin em. You're fixin to find out how hard."

Abbie was right. By lunch, I never wanted to peel or core another apple. Shoot, I didn't want to ever see one again.

Abbie laughed at me as she stirred the water in the half barrel we were using to wash the apples. "It's hard work, but you won't think of that whenever Maggie makes some of her fried apple pies or we have her hot biscuits slathered with apple butter this winter." She took a long, indulgent sniff. "And don't they smell like heaven?"

I had to admit they did even as I stretched the stiffness out of my back and neck. "There has to be an easier way, though." I gestured to the bushel basket of apples sitting beside the table. "And we didn't even use all the apples."

"Nope, not yet. But those won't need to be peeled or sliced. We'll bury them in sawdust in the root cellar for the winter. They might get a little bit mealy by the time spring gets here but they'll still have that fresh fruit taste. And we'll use the culled ones under the trees to make us some sweet apple sauce."

Abbie smiled when I groaned at this. "With apple sauce, you don't have to peel or core em, just cut em up and toss em in the pot to cook. Once they're soft enough, we'll run em through the sieve to remove the peels and seeds. Then we'll have us a great big crock of apple sauce. We had a good harvest this year so we might even have enough left over to make fruit leather."

"What's fruit leather?"

"We spread a thin layer of apple sauce on a sheet and let it dry. Then we peel it off, roll it up and store it in the root cellar over the winter."

"Why? I mean, what do you do with it?"

"Oh, Maggie has several recipes she uses the leather for or you can just peel off a bit and eat it."

"You eat the leather? Isn't it tough?"

"Not if you prepare it right."

"I think I'll reserve judgment on that. Sounds pretty yucky if you ask me."

Abbie shook her head as she clucked her tongue. "Trust me, long about January, you'll be beggin for it just so's you can get a taste of summer." She stepped back, wiping her hands on her apron. "Here, Lizzie, you set the rest of these out on the towel to dry. I'm goin out to the outhouse for a minute. When I get back, we'll cut em into quarters then I'll bank the fire and we'll put em in that big pot with some water and let em start cookin. Maggie and Sarie can run em through the sieve for apple sauce tonight while we're out searchin for poor Mr. Westcott and his people."

I leaned over the barrel, pulled out a couple of apples and set them on the towel Abbie had covered the table with, praying fervently as Abbie walked out the door that I wouldn't be around to taste the apple sauce or the fried apple pies.

I missed my home so much I ached for it, and as I stood there picking the apples out of the water and placing them on the towel to dry, I thought about Halloween, trick or treating with my mom and dad when I was little, dressed up in a costume I had planned for months, and one party when I was sixteen where we bobbed for apples. That was the night I'd gotten my first kiss from a boy named Paul who went on to become my first love. I smiled as I remembered he'd given me a ring he got out of a gumball machine. I jumped as Abbie walked back in the door, jerking me out of my memories. It surprised me as much as her when I burst into tears, as the pang of homesickness washed over me again.

"Oh, Lizzie," Abbie said as she rushed over to give me a hug. "What's wrong, honey? Did you hurt yourself?"

"No, I'm okay. Really I am."

"Then why are you cryin?" She drew away and slipped a handkerchief out of the waistband of her apron, handing it to me.

I wiped my eyes and blew my nose. My voice shook when I spoke. "Oh, Abbie, I'm sorry for losing my cool and blubbering all over you." I crumpled the handkerchief in my hand. "It's just, taking the apples out of the water reminded me of happy memories from home and it hurt so much. I want to go home, Abbie, I want to go now."

Abbie wrapped her arms around me, rocking me gently as she held on. I drew in a deep breath, trying to calm myself down, but as I let it out, it turned into another sob as a terrible thought flew into my mind, almost doubling me over in horror and panic. "Oh, Lord, Abbie."

"What is it, Lizzie?"

"I just had a terrible thought about the lights and Mr. Westcott. What if my light took him or maybe one of his men? Or all of them even. Could it do that?"

Abbie thought for a moment. "I don't know, Lizzie, but I don't think so. Next time we see Pokni, we'll ask her. She knows more about the lights than anybody I know but I ain't never heared her say nothin about that."

I tried to say something, but the thought that it was possible had me so upset, I couldn't get anything out.

Abbie guided me over to one of the chairs we'd pushed back from the table while we were working. She took the crumpled handkerchief from me and replaced it with a small towel which I immediately buried my face in.

"Lizzie, listen to me." She took my shoulders and gave me a little shake. "You listen to me now."

I hitched in a breath as I uncovered my face so I could look at her.

"You hearin me now?" she asked as her hands gentled on my shoulders.

I nodded.

"You're gettin all het up over nothin, honey. You don't know if that's possible. What made you think of it, anyway?"

I shook my head. "I don't know. It just popped into my head."

"We'll go by Pokni's tonight afore we do anything. I don't reckon she knows for sure if somebody else can go through your light, but I don't think they can. I think the light you came through is your light, it only works for you." She smiled suddenly. "You said it took you when you touched the center of the light. Ain't that right, Lizzie?"

I thought for a moment then nodded. "Yes. When I touched the outer rim, the orange part edging the white light, it just gave me a slight shock. But when I touched the dark hole in the center, it sucked me right in and transported me here. Why?"

"Think about it, Lizzie. I was watchin Constable Jackson when he was runnin toward it. When he knocked you down, he put out his hand, tryin to shove the light away or maybe just to stop hisself. He was right in front of it and he touched it in the black center too. And all it did was knock him flat on his backside. If it could take anybody else, why didn't it take him 'stead of pushin him away like that?"

I had to admit she had a point. I hitched in another breath as I wiped my face on the towel then did my best to slow my breathing so I could talk. After about a minute, I nodded. "I guess you're right. Thank you, Abbie."

She smiled. "Ain't no use a'tall wasting all this worry until we talk to Pokni but I'm guessin she can't tell you nothin."

"Yes, you're probably right but I would like to go see her anyway. For some reason, talking to her always calms me down."

"Truth be known, I reckon it's more 'cause you like them nasty smelly tobacco sticks she gives you."

That drew a laugh out of me. I couldn't argue with Abbie's logic so went back to picking the apples out of the barrel.

As Abbie predicted, Pokni didn't have a solid answer to my question, although she too seemed to think that I had somehow laid claim to the light I came through and only I could go back through it. This relieved my mind somewhat but did not ease my anxiousness over finding that light and being gone from this place.

Although many people pitched in and searched the mountain for Mr. Westcott and his two slaves, they were never found. It wasn't long before the searchers gave up but the disappearance was still talked about as time went on. Over the years, the story would become a part of the legends and mystery surrounding the Brown Mountain lights. It was, in fact, one of the stories I heard from the garage mechanic when Ben's van broke down over a hundred years in the future.

Chapter Four

Fall 1859

It's All Over Now

Fall stayed around for a good while that year, showing off her vibrant colors as leaves died and fell to the ground. The weather stayed mild except for chilly nights and mornings, and the air seemed so pure and clean, I thought it a miracle people in my time didn't suffer more from pollution. Winter made itself known from time to time, promising snow and colder weather, but for the most part seemed content to let fall linger a bit more.

I was busy grooming Buck early one morning when I heard a woman's panicked voice near the cabin. I gave Buck a quick kiss between the eyes then hurried out of the barn to see what was going on. When I spied a young woman carrying an unconscious child in her arms, I ran toward her just as the door to the cabin opened and Abbie stepped onto the porch. We reached the woman at the same time as she fell to her knees, the boy almost toppling out of her arms. I caught him and eased him to the ground, noting the drool flowing from his mouth and the way his arms and legs kept twitching. I put my fingers to his neck, felt the irregular pulse, as Abbie said, "Janie, what happened to your boy?"

"I don't know," Janie wailed.

I glanced up at Abbie, who was watching me. "Is he epileptic?" When she gave me a confused look, I turned to Janie, who I gauged couldn't be much older than a teenager, and put a hand on her shoulder to draw her attention. "Is your son here prone to fits?"

Janie shook her head before returning her attention to the boy. "Billy's right healthy. But this mornin, when he come in for breakfast, he said he felt right weak then started shakin like that. I reckon he's done it twice more since." She reached out to touch him, her hands trembling with panic and anxiety.

I lifted his lids to check his eyes, which dilated normally from the light, felt his skin which was clammy and warm. I opened his mouth and examined the tongue. It didn't look like he'd bitten it while seizing. I leaned close and sniffed, wondering if this could be a seizure from diabetes, but his breath didn't smell sweet. "Has he had a high fever lately?"

Janie shook her head. "He ain't been sick in a coon's age."

Brain tumor, I thought, or brain infection or one of a host of diseases that could cause seizing. "Is there a history of epilepsy in your family?"

She shook her head. "I ain't real certain what you mean, but if'n you're talkin about fits like this, I don't know of none." She grabbed my hand. "Please, you got to help my boy. He's all I got in this world and I can't lose him."

"We'll do everything we can, I promise. Let's get him inside, Abbie." I put my arms beneath his shoulders and waited while Abbie grabbed hold of his feet. We lifted him, his mother supporting his back, and carried him like this into the cabin. I was relieved Abbie had cleared the breakfast dishes and the table was bare as we eased him gently onto the wooden surface. I stepped back, watching as the twitching eased and he finally lay still. Abbie used her apron to wipe the spittle from his mouth and chin while I frantically thought through what could be causing the boy's unconscious state and twitching limbs.

I turned to Abbie. "Could it be something poisonous?"

She shrugged. "I reckon it could be. I can't think of anything else to cause somethin like this." She turned to Janie. "Has he eat anything he shouldn't, Janie?"

Janie turned her attention away from her boy and straightened up. "If he did, I didn't see it."

"Drunk moonshine from a galvanized container?" Abbie said. She glanced at me. "We had a man near die after doin that just last year."

Janie shook her head and when she spoke her voice was raw with emotion. "I don't keep any liquor on my land, not after what his pa done."

Abbie didn't pursue that statement and I made a mental note to ask her later what had happened with the boy's father.

"No one else around you has had any fits like this?" I asked her.

She thought about it for a moment and shook her head. "Nary a one." She hesitated as if a thought had occurred.

"What is it?"

"Tweren't a person, but our cow got mighty sick this past week. She was staggerin around, spit comin out of her mouth, a-twitchin all over." She sighed. "I was a-feared she was gonna die on me and didn't know what I was gonna do. I need her for the milk, you see, for my boy."

"She recovered?"

"A day or two later, she was fine. Back to grazin at least."

"Did you give your boy the milk while she was sick?"

She shook her head. "No, I didn't trust what might be wrong with ol' Beulah. I didn't want her to pass it on to my boy."

I walked around the table, watching Billy, thinking hard. First the cow, then the boy. My mind kept returning to poison. I wondered what could be on the mountain that might be toxic to animals and humans alike. "Has he had anything at all lately that you've had to treat, maybe with herbs?"

"Just some nasty ol' head lice I didn't think I'd ever get rid of. We got some larkspur growin in our meadow and I remembered my granny used to use that to treat lice. So I picked em and made up a powder for his head."

My interest pricked. "Larkspur?"

She nodded. "Granny also used oxeye daisies but I couldn't find none of them."

My eyes met Abbie's and I saw the alarm in hers.

"Abbie, what do you treat lice with?" I asked.

"Vinegar mostly. Our granny said to stay away from larkspur and daisies and mums 'cause they do more harm than good."

I nodded. "My mother was a botanist." I noted their confused looks. "She studied flowers and herbs, and if I remember right, she said sometimes the prettiest flowers were the most deadliest." I nodded as it came back to me and I could hear her voice perfectly in my mind. "Larkspur and oxeye daisies were once used to treat lice because they have a chemical, pyrethrum, which is insecticidal but is toxic to humans and animals." I glanced at Janie. "You're lucky your cow didn't die, larkspur is extremely poisonous to cows and horses."

"Oh, Lordy," she said in a low moan. "You reckon it's gonna kill my boy?"

I didn't know how to answer her. "Abbie?"

She chose to ignore the question as she asked, "You reckon if we wash his hair and get that larkspur powder out, it'll help?"

"It couldn't hurt." I went to the long, wooden countertop for a bowl and pitcher of water. "Janie, could he have eaten the powder you made, you reckon?" I asked, thinking how much I was beginning to sound like a mountaineer.

"If'n he did, I didn't see it, but it's right possible. Oh, Lordy," she moaned. "I shoulda throwed it out after I used it but I figured I'd keep it for later, if it happened again." She shook her head. "All the young'uns on this mountain got lice, they just pass it back and forth a-tween them."

While Abbie held Billy's head, I poured water over his hair, watching as dead lice fell into the bowl. When one moved, I screeched and almost dropped the pitcher. I didn't miss Abbie's amused look and knew I'd be scratching at imagined lice crawling all over me the rest of the day.

"Fetch that lye soap over there and wash his scalp with it, Lizzie," she said.

After I lathered Billy's scalp and rinsed with water twice more, we put his head back down. "You think we ought to pour vinegar over his scalp just to make sure all those lice are dead and gone?" I asked Abbie.

She smiled. "If'n it'll set your mind at rest, I reckon that will do it."

So once more I poured a liquid over Billy's scalp while Abbie held his head. I was relieved to see no more lice jumping out at me. After I rinsed and dried his hair, I checked his vital signs. His pulse was still a bit erratic but not as fluttery as before, and he hadn't seized since we'd put him on the table.

"You reckon he's better?" Janie asked, tenderly touching her boy's cheek.

"Maybe so. I wish he was awake so we could give him charcoal."

Abbie frowned at me. "What fer?"

"To absorb the poison in his stomach if he ate any."

She nodded in agreement. "I reckon we'll just have to wait and see how he fares." She went to Janie and took her arm. "Come on over by the fire, Janie, and sit while I make us some tea."

Janie didn't seem to want to leave her son. "You reckon he'll be all right, Abbie?" She looked at me and her eyes were wild with distress. When she spoke, her voice broke. "I can't lose my boy."

I reached over and patted her hand. "It didn't kill your cow and hopefully Billy didn't ingest enough to do anything other than affect him neurologically. If that's so, he should be better by tomorrow."

She grasped my hand with hers. "Thank you both. I knew if anybody on this mountain could help me, it'd be you'uns."

As we sat before the fire drinking our tea, I resisted the urge to scratch, feeling phantom lice crawling on my scalp and all over my body. Of course, I knew they were prevalent on the mountain due to poor hygiene. How could they not be with such primitive conditions and among people who bathed once a month if that and lived packed into a one-room cabin. And I had seen them before, but at other cabins or places, where I left them behind when I took my leave. Here, I worried they might somehow burrow into the table or floor, ready to leap up and attach to me as I walked past. My eyes kept darting to the boy's head, searching for signs of lice jumping onto the table. I was so focused on this, I didn't hear the door open, and it was only when I felt cold air brush across my face that I realized someone had come inside. I looked up, expecting to see Maggie or Sarie, but instead spied an old man leaning against the door, holding his chest and breathing raspily. Abbie jumped to her feet and rushed over to him, managing to catch him as he collapsed onto the wooden floor. I set my cup of tea down and went to join her, both of us kneeling at his side, watching as he struggled for air.

Janie appeared next to me, saying, "If you'uns will drag him on inside, I'll get this door closed. Don't want my boy to catch pneumony on top of what's ailing him."

I looked at Abbie and read the message in her eyes: looked like this would be a day for hauling bodies around. She nodded at me and we both managed to get our shoulders under each arm and pulled him to his feet. We carried him to the rag rug in front of the fire and as gently as we could lay him on his back.

"I need a pillow." I placed my fingers over his wrist, feeling for a pulse, as I watched the rise and fall of his chest while Abbie went into the bedroom to fetch one. I used it to prop his head up, hoping to ease his breathing. He blinked several times then focused on me, watching as I tried to get the shirt loosened around his neck. I imagined it had once been white but was so old and worn, I feared I might tear the dingy material. I smiled at him. "Let's see if we can get you feeling better."

"I don't reckon that's a-gonna happen," he said in a wheezy voice. "I been this way fer a good long while now."

I glanced at Abbie, raising my eyebrows, mentally asking if she knew this man.

She nodded. "This here's Luther Spradlin, he lives about a mile up the mountain."

"Nice to meet you, Luther. I'm Lizzie." I patted his hand, noting his pallor beneath his gray beard which hung down to his chest. "When did you start having trouble breathing, Luther?"

"Oh, I have spells on and off," he managed to wheeze. "This here's the worst one yet. I was a-feared I'd pass out afore I got here, but I'm glad to see I made it."

Thinking it might be pneumonia, I said, "Have you had a bad cold recently, Luther?"

He shook his head, rummaging in his pocket and pulling out a stained, tattered handkerchief which he put to his mouth when he began coughing. He pulled it away and my mouth opened in alarm when I saw fresh blood on the hankie.

"Abbie, we need to cover our faces," I said.

"Whatever for?"

I nodded toward the hankie. Without a word, she got to her feet and went into the bedroom, returning a moment later with a kerchief for her and one for me.

She sat next to me as we tied them, covering our noses and mouths, then leaned close to whisper, "What is it, Lizzie?"

I shook my head. "Could be anything, but coughing spreads germs and we don't want to get whatever he has if he's contagious." I looked around for Janie, relieved to see her standing by her son, rubbing his arm while watching us.

"You don't reckon he's got somethin he can pass on to Billy, do you?" she asked with alarm.

"As long as you both stay over there, you should be fine." I turned my attention back to Luther. He seemed to be in a daze and I had to shake his arm a couple of times to get his attention. "How long have you had these spells, Luther?"

His eyes widened when he noticed our covered faces but he didn't comment. "Like I said, I've had spells like this for a good while now."

"Don't be alarmed by the kerchiefs. We're just protecting ourselves in case you have anything contagious."

He nodded.

"When did you start coughing up blood?"

"Oh, I reckon I've done that on and off through the years but lately it don't seem to stop." He put the hankie up to his mouth when he began coughing again. I leaned away from him, putting out my hand to guide Abbie back as well.

When he finished, I touched his arm to get his attention. "Are you a smoker, Luther?"

He looked confused at this.

"Do you smoke tobacco?"

"I smoked a bit when I was a young whelp, but when I started mining I figured it'd be too dangerous so give it up."

"Mining? You were a miner?"

"Yes'm."

"Coal?"

"No'm, gold."

"Gold?" I looked at Abbie. "There's gold mining around here?"

"Sure is. Back in the '30s, they found gold in the mountains around here and a whole flock of people come down thinkin to get rich from it. They's at least three mines I know of close by. Most of it petered out right quick but they's still some mining done. We hear about somebody findin gold ever once in awhile, although I don't reckon it's worth much."

Luther nodded in agreement. "I come from the Uwharrie Mountains over to the east of here, near Charlotte. That's where I started working the mines when I weren't much older than you, I reckon. Heard there was gold down this away so come on down and worked in the Hercules Mine, 'bout 10 or 15 miles north of here."

Abbie nodded. "Placer mining or lode mining, Luther?"

"Lode it was."

"What's the difference?" I asked Abbie.

"Placer mining's what you'd call panning for gold, I reckon, in streams and such. Lode mining's diggin for the gold that's inside a rock, like in a mountain." She looked at

Luther. "Is that right, Luther? You were a miner inside a mountain?"

He nodded weakly. "Got to where I couldn't work a whole day so I bought ol' Hiram Lydle's place up the mountain and figured I'd live out the rest of my life doing what farmin I could to get by."

Gold dust, I thought, leading to hemoptysis which could mean anything from emphysema to pulmonary tuberculosis to lung cancer. And tuberculosis was highly contagious. I turned once more to Abbie. "Have you had any episodes of tuberculosis on the mountain?"

She raised her eyebrows. I searched my memory for what it might have been called in the past but couldn't come up with anything. "People like Luther here, coughing up blood, feeling poorly, spreading it to others?" I lowered my voice. "Some dying from it?"

Her eyes grew alarmed. "Sounds like what we call consumption. I reckon we get flare-ups from time to time." She shrugged. "Some survive, some don't. But I ain't heared of any lately."

I felt Luther's forehead, hoping for signs of a fever which could mean a respiratory or bronchial infection. He was warm, but not overly so.

"What other symptoms do you have, Luther?"

The look he gave me was one I knew well by now.

"Have you been running a fever? Are you feeling poorly?"

"Oh, yes'm. I shore do feel poorly. Tired all the time."

"Have you lost weight recently?"

He shrugged his frail shoulders. "Mayhap. Don't have no appetite no more."

"Pain in your chest?"

"Oh, yes'm, near about all the time now."

And the cough. My guess was either lung cancer or tuberculosis and, God help me, I hoped it was lung cancer although I knew poor Luther would be in for a bad time of it. But tuberculosis was airborne, easy to catch from being around anyone coughing, and it could sweep through this mountain in no time. But I had no way to diagnose which it could be. No means to do a chest x-ray or sputum test, not even a blood test.

"What about fevers, Luther? Have you had any chills or night sweats?"

"Had a few." He closed his eyes and sighed. "I sure am tired, Miss Lizzie."

I patted his shoulder. "We'll make you as comfortable as we can, Luther. You rest now while we get some medicine for you."

I stood up, watching as Abbie did the same, then motioned for her to join me in the kitchen. "What do you do for consumption, Abbie?" I asked as I pulled the kerchief off my face.

"You reckon that's what it is?"

"I'm not sure. I'd say it's either lung cancer or tuberculosis, what you probably call consumption. We can't really do anything for him at this point except treat the symptoms, help ease his pain. But I think we need to keep our faces covered when we're around him."

She nodded. "If I remember right, Sarie says they's several things we can use to treat consumption." She began to rummage in the cupboard containing their herbal medicines. "We got hyssop we can make a tea from, that helps when a body's got a bad cold and can't breathe too good." She pulled out some roots and showed them to me.

"We'll need something along the lines of an antibiotic, although I fear it's too late for that if he has TB," I muttered to myself. I found cone flower roots and showed them to Abbie, who had gone to the hearth to put the kettle on the hook over the fireplace. "We'll also use these."

I watched Luther while the water boiled, noting his skin seemed even paler as he struggled to breathe. Poor man. I wished for the medical treatments of my time for tuberculosis and cancer, which might not save him but could hopefully make him more comfortable.

We spent the next several hours tending to Luther, who seemed to pass in and out of consciousness. Janie proved helpful, cleaning up the mess we'd made treating Billy's lice, then making us all a late lunch and clearing away the dishes after we'd eaten. Afterward, she kept vigil at the table, staring at Billy, who now appeared to be in a deep sleep. I kept watch for further signs of a seizure but that seemed to have passed. Not long after lunch, I heard Janie gasp behind me and turned around, smiling as I watched her son rise up on elbows and look around the room. I quickly washed my hands and hurried over to them.

"How are you feeling, Billy?" I said, putting the back of my hand against his forehead, checking for fever, relieved to see he wasn't seizing.

"I reckon I'm all right." He turned to his mother. "Where are we, Ma? What happened?"

She put her hands on him, running them over his shoulders and down his arms. "Oh, thank the good Lord you're all right, Billy."

"You're at Miss Abbie's cabin," I told him. "You had a spell and your mama brought you here to us."

He frowned at me. "Why you coverin your face like that?"

I pulled the kerchief down. "We're taking precautions against ..." My voice trailed off when I realized he didn't understand. "We want to make sure we don't get what Luther over there has." I gestured toward Luther, prone on the floor.

Billy shrugged as if it made no never-mind to him.

I helped him sit up. "Billy, did you eat something lately, different from what you normally eat?"

He glanced at his mother before looking down, his face reddening.

"It's all right, Billy, if you did. We just need to know what caused you to be so ill."

"I only ate a little bit. It didn't taste good so I spit most of it out."

"The powder your ma made to treat your lice?"

He nodded then looked at his mother. "I'm right sorry, Ma. I figured if them lice was on my head, they might be in my body too, making me itch all over, and maybe if I took some, like medicine, it'd make me stop itchin so bad."

Janie put her hand to his cheek. "Well, I reckon you thought you was doin the right thing, Billy, but next time ask me afore you do somethin like that."

"Your ma's right, Billy. Next time be sure to ask her, all right?"

He nodded.

"Do you feel well enough to stand?"

Without responding, he slid off the table and stood although he seemed weak, swaying a bit. He glanced out the window. "It's gonna be dark soon, Ma, we need to get on home and make sure Beulah's put up for the night."

Janie's eyes met mine. "Is it all right? Can we go?"

I would have preferred they stay overnight, but with Luther here, possibly contagious, it would be better if they were away from him. "Yes, but if he starts to have fits again, you come right back or send for us." I touched Billy's arm as he began to move away. "You'll probably feel weak for a day or two, Billy, so try to rest as much as you can and don't overdo."

"I ain't got time for rest, I got a farm to take care of," he said, sounding as old as Luther.

Janie pulled me into a hug. "I can't thank you enough for savin my boy."

I smiled at her. "We didn't save him, Janie. I think he would have been all right. Just make sure you dispose of the rest of that powder."

She nodded. "Oh, I'll do that first thing I get home."

"And keep Beulah away from that patch of larkspur."

"Don't you worry none about that, I'll keep her away till we can weed it out," Billy said.

"Here, Billy," Abbie said as she held out two biscuits left over from breakfast, loosely wrapped in a towel. "You ain't had nothin to eat all day and I reckon you're hungry. This should hold you over till you get home."

Billy thanked her as Janie stepped over and hugged Abbie then bade her goodbye, steering her son in a wide berth around Luther.

After I shut the door behind them, I joined Abbie, who was trying to get Luther to drink, but he had either fallen asleep or passed into unconsciousness. "We need to make him more comfortable, Abbie. Lord knows, we can't drag him into the bedroom. You think we can make a pallet on the floor?"

"I reckon so. Why don't you fetch a couple of quilts out of Mama's chest in the bedroom? We'll at least get him off the floor and onto something a bit softer."

I hurried into the bedroom and lifted the lid of the chest, resisting the urge to dig beneath the linen and clothing to my treasures at the bottom. I pulled out two quilts and returned to the living room, where I folded each one and put them on the floor next to Luther. It took some maneuvering but we finally managed to get him onto the pallet. Although he was not a tall man and couldn't have weighed much more than a hundred and twenty pounds, his dead weight was hard to manipulate and we were both sweating by the time we got him on the quilts. I sat back, wiping my forehead with my apron.

"He ain't long for this world," Abbie said in a whisper.

"You think so?"

"Yep. I can feel a force around him, like somethin's come to claim his body."

That gave me goose bumps. "Have you ever felt it before, Abbie?"

"Oh, a few times, I reckon. Liked to scared me to death the first time but I've come to accept it. It ain't an evil thing I'm feelin, just something that's waitin, bidin it's time, I reckon, to take poor ol' Luther's soul away with it."

I shook my head, trying to force out of my mind the image of a winged creature carrying away Luther's immortal soul. "I don't know that there's anything more we can do for him except try to keep him as warm and comfortable as possible." I fetched a large bowl from the kitchen along with a cloth and lye soap. After pouring water from the kettle into the bowl, I knelt beside him.

Abbie said, "What are you gonna do?"

"Wash some of this dirt off his face and hands. It might make him feel a bit better. I know I do when I've cleaned up." I bathed his face as gently as I could, noting the grime

60

embedded in the pores. "Another mountain man that doesn't bathe as often as he should," I observed.

Abbie snorted. "I bet your sweetheart Josh takes a lot of baths. I ain't never seen him dirty even when we was kids."

I was glad the kerchief hid my mouth so she couldn't see my smile at his name. Although I hadn't seen much of Josh since the incident with the light, he was a constant intruder into my thoughts and dreams.

The door opened and we glanced up, both, I'm sure, relieved to see Sarie and Maggie, the two dogs on their heels. When the sisters noted Luther on the floor, they quickly removed their scarves and shawls as they hurried over to us. Billy and Bob joined them, sniffing at Luther before retreating to the kitchen. They know, I thought.

"Don't get close to him," I said. "He's contagious."

Sarie and Maggie both froze, waiting for an explanation.

"He's coughing up blood. I think it's either consumption or lung cancer."

Sarie nodded. "He was a miner, I reckon it's one or t'other. Lord knows, we've seen a lot of sickness like this with miners on the mountain." She retrieved her scarf and wrapped it around her lower face before kneeling beside us. "What are you doin for the poor soul?"

"We been treating him with hyssop and cone flower," Abbie said. "But he don't stay awake long enough to get a good dose in." She shrugged. "Don't reckon it matters now, anyhow," she lowered her voice, "he's well on his way to dyin."

Maggie nodded as if she agreed. "Only thing to do is make him comfortable." She headed toward the kitchen. "I'll fix us some supper while we wait."

Dinner was a solemn affair, each of us continually glancing at Luther, listening to his rasping breaths, waiting for him to either wake up or die, which I found macabre. Abbie finally broke the silence, telling Maggie and Sarie about Billy.

I barely listened, once more grieving my presence in this time and place, wishing to be where death was not so brutal, where Luther would have at least been much more comfortable as he traversed the path from here to there.

After the dishes were washed and put away, Sarie said, "We need to sit with him tonight. I reckon we can do it in shifts."

"I'll sit up with him," I said. "I don't mind, really. I don't think I could sleep anyway."

"Are you sure, Lizzie?" Abbie asked.

"Yes." I squeezed her hand. "It's been a trying day, Abbie." I looked at Sarie and Maggie. "You two have been gone all day, I know you're tired, so y'all go on to bed. I'll let you know if anything happens."

"Holler if you need me," Abbie said.

Sarie gave me a long look before following Maggie into the bedroom.

So I sat on the floor beside Luther that night, occasionally touching him, trying to let him know he was not alone on this journey. Billy and Bob, whom I had found to be wonderful snugglers, kept their distance, lying under the table and keeping watch as well. I got up, stoked the fire, then sat in the rocker, wrapping my shawl around me, waiting. When Luther stirred, I knelt beside him, putting my hand on his forehead. He opened his eyes and stared at me with such clarity it sent a shiver through my body.

"I thought you was an angel," he said, his voice low.

I smiled at him. "Do you think you can take some tea, Luther?"

He shook his head. "I reckon you know by now it won't do no good. I'd just as soon not."

I nodded. "Do you have any family we can fetch for you, Luther?" I asked, dismayed that I hadn't thought of it sooner.

"Oh no, ma'am. I'm all alone in this world 'ceptin for my mule." He sighed, then with a strength that surprised me, grabbed my hand. "Miss Lizzie, do you reckon after I'm gone, you can go fetch ol' Jonah and care for him?" He put the handkerchief to his mouth and coughed into it. After the spell passed, he continued. "He's been my friend and loyal companion since I come to this part of the country and I don't want him to die on his own or at the hands of some ol' mountaineer who might think he'd be a tasty treat."

I squeezed his hand. "I promise, we'll bring him here and take good care of him if anything happens to you, Luther. But you may feel well enough to go home before long."

He shook his head. "I'm goin home, I reckon, but not there." He sighed with such regret, it tore my heart.

Thinking to distract him, I said, "Did you ever marry, Luther?"

He shook his head. "Come close once but I was a fool. Pining for what lay ahead of me instead of being thankful for what I had. She was a beauty, my Dorothy, tall like you, with dark hair and eyes. To me, she was like the sun shinin through the clouds on a rainy day, filled my life with warmth and light. And loved me well enough to tell me she'd wait for me. So off I went to the mines, thinkin I'd strike gold and go back to her a rich man." I waited as he coughed into the handkerchief again. "But the years passed and it never happened and pride got in the way and I never returned to her, shamed that I would go back a poor man and not rich like I claimed I would be."

I patted his hand. "I'm sure she would have understood, Luther."

"She didn't deserve what I did to her. Why, I reckon if I'd married her, I'd have lived a happy life, with a family and love. Instead, all I got was loneliness and a miserly way of life, with nothin to love but ol' Jonah."

I smiled at him. "But you knew love, Luther, at least you had that."

He surprised me by returning my smile. "And I see you have too, Miss Lizzie." His look grew intense. "Don't be a prideful fool like me, thinkin somethin better's ahead of you." He put the handkerchief to his mouth once more, and while he coughed, his words resonated in my mind. How did he know that's exactly what I had been doing since I came to this place, I wondered.

Luther lay back, spent, breathing heavily, and said in a weak voice, "Live your life like you ain't got no future."

I reached over and held his hand. "I wish I could do more for you, Luther."

He turned his head to me. "You've been awful kind to this old man, Lizzie. I hope you don't mind me askin you to look after my things when I'm gone."

"Certainly. Is there anyone you want me to contact, anyone you want me to give your things to?"

He shook his head. "Ain't got no family left and my friends has all died on me." He studied me for a moment. "You've been so kind to me, I reckon I'd like you to have my things, if you've a mind to. A-course, if you don't want em, that's all right too, I reckon. But you're welcome to anything of mine you'd like."

I squeezed his hand. "Thank you, Luther. I promise I'll take good care of your things."

He nodded as he closed his eyes.

"Is there anything I can do for you?" I asked.

He nodded weakly. "Can you say somethin from the Bible?"

Tears stung my eyes as I bowed my head and began, "The Lord is my shepherd, I shall not want ..." and when I finished, I looked back at his eyes, open and staring. I put my fingers on the side of his neck, then my hand over his chest. "God rest your sweet soul, Luther," I said, closing his eyes before taking off my apron and placing it over his face then returning to the rocking chair to wait for morning.

Like dinner, breakfast was a macabre affair, each of us staring at Luther's body, thinking our own thoughts.

Sarie finally broke the silence. "What do you reckon we ought to do with his body?"

"Do you not have a funeral home?" I asked.

The sisters gave me blank stares.

"When—where I come from, when a person dies, a mortician takes the body and embalms it then arranges for the burial."

"I ain't sure what you mean by embalming," Abbie said.

"It's a way of preserving the body, using chemicals ..." My voice trailed off when I realized they had no idea what I was talking about. "Does Morganton have an undertaker who buries the body?"

Sarie shrugged. "I ain't got no idea. Up here on the mountain, it's generally left up to the family. They dig a hole, wrap the body in a sheet and drop it in."

"Luther told me he didn't have any family."

Abbie nodded. "He's been alone as long as I've known him."

That reminded me of Jonah. "He asked that we go fetch his mule and take care of him after he passed. He was afraid he might die from neglect or as someone's next meal."

Abbie grimaced at this. "I'll go right after breakfast."

"I'll go with you." I looked at Sarie. "In the meantime, do you think we could bury him, maybe say a prayer over his grave?"

Maggie gave me a look of disbelief. "In case you ain't noticed, it frosted last night. The ground's liable to be too hard to dig."

"Maybe not. We've had some nice weather lately. I'm happy to dig the grave myself."

Sarie surprised me by nodding. "It's only right and proper we see the man has a resting place." She looked at me. "We can bury him on our land in a plot alongside our mother. The sun hits that spot nearly ever day it shines, so the ground shouldn't be too hard." She gathered up her plate and stood. "Maggie and me'll take care of his body while you and Abbie go fetch that mule."

"Thank you, Sarie," I said, rising to my feet, anxious to get this day behind me.

As Abbie and I walked toward Luther's cabin, I was glad the weather of the past few days held and it was relatively mild. I told Abbie what Luther had said to me about holding on to a possible future.

She studied me for a moment. "I reckon what he said makes some sense," she finally said.

"It does. I guess I need to stop hoping for something that might not happen and start living more in the moment."

She smiled. "I reckon Mr. Josh might like that as well."

65

I didn't reply to this. By this time, I knew I was in love with him but had put up a wall between us, trying to distance myself for when I would step through the light into my time and leave him behind. At times, I had had to force myself not to seek him out and relay to him where and when I came from. I wasn't sure if he would believe me or think me depraved and didn't think I was ready to find that out.

When we arrived at Luther's cabin, it surprised me how neat and tidy it appeared from the outside and I wondered if it was the same on the inside. Poor Luther hadn't kept himself clean but I'd only met him the one time and he'd been terribly sick, which could have accounted for his unkempt state. If the way the cabin looked was a reflection of the miner, I figured when he was healthy and felt well, he probably kept himself as neat and tidy as his home.

Abbie drew me out of my thoughts when she said, "Shore is a purty thing, ain't it?"

I smiled. "It is." Not sure if I even had the right to this cabin, I hesitated before going on. "Abbie, Luther told me before he died that I was welcome to any of his things I wanted. Do you think he meant the cabin as well?"

"Well, I reckon so. He said he didn't have no family, and if he give his things to you, they're yours to do with as you want."

"Is that the mountain way? When I came from, family inherits unless there's a will."

"What's that?"

"A Last Will and Testament, a piece of paper, a legal document saying who the deceased wanted to leave his belongings to."

Abbie shrugged. "They might do it that away in Morganton, but up here on the mountain, one man's word's good enough."

I smiled as I looked back at the cabin. "I'd love to see the inside."

She shrugged. "We'll take a look another day. Right now, we best get on with what we come here to do. Sarie and Maggie'll be waitin on us."

We found Luther's mule in a crude makeshift barn that didn't offer much cover from the harsh elements of winter or summer. I stepped into the narrow stall, talking softly to Jonah, thinking what a beautiful animal he was with a body like a horse and ears like a donkey, reddish in color with a blond mane. He put his muzzle into my hand and snorted into it as I stroked it, thinking how soft it was, much like Buck's. Abbie fetched a rope and put it around Jonah's neck and we led him out of the barn and toward home. He followed along docilely enough, occasionally looking back as if searching for Luther.

"Is there any way we can let him know about Luther?" I asked Abbie, watching as Jonah turned his head to look behind us once more.

"We'll let him see his body." She glanced at me. "Animals ain't like us, they don't know they're gonna die one day, but they know death all right." She sighed. "Lord knows, they live with it day and night in these times. Is it the same in your time, Lizzie, are animals still ill-treated?"

I nodded. "I hate to say it is. Dogs, cats and horses are prized by some but not all. Since I've come here, I've begun to think there's something terribly wrong with a person who doesn't look upon animals with kindness and compassion, if not love. I wonder if there isn't a part of their soul missing."

"If truth be told, I think animals are a cut above folks, at least most of the ones I know."

I nodded. "Especially dogs and horses."

"Yep."

When we arrived back at the cabin, we found Sarie and Maggie marking the place for Luther's grave. After cleaning his body, they had wrapped it in a coarse sheet and carried it to the small cemetery. Abbie led Jonah to the corpse, dropping the rope and bending down to unwrap the sheet from around Luther's face. I watched as the mule placed his muzzle on Luther and nudged his chest. He did this a few times before releasing such a sound of grief and agony, goose bumps broke out along my body. Billy and Bob trotted over and began nuzzling the mule as if commiserating with him. I watched this, wiping tears and trying not to cry.

"I'll put him in the barn with Buck," Abbie said, leading him away. "Ol' Buck will help him feel better."

I picked up the shovel next to the marked area and jabbed it into the hard ground. It took several tries before it penetrated. Maggie watched me for a moment then shook her head. "Be right back," she said, heading to the barn. She returned with a spade and began hacking at the ground. An hour later, we hadn't made much progress when I heard Josh's voice nearby. I straightened up, wiping sweat off my forehead with my apron, trying to hide the smile that came to my face unbidden.

"Mornin, Lizzie, Miss Maggie," he said, joining us.

"Good morning to you, Mr. Josh," Maggie said. "You got trouble out your way?"

"Nah. Papa sent me for some of that rheumatiz salve y'all make. This weather hasn't been too kind to his body, I'm afraid. He seems to be in pain more times than not."

Maggie put down the spade. "I'll go fetch you some." I didn't miss the knowing look she gave me before she left.

Josh waited until she was out of hearing distance before speaking. "How are you, Lizzie? I haven't seen you in a good while although I have to tell you you're on my mind near about every minute of the day."

I couldn't stop my smile at that. "And you me," I admitted.

He glanced at the body on the ground. "Who you got beneath that sheet?"

"Luther Spradlin. He died last night. Told me he doesn't have any family so we thought it best we bury him ourselves here in the sisters' family's cemetery."

He nodded. "Christian thing to do. Long as I'm here, I reckon I'll help." He picked up the spade and began chopping away at the ground. I watched him work, noting the musculature of his arms and back, amazed he made more progress in ten minutes than we had in an hour. He glanced up and caught me looking, and I cast my eyes away, embarrassed. When the hole was deep enough, Josh handed me the spade and held out his hand for the shovel. After he smoothed the sides of the grave and leveled the bottom, he put it down. "If you want to go get the sisters, I'll put him in the grave and we can say a prayer over his soul before we bury him."

I put my hand on his forearm. "Thank you, Josh."

He smiled, his beautiful green eyes gleaming. "I reckon I'd do anything for you, Lizzie."

Although I was pleased more than I could say at this, I felt self-conscious and ill-at-ease as my gaze met his. I had seen Josh several times at church since the incident with the light but hadn't really talked to him at length. I realized with a feeling of guilt that I had never explained my behavior to him. We shared an awkward silence before I said, "I know it's been a good while since it happened, but I've been meaning to apologize to you about what happened that night with the light, Josh."

He waved his hand in a dismissive gesture. "Oh, now, don't you worry about that."

"No, I was upset and took it out on you when I shouldn't have."

He studied me for a moment. "Were you trying to get to the light, Lizzie? Is that why you were so upset because Jackson kept you from touching it for some reason?"

How could I explain to him about the lights, I wondered. What could I say?

As if sensing my unease, he shook his head. "It doesn't matter. You had your reasons and you don't need to tell me."

"I do have a good reason. I'll tell you one day, Josh, I promise."

"Well, that's good enough for me."

I sighed with relief, thankful I had a friend in this man. I left to fetch the sisters, and upon our return, we all stood over the grave, staring at Luther's sheet-wrapped body. Sarie led us in prayer then we watched as Josh shoveled the dirt he had removed from the hole back in and packed it down tightly. We gathered rocks from nearby and placed them on top to discourage animals from rooting, then stepped away from the grave.

Abbie wiped her eyes. "I'll make him a headstone."

I squeezed her hand, thinking there was no better soul on earth than our sweet Abbie.

Maggie held out a bundle for Josh. "I reckon we don't need to tell your pa how to use this, since he's used it before."

"No, ma'am, I don't reckon you do." Josh dropped coins into her hand, and I realized I had no idea what currency was used in this time. "I do thank you."

"We thank you," Sarie replied in her brusque manner. "I reckon it would've taken Lizzie and Maggie a week or more to dig that grave, the progress they were making." She looked at Maggie, who, seeming to understand, held the coins out to Josh. "You don't owe us a thing, Mr. Josh," Sarie said.

"I insist you keep the money, Miss Sarie. Lord knows, your salve sure does help my father, and when he feels better physically, we all benefit. He can be a monster when he's in pain." Josh nodded his head to each of us. "I reckon I best get on home with this and tell Papa the sad news about Luther." He looked at me once more, smiled widely, then turned and left.

Abbie nudged me. "Well, I reckon I was wrong. Looks to me like Mr. Josh does get dirty from time to time."

I shook my head, trying not to smile.

Chapter Five

Fall 1859

You Can Make it if You Try

The next day I indulged myself by sleeping late, snuggling under the quilts and enjoying memories of home. I had spent the night lost in dreams about Ben, my father and Thanksgiving. We all sat around the table in Dad's formal dining room, sharing jokes and laughing, eating the wonderful feast his maid, Jessica, had prepared before going home to spend the rest of the day celebrating with her own family. When I woke up, I had a smile on my face despite the fact my cheeks were damp with tears.

I lingered over my morning ablutions until Abbie called me down for breakfast. Her voice cheerful, she yelled, "Come on Lizzie, you don't want to miss a second of this day."

Wondering why this day should be different from any other, I climbed down the ladder. I didn't notice the warmth until I was all the way down and saw the front door standing wide open. Abbie giggled as she watched me rush over to the door, thinking to close it before all the heat in the cabin escaped. When I felt a warm breeze blowing in, I stopped for a second and just gaped.

Abbie giggled again. "Go on Lizzie, go outside. We've

been given a blessin from God."

I walked out and kept going until I was in the yard. Then I just stood there enjoying the feel of the warm breeze blowing gently on my cheeks. I looked up to the sky, threw my arms out and started spinning in circles. When I stopped, I was so dizzy, I would have fallen if Abbie hadn't been there to steady me. I wrapped my arms around her and squeezed. "It's wonderful. It feels like summer again. How long will it last?"

She shrugged. "Probably just a day, maybe two. God sends us these warm spells ever once in a while during the winter. Sarie says it almost makes the cold and snow bearable."

"I don't know about that, but I'll take every day like this I can get."

Maggie stepped outside on the porch, smiling. "Them chickens ain't goin to put the eggs in the basket and bring em to us, Lizzie."

I laughed. I could face even the pecking chickens that day.

Later, after gathering the eggs, eating breakfast, and finishing the many other morning chores, Abbie and I went out to see Jonah.

"He was kinda sad this mornin when I was feedin him and Buck. I just want to check and make sure he's all right," she said as we walked into the dark coolness of the barn.

Abbie went into Jonah's stall and moved over to stand in front of the mule. Facing him, she put her hands gently on either side of his face, laid her forehead against his and closed her eyes. I draped my arms over the stall door, watching the two of them. It was a sight to see and I marveled at her ability to communicate with the animal.

She drew back, opened her eyes and looked into the mule's soulful brown ones. His ears pricked forward as her lips moved. I strained to hear but didn't have any luck. If she'd spoken at all, it was for Jonah's benefit, not mine.

The whole thing put me in mind of a scene from one of Ben's favorite television shows, *Star Trek*. I'd never been a big science fiction fan but had watched several episodes with Ben. There was a character on the show, an alien with pointy ears. I think his name was Speck or Spock or something like that, and he had the uncanny ability to read people's thoughts if he placed his hand on their face, fingers spread from beside the ear to right over the eyebrow, the thumb resting on the chin. When he did that, he could search their mind for whatever he wanted or needed to know.

Abbie's lips moved again, and this time, Jonah raised his head up then lowered it again. It looked as if the mule was agreeing with her. I knew Abbie said she could feel what the animals felt—which was why I would never eat meat again, even if I did return to my time—but I'd never seen this particular performance before.

She slipped her hand under Jonah's mane, gave him a good scratch then turned to me with a smile. "Jonah misses Luther but he understands that his friend has passed on to a better place." She kissed Jonah on his soft muzzle. "I know you're sad but you'll be all right. I promise it will get better with a little more time."

The mule snorted. Abbie smiled then turned to me. "I'm gonna take him up to visit Luther's grave then I'll turn him out with Buck for today. Buck's a big help to him."

I followed behind her as she led Jonah out of his stall and took him outside. Buck stood by the pasture fence watching her and Jonah, and I wondered if he already knew what Abbie had in store for him today. Was she able to communicate with her animals from a distance? Before I could ask, she nodded toward the woods. "Will you go and see what they need, Lizzie? I won't be very long."

I turned and saw an old woman and a young girl emerging from the woods, heading for the front of the house.

I ran across the yard to greet the visitors, hoping they were here for medical reasons. I always enjoyed discovering how the sisters treated different illnesses. Over the past few months, I felt I had learned enough from them about healing with the myriad of plants that grew on the mountain that maybe I could help the visitors myself.

"Hello," I called.

The two stopped and waited for me to catch up to them.

I smiled. "I'm Lizzie. Can I help you with something? Do you need to see one of the sisters?"

Even from several feet away, I could hear the old woman's breath rattling in and out of her chest and looked at her with concern. I had no doubt she was old but couldn't gauge her age. Her hair, though dark, was liberally threaded with white and pulled back into a bun that rested at the nape of her neck. The wrinkled skin on her face was darker than mine, more the shade of Pokni's. I wondered if she might be Cherokee or from some other Indian tribe before I got a good look at her eyes. They were the loveliest shade of blue, almost crystalline.

It took her a few seconds to catch her breath, but when she answered my question, it was in a strong and commanding voice that surprised me. "We's here to see Miss Sarie Collins. We heared she might be able to help us."

Her voice, though powerful, was labored and hoarse like her respiration. I reached out to steady her when she wobbled on her feet.

The young one, who couldn't be more than twelve or thirteen, wrapped her arms protectively around the older woman. "Here, Nonna, lean on me."

When the girl looked up at me, her eyes, the same blue as the old woman's, were full of worry. She looked like a younger version of the older woman, with the same black hair, though hers wasn't streaked with white, pulled back in the same practical bun. She was slim, enough so that she reminded me of a British fashion model, Twiggy, whose picture was splashed all over the magazines in my time.

I smiled reassuringly at her. "Come on, let's take her inside where she can sit. I'll make her some hot tea to drink while she rests. Is she your grandmother?"

The girl didn't respond, watching carefully as the woman straightened her shoulders and moved away from the girl. "Shush, Amanda May, don't carry on so. I'm all right." She turned to me. "The girl's always fussin over me. Law, Manda, I just need to get out of this heat. I swan, it's hot enough out here to roast a cat." She tempered the words with a smile at her companion then turned those amazing eyes on me again. "We need to see Miss Sarie, if'n you please. It's important."

Amanda May moved closer. While she didn't put her arms around the older woman again, I could see she was braced to do so if the woman so much as shivered.

I gestured to the porch as Abbie approached from the pasture. "Can she make it inside, do you think?" I asked Amanda May. "Abbie and I can help if you want." I looked at the old woman. "I mean, if you would allow us to, ma'am."

The woman waved a hand in clear dismissal. "I can walk, been doin it for nigh on ninety years now without any help. Manda'll help if need be."

With that, she turned and proved she could do just that, making it up the two porch steps with only the assistance of the handrail.

Amanda May looked at us, mumbling, "Sorry, she's 88 years old and hates it when she needs help."

"What's her name?" Abbie asked.

"Lily Gibson. She's my great-granny. I call her Nonna."

"Is she sick?"

"No, or at least she says she ain't. She's here to see Miss Sarie about somethin. She won't tell me what it is, though. All she'll say is that she needs to talk to Miss Sarie Collins. Is she here?"

I shook my head. Sarie and Maggie had left earlier for Morganton to check on one of Maggie's pregnant patients. "Sarie isn't here right now but Abbie knows an awful lot about healing and I've learned some too. We'll do whatever we can to help."

Amanda May only shook her head as she stepped up on the porch. "They says Miss Sarie ain't here, Nonna, but they know some healin and might can help."

The old woman glanced at us. "I don't need no healin, Manda. I didn't come here for that. I need to see Miss Sarie. When will she be back?"

Abbie answered, "Shouldn't be long now, she and Maggie left d'rectly after breakfast."

"Can we wait for her? We won't be no trouble to y'all. We'll sit ourselves down on the step there, if'n you don't mind."

Abbie shook her head. "I won't hear of it. It's too hot out here. You can come inside where it's cooler. I'll make you some ginseng tea, that should perk you right up. If you like, you can have somethin to eat too."

"All right. We're much obliged to you."

"Why, it ain't no trouble a'tall." Abbie opened the door wide and waved them inside.

With only a bit of help from her great-granddaughter, Lily made it to the table, taking Sarie's traditional spot at the head.

Abbie stopped me at the door before I could go in. "Sit with them, Lizzie, and keep your eye on the old woman while I make the tea. I'm afraid somethin bad's about to happen to her."

"All right. Can you tell me what I should watch for, Abbie?"

She shook her head. "I only know that somethin's wrong and she'll need our help."

"Okay, um, all right." I went to sit at the table on Miss Lily's right-hand side and across from Amanda May. "Abbie will have the tea ready soon. Would you like something to eat?" I said, addressing both of them.

Miss Lily narrowed her eyes at me. "Did I hear you sayin you been learnin from Miss Sarie?"

I smiled. "Why, yes, I have, from her and Miss Maggie and Miss Abbie too."

"You bound to em?"

"Bound? I'm sorry, I don't know what that means."

She started coughing, almost doubling over with the effort. Abbie rushed over with a cup of water but Miss Lily waved it away.

I watched her carefully as she got the coughing under control then wiped her hand across her mouth. Her breathing had gotten much worse, filling the small cabin with a raspy sound, reminding me of Luther just before he died. She had her eyes closed as if concentrating on something. Or maybe it was just that hard for her to draw in a breath.

My eyes darted to Amanda May when she laid a hand

on Miss Lily's shoulder. "Nonna? Are you—"

Without warning, Miss Lily slumped in her chair. I reached out to keep her from falling. She was as limp as a cooked noodle, gasping for air as she clutched her chest.

Amanda May and I jumped up at the same time. "Abbie, get us a quilt and pillow off the bed," I said. "She needs to lie down." I didn't want to put her on the hard wooden floor of the cabin without anything to protect her from the dampness.

Abbie ran into the other room and grabbed a folded quilt that lay on the chest at the end of the bed. Bringing it back, she snapped it once and allowed it to float down to the floor.

"We need to stretch her out on the quilt," I said to Amanda May. "Gently, gently."

"What's wrong with her?" Amanda May's voice shook.

"I'm not sure. I'll know more after I examine her."

Abbie supported Miss Lily's head as Amanda May and I guided her carefully to the floor.

"What do you think it is, Lizzie?" Abbie whispered as she placed the pillow under the old woman's head.

"I don't know," I said as I felt for a pulse in her neck. Not finding one, I lowered my head to her chest, hoping to hear her heartbeat or feel the rise and fall which would mean she was still breathing. She wasn't.

After a few seconds, I raised my head. "She isn't breathing and I can't feel her heart beat. I think she's had a heart attack." Looking at Amanda May, I asked, "Has she ever passed out like this before?"

Amanda May shook her head as tears ran down her face. "Is she dead? Oh, Lord, please don't let her be dead. She's all I got."

I looked at Abbie. "Any idea what to do?"

Abbie shook her head, "Not if she's dead."

I laid my right hand over her heart, stacked my left one on top and laced my fingers together before I started doing compressions.

"What are you doin, Lizzie?" Abbie asked.

"C ... P ... R," I gasped in between compressions. On the count of five, I tilted Miss Lily's head back, pinched her nose shut with my left hand then leaned down and blew into her mouth. Remembering I should've checked her airway first to make sure it was clear, I scooped my fingers inside her open mouth, relieved to find no blockages. Then I went back to the compressions.

I felt Abbie's hand on my shoulder and looked up. "What can I do to help?"

I started to shake my head. "Noth—yes, there is. Do what I did, pinch her nose shut and blow air into her mouth … now."

It shouldn't have surprised me when Abbie copied my movements exactly, even scooping her fingers in Miss Lily's mouth after she'd breathed into it.

I smiled. "Good. Do it again … now. Just give her your breath every time I say five. You don't need to stick your hand into her mouth again."

I counted the compressions out loud and Abbie breathed on the count of five. I tried to keep count the total number of compressions in my head in order to gauge the time but kept screwing it up. I knew I should be doing about one hundred per minute but without a clock or a watch—how I wished for my Seiko right at that moment—it was hard to judge.

"Ain't got no idea what … in tarnation you're doin but I … sure hope it works," Abbie said in between breathing for Miss Lily.

I looked up. "Tell you later. Just keep breathing."

"All right."

"Will she live?" Amanda May asked. She sounded as breathless as Abbie and I did.

"I surely … hope so … Amanda May," I gasped.

"Can I help? Let me help, please," she sobbed, "She's my Nonna, I need to help."

In between compressions, I showed her where to feel for a pulse, both on the neck and wrist. "Check for a pulse, a bumping here and here. Tell me when you feel one."

She nodded and I prayed she knew what I meant by a pulse.

And of course with all that I lost count of the compressions again. I had no idea how much time we worked on Miss Lily but it was long enough that my arms and back ached with each one and sweat was running down my face.

"Amanda May, can you reach that towel on the table there and wipe Miss Lizzie's face?"

I looked up and smiled at Abbie, silently giving thanks that she was here with me. Amanda May grabbed the towel and hesitantly swiped it across my forehead. "Wipe my whole face, Amanda May. I'm sweating like a stuck pig here." After she did as I asked, she draped the damp towel over my shoulder and went back to searching for a pulse.

After what seemed like hours but was probably only ten minutes or so, my back and shoulders ached more with every compression and my arms began to shake. My own breathing sounded a lot like Miss Lily's before she had the attack and I wondered how much longer I could continue. Although I longed to quit, I kept on until finally, Amanda May gasped. I stopped immediately and put my fingers on Miss Lily's neck. "Stop, Abbie. She has a pulse. It's thready and weak but her heart's beating." Sitting back on my heels, I smiled as I watched Abbie wet her finger and place it under Miss Lily's nose.

"She's breathing. You did it, Lizzie. I ain't never seen nothin like that. It's a miracle is what it is." She looked up at me and smiled. "You brought her back to life."

"With a little help from my friends." I sang the words to a song that wouldn't be written for at least another one hundred years. My eyes filled with tears at that and I buried my face in my hands.

Abbie moved quickly, pulling me into her arms. "Shh, Lizzie, you saved her. You should be dancing a jig, not crying."

I lifted my head, drying my cheeks with my hands. "I'm not crying because I'm sad, Abbie. These are happy tears. Well, actually, they're tears of relief. I've never done that on a real person and didn't know if it would work. Thank God it did."

Abbie smiled. "Yes, thank God."

"Nonna?" Amanda May still held her great-grandmother's wrist only now she was pressing it to her lips as she whispered, "Nonna, Nonna," over and over again. She'd started crying again but I would stake my life that these were tears of joy and not sadness.

Miss Lily's eyes were fluttering. It appeared she was waking up. When she opened her eyes completely, I knew it wouldn't be long before they closed again. Where before they had been a startling bright blue, now they were dull and clouded. Even without Abbie's special ability, I saw this as a sign of death. That was confirmed when I looked at Abbie. I could see we shared the same thought.

"Nonna? Oh, Nonna, are you all right?" Manda asked.

Miss Lily only said, "Miss Sarie?"

Smiling through her tears, Amanda said, "No, Nonna, it's me, Manda May. Lizzie and Abbie saved you."

Miss Lily looked around, and when her eyes settled on Abbie, she said, "Tell Miss Sarie." She stopped to draw in a raspy breath. "She's your'n now … keep her safe … teach her."

I had no idea what she was talking about but Abbie seemed to. She nodded as she took the woman's hand in her own. "I promise we will, Miss Lily."

She closed her eyes, inhaled a deep breath then let it out. We waited for her to breathe again, and when she didn't, my eyes met Abbie's, who gave me a questioning look. I debated whether we dared try CPR on her again.

"Nonna, Nonna," Amanda wailed as she collapsed on her great-grandmother's chest. "Please, Nonna, don't go. What will I do without you?"

"Lizzie?" Abbie said. "Should we try … whatever you called it?"

"CPR. It's short for cardiopulmonary resuscitation. I'm not sure if we should. She was down so long before and there's a chance if we get her back again she'll have brain damage."

Still, we tried but weren't able to bring her back this time. After about 30 minutes, I stopped and put my hand on Abbie's shoulder. "I think we'd best let her go now."

Amanda May collapsed on her great-grandmother's chest again, sobbing and begging her to open her eyes.

After several minutes of this, Abbie reached out and pulled her away and into her arms. She murmured soothing things to her until Amanda May settled down a bit and pulled away. She bent to her great-grandmother and gently kissed her cheek, whispering, "Good-bye, Nonna, I love you very much. I'll miss you."

I gently folded the quilt over the body. When I got to her face, Amanda let out one sorrowful sob then said, "No, I should do it." We watched as she lovingly draped the soft fabric over Miss Lily's face, kissing her again through the folds of the material.

I turned to Abbie to ask her what we should do with the body when the door opened behind us.

Sarie and Maggie both stopped short then Sarie rushed over to us. "What's goin on here, Abbie?" Her eyes cut to me. "What have you done, girl?"

Abbie sighed. "She ain't done nothing, Sarie, 'ceptin try to save this poor woman's life. She did it too, brought her back from the dead, but then we lost her again."

"Who is she?"

"Miss Lily Gibson and that's her great-granddaughter, Amanda May."

"Where did they come from?"

"Don't know. They showed up here a coupla hours ago. Miss Lily said she wanted to see you, that she'd been told you could help them."

"Help them with what?"

"She never got a chance to say. Right afore she died, she told me to tell you, 'She's your'n now, keep her safe and teach her.' Not sure what that means exactly but that's what she said."

"Well, what in the Sam Hill am I ..." She held up her hand like a traffic cop as Amanda May lifted her head. Her blue eyes were so terribly sad and drenched with tears. I hoped Sarie would cut her some slack and curb her usual bitchiness while she dealt with the girl. She'd just had a heartbreaking loss.

"What's her name again, Abbie?"

"Amanda May. Didn't catch her last name but I reckon

it's Gibson like her great-grandmother's. She called the girl Manda May."

Maggie handed Amanda May a handkerchief then patted her on the shoulder. "I'm so sorry, child." She straightened up. "I'll make her some St. John's wort tea."

Abbie stood up with her. "The kettle's beside the fire but it's probably cold by now. I moved it off the fire when Miss Lily collapsed."

Sarie reached out and lifted Amanda May's chin then simply sat there and stared at her. After several minutes, she said, "Where did you and your great-grandmother come from?"

Amanda May sniffed then wiped her cheeks with the handkerchief. "Pert near up to the Virginia border. We been walking fer awhile, nigh on a week, I guess."

"Did your great-grandmother tell you why you made the journey, why she wanted to see me?"

"No, only thing she would tell me was she had to see you afore it was too late."

"How did she know my name?"

Amanda May shrugged. "Must'a got it from somebody in town. All I know is she come home one day from treating Mr. Shepherd's bursitis and said we was goin on a trip. When I asked her where and why we had to go, she would only say she needed to see Miss Sarie Collins on Brown Mountain, outside of Morganton, that you could help her."

Sarie frowned. "Your great-grandmother was a healer, then?"

"Yes'm, she was. She took care of pert near ever'body in our town."

"Had she been teachin you?"

"Little bit but not for long. She didn't really have the chance."

Sarie nodded. "You sit here with your Nonna and drink the tea Maggie's gonna bring you soon as its ready." She laid a gentle hand on Amanda May's shoulder then stood up. "I need to talk to my sisters for a minute. Lizzie, you come too."

That surprised me. It wasn't often that Sarie included me

in the pow-wows she had with her sisters. In fact, she had a rather annoying habit of shutting her mouth whenever I came into the room which always made me think she was talking about me.

She led me over to the fireplace where Maggie and Abbie were waiting for the kettle to boil. We huddled together and Sarie said, "I think her great-grandmother brought her here so she could leave her with us as a bound girl."

Abbie gasped while Maggie clicked her tongue and shook her head.

I had no earthly idea what Sarie was talking about. Miss Lily had wanted to know if I was bound to the sisters. Could this be what she meant? "Bound? What does that mean?"

"It's a girl or boy whose parents or guardians turn over to others when they can't take care of em. They give em to another person, usually a businessman or some kind of tradesman, for seven or so years so the child can learn a trade. I reckon her great-grandmother was a healer and was tryin to teach her but knew she was runnin out of time so she brought her here for us to train. If we accept her, she'll live with us and we'll have to feed and clothe her too."

I wasn't sure I was hearing right. "Wait, she's going to stay here and work for us?" My mind seemed to be stuck on only that fact. "Why, that's a form of slavery, isn't it?"

Sarie frowned. "No, it ain't like slavery in the least."

"But she has to stay here and work for you as she's learning without being paid. That sure sounds like she'll be your slave to me."

Abbie put her hand on my shoulder. "Hold on, Lizzie. Hear Sarie out."

Sarie gave me a disgruntled look. "It's a common enough practice these days. She'll be fed, clothed, and she'll learn a trade she can use to support herself for the rest of her life."

"But if she has to stay—"

"Ain't said nothin about her havin to stay here, girl, so climb down off'n your high horse and listen. She's free to leave anytime she wants."

"But where would she go? She said they've been

walking for over a week. It isn't safe for her to travel on her own."

"No," Maggie said, "especially since she's Melungeon."

"She's what?"

"Melungeon," Abbie said. "They're frowned on. Nobody knows where they come from but they're all over these parts, up in Virginia and over in East Tennessee too. Most of em try to stay away from other people 'cause they treat em bad, as bad as they do the Indians or free Negroes, sometimes even worse. If she tried to travel back to her home, she probably wouldn't make it. They's a lot of mean people out there, and if they see a Melungeon girl travelin on her own, they's just no tellin what they'd do to her."

My mind was spinning. I had never heard of Melungeons or bound girls or bound boys for that matter. I thought I had seen everything this time had to offer but it seemed I hadn't even scratched the surface.

"If she's to stay, we all have to agree to do what her great-grandmother wanted," Sarie said. "We have to teach her our trade, and that means all of us. You too, Lizzie."

I sputtered out an agreement, wondering what I could teach her except to wash her hands before treating someone. I certainly couldn't let her know that I'd come from over a hundred years in the future. The fewer people who knew that, the better.

Chapter Six

Fall 1859

Good Times, Bad Times

The differences between my time in 1969 and this time in 1859 were innumerable and vast, but one of the most unsettling to me was that the sisters had no printed calendar to tell us which day it was. It didn't seem to bother them overly much but I found it frustrating. The times I visited plantations or homes, I would always ask the date then try to remember when I returned to the sisters' cabin to record it and mark days forward from that point on. But we were so busy, most times I forgot, so constantly found myself trying to figure out what day, let along month, we were in.

After a visit to the Adams' plantation to treat a slave suffering from a broken arm, where I was told the day was November 13th, I asked Abbie if Thanksgiving was celebrated on the mountain. I vaguely remembered it wasn't official until President Lincoln proclaimed it a federal holiday to be regularly observed on the fourth Thursday of each November, but that was in 1864, five years in the future.

Abbie gave me a confused look. "Well, a-course we give thanks, Lizzie, but I ain't never heared of Thanksgiving. What's that?"

I told her the story about how the Pilgrims and Indians began the tradition of Thanksgiving after the Pilgrims' first harvest in the New World in October of 1621 and how it would come to be celebrated in November in the future. "So I take it you don't celebrate Thanksgiving here?"

"Nope, but if you want, I reckon we can do it, Lizzie."

I thought about it for a long moment then shook my head. "I'm afraid it'll bring back too many memories of my time before."

Abbie nodded in sympathy then her eyes brightened. "But we do celebrate Christmas. A-course it ain't much. Maggie fixes up a fine meal and we exchange one present apiece 'cause Sarie don't see the need for glad tidings and such. You think you'll be all right with that, Lizzie?"

I smiled at her, my thoughts racing about what exactly I could give as gifts. I had always loved Christmas with all its trappings; decorating, shopping for the perfect present and going downtown to watch as the lights were lit on the big Christmas tree that always stood outside of Miller's, a large department store on Henley Street. When I was really small, my dad would pick me up and sit me on his shoulders so I could see over the heads of the crowd.

I couldn't go shopping now because I had no money nor means, but I was determined to come up with something in the limited time I had. There would be no tree-lighting but I could cut down a small pine or fir tree out in the forest and find something to decorate it. I felt despondent when I realized it wasn't nearly enough, not compared to Christmas in my time. "It'll be fun," I said, forcing a brightness in my voice.

It was a rare occasion for me to find myself alone at the cabin with nothing to do. After breakfast, Abbie had gone off with Maggie to help with a delivery followed shortly thereafter by Sarie and Amanda May to make rounds on the mountain. The recent flu epidemic had affected more than a few families and Sarie felt it her duty each day to check on the old and young, who were more susceptible to pneumonia and death. I was glad for the time by myself, hoping that without distractions, I could finally decide on what to give the sisters and Amanda May as Christmas gifts. After grooming Buck and Jonah, and making sure each had enough hay and water, I headed back to the cabin, my thoughts turned toward savoring a hot cup of tea to warm me up. Although winter hadn't yet officially arrived, was, in fact, only days away, the frosty mornings were testament that it was on its way and would be here soon.

The sound of someone stepping on a broken branch drew my attention toward the surrounding forest. I stood frozen, waiting for whomever was nearby to reveal themselves, praying it wasn't that hateful Constable Jackson.

A young stable boy I recognized from the Hampton Plantation stepped into view, lifting his hand in a wave as he walked toward me. Crossing the small yard to meet him, I wondered if Little Jack was his real name. The little part was obvious, he stood no more than five feet two, if that, although the stubble on his face told me he was well past puberty. I mentally ticked off reasons for his small size: heredity, perhaps his African tribe shared the same gene for short stature; or malnutrition could have possibly stumped his growth. As for Jack, I knew some slaves were given new names when they were brought to a plantation so he possibly could have had a different moniker before Mr. Hampton bought him. I mentally made a note to ask Little Jack what his real name was.

"Mornin, Miss Lizzie," he said when we met.

"Good morning, Little Jack. Is there trouble at the plantation?"

"Yes'm, one of the kitchen maids has got a burnt hand and is in an awful lot of pain. Miss Tillie sent me to see if y'all'd come tend to her if'n you wasn't too busy."

"The sisters are gone but I can come. I'll leave right now."

"Thank you, ma'am. I'll go tell Miss Tillie you're comin."

As he began walking away, I said, "Little Jack, you can ride with me if you'd like. I figure there's plenty of room on old Buck for the both of us."

He backed away, looking stricken, as if I'd offended him. "Oh, no'm. That won't do at all. Mr. Eustus would whip me bloody if I got on that horse with you." And with that, he turned and ran back into the forest.

Thoughts of doing physical harm to Eustus ran through my mind as I placed a saddle blanket on Buck and fitted his harness, then threw myself over his back. As he picked his way down the mountain trail, I tried to calm down by looking around at the leaf-barren trees. Although the naked branches spearing up into the brilliant clear blue of the late autumn sky held a certain magnificence of their own, I found myself mourning the loss of all that glorious color. I wondered if during my time the fall trees had ever seemed so bountiful, so beautiful, so vibrant as they had here. Or was I actually seeing them for the first time, through another time and era, one that was foreign to me. The wind picked up and I drew my shawl closer around me, wishing now I'd brought along a blanket to wrap myself in. But the cool air seemed to invigorate Buck, and once we reached flat land, at my cluck, he leaped into a full gallop. I bent over his back, close to his body, feeling the wind rushing around me, startling myself when I yelled out, not from fright but from sheer joy. I'd never had such a feeling of freedom, such a feeling of oneness with another being.

I reined Buck in at the drive to the Hampton place and we trotted down the dirt lane, branching off to go to the barn behind the plantation house. As we neared, I spied Samuel hammering away on the outside of the barn. He smiled when he saw me, putting down the hammer and crossing over to us to hold Buck while I slid down off him.

"Miss Lizzie, you look plumb happy," he said.

I couldn't help but laugh. "I feel so alive, Samuel. Buck was really booking it after we got off the mountain. It was a blast."

He frowned at me.

"Um, I mean, Buck and I just had ourselves a thrilling run." I shook my head. "I don't think there's a better feeling in the world."

Samuel smiled widely. "I reckon you're right, Miss Lizzie. And you got a fine horse here to enjoy that feeling with."

"Yes, I do, Samuel." I patted Buck on the neck. "Can you see to him while I go to the kitchen? I've been called to take care of a painful burn."

He nodded. "Sure hope you can help young Sally. She shore is in a world of hurt."

"I'll do my best," I promised as I walked toward the back of the plantation house.

When I stepped into the kitchen, I hesitated, appreciating the warmth from the huge fireplace and the different cooking smells floating in the air around me. Tillie joined me, asking if I'd like anything to eat or drink.

"I'm fine. I've come to see about Sally, I think Samuel said her name was."

Tillie gestured to a young woman sitting on a stool near the fire, her left hand wrapped in a rag. Her face was pure misery as she got up from the stool and walked toward us, holding her hand close to her body.

When she joined us, Tillie said, "Miss Lizzie, this here's Sally. She burned her hand on an iron skillet and didn't do nothin but put butter on it, thinking it'd get better right quick. But it's been painin her somethin fierce and don't look too good so I thought maybe you ought to tend to it, see if you can help her feel better."

"Has Viola taken a look?" I asked. She was an elderly slave who had been a big help during the smallpox outbreak and usually saw to injuries such as this.

"She been busy helpin Mrs. Hampton, who's down with one of her bad headaches. She give me some salve to use but Sally here said it don't help."

I smiled at Sally. "I'll be happy to see what I can do. Let's go back to the fire where the light's better." I had her sit on the stool while I unwrapped the rag from around her hand, trying not to grimace when I saw the angry, puss-filled blisters covering her palm. "Bummer," I muttered to myself.

"Ma'am?" Sally said, peering at me curiously.

"That must hurt terribly."

"Yes'm, it shore do. I can't sleep it hurts so much. I been putting it in cold water, hoping that'd ease the pain, but it starts hurtin again when I take it out."

"I imagine. But I think I can help with that. I have some salve that should do the trick."

"Do the what?" she asked.

I mentally shook my head. What was the matter with me today, I wondered. I seemed to have 1960s slang on my mind. "Make it better."

"Oh, yes'm."

As I placed an ointment made from lilac on the puss-filled blisters, I noticed the other slaves seemed to be in a high state of agitation, huddling together and whispering to one another. Some wove their hands together while others smiled and laughed as with great excitement.

"What's happened?" I asked Tillie, who stood nearby, watching me.

She shook her head, whispering, "We ain't supposed to be talkin about it."

I began wrapping the hand. "This salve should bring you some relief fairly quick. Lavender is also an antibacterial and analgesic." I looked up at Tillie, noticing her furrowed brow. "It should fight the infection and help with the pain."

"Oh, praise the Lord, Miss Lizzie, she been in an awful lot of pain."

"Burns are horrible to deal with." I smiled at Sally, who was watching me carefully. "Remember next time to use a pot holder before grabbing a hot skillet."

"Oh, I reckon she'll remember," Tillie said, giving the young lady a hard stare.

The words John Brown seemed to hiss in the air and I looked up. Where had I heard that name? And then it came to me, sitting in history class during high school, bored out of my mind—history had never really interested me then—reading about the incidents leading up to the Civil War. One of the first harbingers: abolitionist John Brown's raid on Harper's Ferry. I looked at Tillie, noted her concerned look.

"Please don't tell what you heard," she said, her voice shrill. "Mr. Eustus said he'd whip anybody talkin about it."

"I didn't hear a thing, Tillie," I said as I gathered up the detritus and stuffed it in my saddlebag. "Don't you worry about Mr. Eustus. I don't have a thing to say that vile man."

After giving Tillie instructions for treating the wound, I left through the kitchen door, heading for the barn to fetch Buck and go back home, looking forward to letting him gallop along the flatland. Josh waylaid me as I drew closer to the barn, joining me on the path with a wide smile.

"Lizzie, I was hoping you'd be the one to come treat Sally's hand."

Since he caught me off guard, my smile was wider than I wanted it to be. Although I kept trying to distance myself from Josh, I was having a hard time of it.

"It's good to see you," he said, his eyes warm.

"It's good to see you as well, Josh. I can't thank you enough for helping us with Luther."

Josh waved his hand in a dismissive gesture. "It was the least I could do. Luther was a fine man."

"Although I didn't know him long, I would agree. I just wish I could have made his last moments more comfortable."

"I'm sure you did all you could for him, Lizzie." He glanced around before lowering his voice. "Have you heard the latest news?"

"About the raid?"

He looked at me with interest. "I reckon word travels fast over this mountain."

I shrugged. "Don't say anything, but I heard whispers about it in the kitchen."

"I hope it didn't upset you, Lizzie." He shrugged. "This was bound to happen with all the turmoil over slavery."

I nodded. "I'm afraid this is ..." I stopped myself before I could tell him my true thought, that this would prove to be a harbinger to the Civil War. "Can you tell me what happened?"

"Have you heard of the abolitionist John Brown?"

I shook my head no, hoping my eyes didn't give me away.

"He's a noted abolitionist, Lizzie, fought against the proslavery forces over in Kansas before coming back East and trying to raise money for his cause." He shook his head. "He supposedly envisions a mass uprising of slaves and managed to procure the backing of six prominent abolitionists who call themselves the Secret Six. On the night of October 16th, he and 21 other men overran the arsenal at Harpers Ferry and took hostages."

"What were they after, armory?"

"I'm certain that's what he wanted but it didn't fare well for him. By morning, they were surrounded by a company of marines led by Colonel Robert E. Lee and Lieutenant J.E.B. Stuart."

I started at that. I didn't recall Lee and Stuart being involved as early as 1859. And on the opposite side at that point.

Josh, noticing this, said, "Do you know either of those men, Lizzie?"

I shook my head. "Go on, Josh, tell me what happened next."

"The soldiers overran Brown and his men on the morning of the 19th. I heard that ten of his men were killed, including two of his sons."

"What happened to him, Josh?"

"He was tried by the state of Virginia for treason and murder and found guilty on November 2nd. They hanged him a week ago, on the 2nd of December." He stopped and turned to me. "Before they executed him, he handed his guard a slip of paper that said something to the effect that the crimes of this guilty land will never be purged away but with blood."

A prophetic statement, I thought to myself. "Some of the slaves seemed excited, do you know why?"

"Why, I imagine they're feeling what I do, that this issue of slavery is not one that is going to die a silent death. People are beginning to talk of war." He leaned close to me and lowered his voice. "Don't you feel it, Lizzie, the tension in the air like we're waiting for some great, horrible thing to occur?"

"Yes," I said, but I didn't feel it, I knew it.

As I rode home, I tried to remember what I had read about the Civil War. Did it touch the Appalachian Mountains or were we protected by rough territory and barely traversable roadways? I could feel my anxiety increase as I began to panic, so desperately wanting to go back home, for I knew one thing for certain. I did not want to be in the South when the war began. I wanted to be away from this place, from all that horrible, brutal death coming this way.

Chapter Seven

Fall - Winter 1859

I'm Alright

Josh's comment about the John Brown hanging taking place a week prior, on the 2nd of December, told me the day we talked was the 9th, a bit over two weeks away from Christmas. This put me in a near-panic as I still had no idea what to give the sisters and Amanda May as Christmas gifts.

A week or so after I saw Josh, a man who introduced himself as Bill, a servant from one of the homes in Morganton, arrived in a small horse and buggy, asking for our help. Sarie and Amanda May were once more making their rounds on the mountain and Abbie had gone off with Maggie to check on the baby they had delivered the week before, so I told him I would get my medical bag and go with him. As we traversed the narrow trail down the mountain, I asked what the problem was. He shrugged before saying, "All I knows is the mistress ain't been feeling too well and Mr. Peterson asked me to fetch one of the sisters." He slid a glance my way. "The doctor ain't been able to help her so he thought maybe y'all would know what to do."

"I'll try my best," I said, wondering what illness had befallen the woman that a doctor couldn't do anything about. As we rode along, I stole glances at this man. He was white, which told me he wasn't a slave. Curiosity finally got the better of me. "You work for Mr. Peterson?"

He nodded. "I been with his family since he was a young'un and liked it well enough to stay long as I have. They's just the two of us, my wife Hannah and me." He darted a look my way. "The Petersons don't believe in slavery like some folks around here. Me, I take care of this here horse, the garden, and do what work needs to be done to the house. My wife cooks and does the cleaning. They give us a place to live, food in our bellies and pay us for our work, so I figure we ain't doin too bad."

"They sound like very nice people."

"They is that," he said, pulling on the reins and stopping the horse in front of a dwelling that looked impressive enough, but I knew if it had been standing beside a plantation house, would have appeared miniature and understated.

I studied the building as I stepped down from the buggy, thankful for once I wouldn't be dealing with plantation owners and overseers. It was a two-story clapboard neatly painted white with dark gray shutters set close to the road with a small lawn in front. Bill led me up a brick walkway to a small portico leading to a massive wooden door. When he stopped, not seeming disposed to open the door for me, I looked at him, noting he seemed as confused as I about what to do. With a shrug, I turned back to the door and knocked as loud as I could.

A man not much older than me opened the door. He was dressed in a rumpled white linen shirt with black trousers and looked a mess, frankly. His eyes were bloodshot, his hair disheveled and he needed a shave. When he saw me, he gave me a questioning look then noticed Bill standing behind me. "You're not one of the sisters," he said.

"No, I'm their cousin Lizzie Baker."

His face immediately relaxed into a smile of relief. "Josh has told me all about you, Miss Baker. Please, come in."

Once inside, he introduced himself as James Peterson, esquire. I smiled at him, thinking, another lawyer. They were prevalent in Morganton, for some reason. Josh himself was an attorney but kept busy dealing with his father's legal issues and didn't practice law. I vaguely wondered how all these attorneys managed to make a living as I waited for him to close the door.

"Josh told me about how you stopped that smallpox outbreak at the plantation," he went on, taking my arm and guiding me toward the staircase. "Outstanding work." He looked at me as if waiting for my thanks.

"I only did what needed to be done." I stopped before stepping on the first stair. "What seems to be the problem, Mr. Peterson?"

His expression crumpled. "Oh, so sorry, so sorry. I'm so distracted, it seems. It's my wife." He ran his hand through his hair, his face reddening. "She's, well, she's with child, and can't seem to keep anything down. I've had the doctor here but he hasn't been able to help at all so I thought maybe a healer like you would know what to do for her."

"How far along is she?"

His attention was focused on the second story and he didn't seem to hear me. When I cleared my throat, he reluctantly brought his eyes back to me.

"I'm sorry?"

"How far along is she? One month, two?"

"Oh, almost three now."

"Morning sickness," I said.

"I'm sorry?"

"It's called morning sickness, caused from increased hormones in the body due to the pregnancy. It's actually a good sign the placenta is developing well."

"But she's so sick. She's lost weight, stays in bed all day. I'm afraid she won't make it through if something isn't done." He grabbed my hand. "Please, you're my last resort. She's just wasting away."

"I can understand your concern and I'll do my best to help." I gestured up the staircase. "Lead the way."

He led me up the stairs and down a long hallway. We stepped into a darkened bedroom but there was enough light I could see a figure reclining on the bed. "Beatrice," he whispered, "are you awake?"

A moan answered him.

"I've brought someone to see you, a healer." He turned to me and motioned me inside the bedroom.

I immediately went to the window and drew back the dark curtains. The woman on the bed squinted her eyes as she looked at me.

I smiled as I approached her. "Hello, Beatrice. I'm Lizzie Baker. I understand you're having a problem with nausea."

She nodded, scooting up to sit. Her husband rushed to plump pillows behind her. She was very pretty with black hair and eyes, although her pallor was concerning.

"Have you tried eating small bites of bread, taking small sips of water?"

"The doctor said the same thing," she said in a weak voice. "I can't keep it down."

"What about teas? There are herbs that can help with nausea."

"The doctor said not to take any herbs, that it could be bad for the baby."

"I assure you there are some we can use that are not." I rummaged in my satchel for ginger root. "If you'll agree to ginger tea, I can make some for you. It's good for nausea, especially during pregnancy, and shouldn't be harmful to your baby."

She looked from me to her husband.

"It's your body, your decision," I said.

She turned back to me, a shocked look on her face. I glanced at the husband and noted the same expression. I inwardly sighed, thinking it a terrible shame it would be another century before this fact was finally acknowledged for women. I didn't say anything more, simply waited them out.

Finally, she said, "I think I'd like to try it." She sat up straighter. "I'll try anything if it'll get me out of this bed and back to my life the way it was before." This was said with a glare at her husband, meant to convey, I'm sure, that she wouldn't be in this mess if not for him.

I was glad to see he took her meaning and was gracious enough to look contrite.

"Just point me to the kitchen," I said.

Peterson was still looking at his wife. "It's downstairs and to the right." He seemed to realize something more was required and glanced my way. "Should I come with you?"

"I'm quite capable, thank you," I said and took my leave.

I found the kitchen easily enough and was glad to see they had a woodstove. An older woman was kneading bread when I came in. She gave me a curious look. I smiled at her. "You must be Hannah. I'm Lizzie Baker. I'm a healer, here to treat Mrs. Peterson's nausea."

Her shoulders visibly relaxed. "I pray you do, miss, she's been awful miserable and the mister's been running around here, driving ever'body insane, trying to figure out what to do for her."

"All I need is a tea kettle and some water."

At my direction, Hannah put the water in the kettle and placed it on the woodstove to boil. While we waited, I removed a ginger root from my bag, peeled it, and began to slice it as thinly as possible into the teapot she provided. I then poured the boiling water into the teapot until it was near full. "Now we wait while it steeps," I told her. Once the tea was tepid enough to drink, I asked for honey and a tray. After placing the teapot, honey and a china cup on the tray, I thanked her and proceeded upstairs where I found Mr. Peterson sitting in a chair next to the bed, holding his wife's hand. They both perked up when I appeared. "Let's see if this helps," I said as I placed the tray on a table beside her. I poured the tea into the cup, added a teaspoon of honey, and handed it to her. "Sip slowly, one or two sips to start, and we'll wait a bit to see if you can tolerate it."

She took a small sip, smiling a little. "It tastes good."

"Try another one."

She did as I suggested then sat back against the pillows. I took the cup from her and placed it on the tray. She looked so frail and weak, and I hoped the ginger root would help. If not, I wasn't quite sure what to do, thinking maybe wild mint or raspberry leaf might work.

Mr. Peterson watched his wife closely. After a couple of minutes, he said, "She usually gets sick right after she eats or drinks anything."

"Let's give it a little more time. Let's try for half an hour."

We made small talk while we waited. Both seemed to know much more about me than I did them, constantly telling me what Josh had said about my skills as a healer and the work I had done for others. "If not for the sisters, I wouldn't have been able to help anyone," I told them.

Mr. Peterson squeezed his wife's hand. "Perhaps we need to call on them more often and not depend on the doctor so much."

"I agree," she said, her lips tilting in a smile.

"Not feeling like you're going to be sick?" I asked.

"No, not at all. In fact, my stomach feels steadier now."

"Good. Why don't you see if you can finish the tea and perhaps a little bread?" I looked at the husband.

"I'll be right back." He was gone before I could turn back to his wife.

"He worries himself sick about me," she said with fondness.

"The sign of a good husband. Go on now, finish it up but remember to take small sips."

After she finished, I took the cup from her and returned it to the tray, both of us glancing up when we heard Peterson's steps on the stairs. He returned with a small piece of cornbread on a china plate which he handed to me.

"How is your stomach now?"

"Better. I think I can eat something."

"Just a bite." I held the plate out to her.

"She picked up the cornbread and took a small nibble, waited a moment then stuffed the whole thing into her mouth.

"Beatrice," Peterson said, sounding shocked.

I couldn't help but laugh. "Well, we'll know if this is going to work or not fairly shortly."

So we waited another half-hour, and when it appeared she was going to keep that down, I began to latch my satchel. "No more than three cups of ginger tea a day and small meals until you feel you can tolerate more," I told her. "I showed Hannah how to make the tea and I'll leave more ginger roots with her." I took Beatrice's hand. "The good news is this usually subsides past three months and I understand you're close to that mark."

"Yes." I noticed she had color back in her face once more and her eyes seemed brighter. "I can't thank you enough, Miss Baker. You've saved my life."

"Please, call me Lizzie."

"All right, Lizzie. And you must call me Beatrice."

"Be sure and let me know if this doesn't help. There are a few other herbs we can try, like wild mint or raspberry leaf, if it doesn't," I said, walking toward the doorway.

"Here, let me show you out," Peterson said, rushing to catch up with me. At the bottom of the stairs, he took my hand and shook it. "I am so appreciative, Miss Baker."

"Lizzie, please."

"Lizzie. How much for your services? I'll pay anything, anything you demand."

I thought about it. Usually we were given produce or eggs for our services from the mountaineers. Sarie handled any money paid to us from the plantation owners. But I needed something to make Christmas presents. "Do you happen to have any jute?"

"Jute?"

"Yes, a rough twine or rope?"

"We have twine, I believe. Let me check." He walked toward the kitchen and when he returned had a long cord of twine in his hand. "Will this do?"

"Yes, thank you. And I have something for you, if you'll be so kind to give it to Hannah," I said, handing over several ginger roots.

"May I ask what you intend to do with the twine?"

"Make presents," I said, ignoring his confused look. When I didn't explain further, he reached into his pocket and pulled out several silver coins, then pressed them into my hand. "I can't thank you enough. If there's anything you ever need, please, consider us friends and feel free to ask."

"Thank you. And be sure to let me know if your lovely wife has any further problems."

"I will." He gestured to Bill, who was standing nearby. "Please take Miss Lizzie home, Bill." He was beaming when he shut the door behind me.

On the way back to the cabin, I ran my fingers over the coins and jute in my apron pocket. I'd give the coins to Sarie but I had plans for the twine.

On Christmas Eve, I asked Abbie to go out into the woods with me. I had spied a small perfectly formed fir that I wanted to use for our Christmas tree. I didn't have anything to decorate it with so had taken a faded red rag out of the rag pile, torn it into strips and planned to tie little bows on each of the branches. Not as festive as trees in my time but it would do. If I could manage it without getting caught, I planned to slip downstairs when everyone else was asleep and place the presents I'd made under the tree.

And on Christmas morning, I was happy to give Sarie shampoo scented with lavender I had made from Pokni's recipe, body lotion scented with jasmine to Maggie, and a macramé friendship bracelet made from the twine to both Amanda May and Abbie, both exclaiming over them and swearing they'd never take theirs off. Sarie gave each of us a silver coin, which I pocketed for future use. Maggie made apple tarts for everyone, and Abbie had embroidered handkerchiefs for all, while Amanda May gave each of us colorful bouquets of dried flowers. As we ate a fine Christmas lunch, I had to admit to myself it wasn't so bad. But I couldn't help but think back on past Christmases with my family, so much happier when my mom was alive, filled with love and an abundance of gifts. But this would do, in this simpler time, when our lives weren't about material things but surviving day to day as best we could.

After lunch, Abbie and I went to visit Pokni, taking her food from Maggie's delicious lunch. Although Pokni told me the Choctaw didn't celebrate Christmas, I wanted to spend time with her. It just didn't seem right to me for someone to be alone on this special day. Abbie had been teaching me how to sew and during the long evenings we worked on a pillowcase for Pokni, made from a white flour bag on which I had drawn a blacksnake to match the tattoo on Pokni's shoulder and neck. We embroidered the snake in black and purple thread and I thought it turned out beautiful. Pokni seemed to agree, as she clutched it to herself, tears coming to her eyes.

As Pokni ate the lunch we provided, she gestured to the corn Maggie had made. "I will tell you about Ohoyochisba."

Abbie and I smiled at one another. "Who is that, Pokni?" I asked.

"She is the Choctaw corn goddess, daughter of the sun god and moon goddess. Ohoyochisba was a beautiful woman who dressed entirely in white. Long ago, she roamed the Choctaw lands disguised as a feeble, wasted woman without a family. Most of the people shunned her and refused her pleas for food and drink. The only ones who would take her in were two Choctaw brothers who were themselves orphans and very poor. They shared their meager meal of hawk meat with this wandering old woman and let her sleep in their home overnight, sheltered from the rain.

"The next morning, Ohoyochisba revealed her true self to the brothers and before leaving told them to go to the spot where they first saw her the day before. When they did, they found strange seeds that when planted produced the first harvest of corn. From then on, this gift of Ohoyochisba became a staple of the Choctaw people, and from time to time, Ohoyochisba can be seen wandering the cornfields in her white gown."

I leaned against Pokni for a brief moment. "I could listen to your stories all day."

"Me too," Abbie agreed.

We stayed an hour more, Pokni and me smoking her hand-rolled cigarettes while Abbie questioned me about Christmas during my time. I tried to downplay how wonderful it had been but I could tell I wasn't truly successful. I grew sadder with the telling until Pokni put her hand on my arm.

"You are here for a reason, Daughter, remember that. And if you are meant to go back, you will return to your time. Until then, all you can do is be happy you are alive and helping others."

That reminded me of Luther and what he'd said about living as if you don't have a future. It seemed someone somewhere was sending me a message. I kissed her cheek. "Thank you, Pokni."

Josh paid us a visit that afternoon, bringing gifts of his own. Knowing Sarie's love for coffee, he gave her a bag from the plantation's larder and Maggie received a pound of sugar for baking. Sarie favored him with one of her rare smiles while Maggie laughed with delight, already planning foods she would make. Abbie was given a large spool of dark-green thread for embroidering, which she immediately placed in her sewing basket for future use. For Amanda May, he had a delicately scented posy of dried flowers he said his sister made. And he surprised me with a printed calendar.

"Thank you, Josh, thank you so much." I hugged him hard, then realizing the others were watching, moved away, my face reddening.

Josh laughed. "Looks like I made the perfect choice."

"How did you know I wanted a calendar?"

"'Cause you're always asking me what day it is."

"I have a gift for you." I pulled out the macramé bracelet I had made for him, one that was thicker and looked more masculine than those I made for Amanda May and Abbie. I had searched the ground around the creek for quartz rocks to place in the bracelets and had been lucky to find a beautiful rock in the shape of a wolf's head for Abbie, one that resembled a butterfly for Amanda May and one that reminded me of a running horse for Josh. "It's a friendship bracelet," I told him as I tied it on his wrist.

Josh looked at it, running his hands over the rough material which I had dyed a dark brown using the shells of chestnuts. "Did Pokni make this?"

"No, I did."

"It's beautiful, Lizzie. Why, I reckon I won't ever take it off."

"I said the same thing, Mr. Josh," Abbie said, showing him hers.

I smiled at both of them. "My two closest friends in the world."

Abbie's brow furrowed. "Mr. Josh, we didn't think to get you anything," she said, with regret.

Josh smiled at her. "Why, I don't reckon I need anything except maybe y'all's friendship."

"Well, you can at least stay for supper," Maggie said, heading toward the kitchen. "I'm of a mind to make some fried apple pies with this sugar you brought us."

"That I won't say no to," Josh answered, "and that's a good enough gift for me, eating Maggie's delicious food and spending time with you young ladies."

Even Sarie smiled at that.

Chapter Eight

Winter 1860

I'm Free

Abbie and I were once more walking the mountain, searching for the lights. These jaunts had become few and far between as winter progressed, due to cold weather and at times snowy conditions. But on fair nights such as this, we would wrap ourselves in coats and scarves and roam the mountainside. It had become our habit to start with where we had last seen my light, when that dreadful Constable Jackson had pushed me away from it and gotten himself electrocuted. Although we had searched countless nights, we rarely saw the lights, and when we did, they were always too far away to reach and disappeared almost as quickly as they appeared. By this time, my despair over finding my light had become so deeply ingrained, I accepted it as part of my mindset.

We were talking about calling it a night and returning to the cabin when I heard a rustling nearby. I stopped, reaching out and grabbing Abbie's hand. We stood silently, waiting to see if it revealed itself and whether it was animal or human. I prayed it wouldn't be another confrontation with Jackson, who turned up far more often than he should.

We stiffened when a man's shadow stepped onto the path and came toward us, walking fast. I sighed with relief when I realized the build and walk were much like Josh's.

"It looks like Josh," I whispered to Abbie, who nodded her acknowledgement.

When he reached us, he tilted his head in greeting then reached out and squeezed my hand, speaking in a whisper. "I was on my way to the cabin to fetch you, Lizzie. I'm afraid I have a huge favor to ask."

"Of course. What can I do?"

He glanced at Abbie. "Miss Abbie, I don't want to get you involved in this, so it might be best if you go on ahead of us while I talk to Lizzie in private."

Abbie straightened up. "I reckon I'm just as able to help as Lizzie is, Mr. Josh. I'll stay if'n you don't mind."

He nodded his thanks. "I've got a slave down at Scarbrough's barn, a young woman with a small child. She's, well, she's expecting a baby and I'm afraid to travel with her like this. I wouldn't know what to do if she, well, if she, you know …" He trailed off, giving me a helpless look.

I immediately turned around and began walking back down the mountain. "Do you know how far along she is?"

"She won't tell me but I can tell she's having a hard time of it walking these trails. She looks awful big to me and I was hoping you could look at her and tell me whether I should continue on with her or wait until …" He looked around as if expecting to see someone behind us. "Since that incident with Zebediah, Jackson's been following me around like a faithful dog, hoping, I'm sure, to catch me at something. I don't think it's safe to keep her in that barn for long, especially if he sees me going in and out."

I looked at Abbie. "Is there any other place we can keep her, Abbie?"

She shrugged. "Let's check her first, see if she's close. If'n she is, we're gonna have to keep her somewheres till she has the baby."

"We can't keep her at the cabin," I said, more to myself than anyone else. "Sarie would know."

I hesitated long enough for Abbie to ask, "What?"

"What about Luther Spradlin's cabin? You and I keep talking about going up there and clearing it out but haven't had time to do that yet. It should still be empty since he said there was no one to pass it on to. Plus it's pretty secluded and hard to get to. No one would know she was there unless they actually went there. I can stay with her, tell anyone who stops by that I'm clearing out the cabin."

Abbie pondered this. "I'll stay and help you, Lizzie."

"But what will we tell Sarie?"

"Why, we'll tell her the truth, that right afore he died, Luther told you to take anything of his you wanted, which we reckon included the cabin. Said he didn't have nobody else to give it to so he wanted you to have it."

"Or we could say us."

"We'll say you since you're the one he left it to. 'Sides, if we tell her he give it to us, Sarie'll be over there tellin us what to do. I'll tell her I'm gonna stay with you while you clear it out, so we can both be there to help that poor woman."

I looked at Josh. "What do you think?"

"I think that's a right good idea," he said, relief evident in his voice.

We walked as fast and as quietly as we could the rest of the way to the barn, checking around us constantly. When we got there, we hurried inside, following Josh to a wide stall in a corner of the barn where he had hidden the pregnant slave and child. After Josh pushed aside the hay bales he had piled in front of them, I stepped closer, wishing we had a light to see by. But the moon was full and enough light shone through the large window above that I could make out two shapes, one far smaller than the other. The woman put the child behind her in a protective measure as we drew closer.

I knelt beside them, whispering, "We're here to help you."

The woman looked at Josh for reassurance and at his nod returned her eyes to me.

"Mr. Josh says you're expecting a baby." I reached my hand out to her swollen belly.

"Yes'm, I reckon I am," she said.

"Do you know how far along you are?"

She shook her head. "It ain't time yet, I don't think."

"Mr. Josh says you're having some trouble."

"I just ain't too comfortable, but I can travel well enough."

"Not very well," Josh said.

"I can travel," she insisted stubbornly. "We got to get up north afore this baby comes, there ain't no other way."

"Do you mind if I examine you, make sure the baby is alright?"

"If you've a mind to," she said with reluctance.

Josh cleared his throat and when I looked at him said, "I'll go check around outside, make sure no one saw us come in here."

I nodded. Abbie knelt beside me, smiling at the woman. "My name's Abbie and this here's Lizzie. Is that your young'un there?"

The woman glanced at the child, cowering behind her. "This here's Melody and my name's Emma."

Abbie smiled at the young girl. "Howdy, Melody. We're just gonna check your ma and make sure she's up to traveling. You reckon that'll be all right?"

The little girl nodded shyly.

I did a quick cervical exam, relieved that Emma hadn't begun to dilate. I put my hand over her belly, marveling as always when I felt a small foot push against my palm. "Your baby's active. That's a good sign. Have you had any contractions? Felt your belly harden like it's time for it to come?"

"No'm, not today. Last night, I thought I was havin em but it went away."

I nodded. "That was probably Braxton Hicks."

Abbie gave me a confused look. "Who?"

"That's what they're called, Braxton Hicks, also known as false labor. They're like practice contractions but not actual labor. I wish I had some way of knowing exactly how far along she is but I can't tell, although she looks to be close. She isn't dilated yet but I think the baby has dropped which means it can be a few weeks or few hours."

Abbie moved restlessly. "We need to get her up the mountain tonight, Lizzie, afore she goes into labor."

"I think so." I looked at Emma. "Do you think you can travel a little while longer? We have a cabin we can take you to that will be safer than this place."

She nodded as she struggled to get to her feet. "I'll make it, don't you worry about me." She reached down and grabbed the little girl's hand.

"We need to be as quiet as possible," I said, leading the way to the door. "Let us know when you need to stop and rest. We'll go at your pace. We certainly don't want to bring on an early labor."

"I'll keep up, don't you worry," she said, following me.

We found Josh standing guard outside. "We're going to Luther's cabin," I said in a low voice. "I'll let you lead the way and I'll take up the rear. Abbie can walk with Emma and her little girl."

Josh nodded and without saying a word began the long trek to Luther's place.

It took several hours to walk to the cabin. The night had become cloudy and there was very little moonlight to see by. Josh, however, managed to keep to the trail as we meandered our way up the mountain. We had to stop more times than I felt it safe to let Emma sit and rest. I could tell the trek was hard on her, as I watched her move along, her hands under her belly, supporting its weight. Melody trailed along behind, clutching her mama's skirt until she began to lag. Josh, seeing this, picked her up and carried her and she immediately fell asleep in his arms.

I breathed a sigh of relief when the one-room cabin came into view. Stepping inside, I was glad to see a bed in the corner, which Luther had apparently neatly made before going to the sisters' cabin. After Abbie and I helped Emma lie down on the bed, Josh placed Melody beside her, then picked up a quilt at the bottom and spread it over both. Emma was so exhausted she immediately began to doze.

"I'll get a fire started," Josh said, going to the hearth.

While he did that, Abbie and I searched for a lantern to light. Abbie finally found one on the mantle and lit it, along with several candles which we placed on the wooden table.

"At least Luther kept it clean and neat," I said, looking around the small cabin.

Once Josh got the fire going, the cabin began to heat up. I stood in front of the hearth, warming my hands while Josh picked up a bucket and went outside, returning with fresh water. "Luther's got a well out front," he said, putting the bucket on the table.

I turned to Abbie. "I reckon you best go on home and in the morning tell Sarie and Maggie I'll be staying here for a few days."

Abbie nodded. "I'll tell em you left afore daybreak so you could get up here and get started. If'n they don't have anything of necessity for me to do, I'll come on up and join you."

"You might bring our medical bags."

Abbie nodded as she wrapped her scarf around her throat.

"I'll escort you home, Miss Abbie," Josh said.

"I thank you, Mr. Josh."

Josh reached for my hands. "I'll come when I can and I'm sure I'm not being followed."

"Don't endanger yourself," I warned. "We'll be fine here. I'll stay until after she has the child and is well enough to travel, then I'll send word to you."

"I can't thank you enough, Lizzie. I'm so sorry to have drawn you into this."

I stepped closer to him and lowered my voice. "You don't understand, Josh. I am happy to help you. What you're doing is so noble and good, and I want to be a part of it."

He leaned forward and kissed my cheek. "Bless you," he said before leaving with Abbie.

Luther's mattress was a spacious one, and after I blew out the candles and lantern, I crawled into bed beside Melody. Recalling how unclean Luther had been, I tried to remember if I had seen any lice on his body. I fell asleep, hoping Luther didn't have that problem.

Light shining through the one window in the cabin woke me the next morning. I glanced at Emma and Melody, curled into one another and still sleeping, before easing out of bed and stepping outside to the privy. The frigid weather had me hurrying up the path and then back into the cabin, where I stoked the fire, shivering and holding my arms close to my body. I heard movement behind me and glanced at the bed. Melody was sitting up, watching me.

"Are you hungry?" I said in a low voice.

She nodded.

"Let's see if we can find something to eat."

Apparently her hunger outweighed her shyness as she climbed off the bed and came over to join me by the fire. I smiled at her then forced myself away from the warmth of the flames and over to the small kitchen, where I began to search for food. Luther had told me he didn't have much of an appetite near the end and this worked to our advantage, as I quickly found a bag of oats and a loaf of sour-dough bread that had frozen and looked to be on the verge of becoming moldy. "How about oatmeal?" I asked Melody.

Her smile was answer enough.

By the time Emma woke, the oatmeal was ready to eat along with bread I had toasted over the fire. I found a jar of honey to sweeten the oatmeal and wished for butter for the bread but the meal was filling. The three of us ate in silence, alert for sounds from outside. After breakfast, when the two expressed a need to use the outhouse, I advised them to wrap a scarf around their heads in a hood-like way so they wouldn't be recognized if anyone happened to see them. When they returned, I examined Emma then encouraged her to go back to bed to rest. I didn't think it would be long before she had her baby and by this point was beginning to panic, afraid I would be alone with her when she did.

Once the sun had melted the frost off the grass, I stepped outside to acquaint myself with Luther's homeplace, walking around the small cabin and barn. I smiled when I saw a chicken coop attached to the back of the rustic barn then became alarmed as I watched the hens and rooster peck weakly at the dirt. In the barn, I found feed and scattered it over the ground for them, wondering how long it had been since they had eaten anything other than bugs and worms. I fetched water from the well and poured it into their small trough before checking for eggs in the coop. Not finding any, I hoped once they began to eat steadily, they would produce once more.

When I returned to the cabin, Emma was relaxing in bed while Melody played with a doll made out of corn husks on the floor near the fire. After I made sure Emma was comfortable, I looked around the small cabin, finding it quaint and charming. Luther apparently had woodworking capabilities and had made a fine pine table and chairs. The mantle over the large fireplace matched the table and chairs and had ornate carvings along the front. The bed featured a headboard and footboard made from the same wood and with the same carvings as the mantle. I wondered if Luther had done this when he still had hopes of marrying his lady friend and thought how pleased she would have been if only she could have seen his handiwork. I walked around, noting the wooden planks on the floor looked relatively clean and the kitchen was neatly organized.

As I set about clearing our breakfast dishes, I began to entertain the idea of actually moving into the cabin. It would be nice to live in a place of my own where I wouldn't be under Sarie's constant scrutiny. Maybe I could even convince Abbie to move in with me. I wondered how hard it would be to convince anyone who questioned my taking possession of the cabin that I had the right to stay here. And then it hit me. I was planning a future here. When did that happen? When did I come to the conclusion I would be staying in this time and place the rest of my life? I didn't want to think about that.

As the day progressed, I busied myself cleaning the cabin of dust that had settled on the furniture and floor since Luther's absence while keeping an eye on Emma and Melody. Melody was a sweet girl who, once she got used to my company, proved to have a fondness for singing. Her voice was high and so innocent and pure that I would pause to listen to her, finding myself smiling. I had her nap with her mother in the afternoon while I once more went outside to see if I could find anything else to eat other than oatmeal and bread. In the barn, I found a potato bin in the back corner, along with another one that held apples. I wished again for butter and added a roll of aluminum foil to my list to wrap the potatoes in so they could be roasted in the fire. My mouth watered just thinking of steaming hot baked potatoes with lots of melted butter. I shook my head, dispelling this fantasy, deciding fried potatoes and stewed apples didn't sound too bad for dinner. After loading my apron with potatoes and apples, I returned to the house, trying to remember Maggie's recipes. She was an outstanding cook and I feared I would not match her in the slightest, but if I could produce something edible, I would count that a success.

I had just begun to cut up the potatoes when the door opened. I hesitated, knife in hand, terrified someone from the mountain had found us out or that Constable Jackson had somehow tracked us here. Seeing Abbie's face, I smiled with relief. "Thank goodness it's you," I said, going to her and hugging her.

"I didn't think I'd ever get away," she said, as she unwrapped her scarf from her lower face and neck after putting our medical bags on the table. "Sarie was suspicious and kept askin me all kinds of questions about the cabin and why you didn't say nothin when Luther died about him tellin you to take anything of his you wanted. I told her it was cause you weren't for sure you was willin to do that but after thinkin about it figured you might as well check it out and at least clean it while you was doin it. She then wanted to know why you picked now to come up here to clear it out. I told her 'cause she don't give us a moment's peace durin the day, always sayin do this or do that, so you just took it upon yourself to leave early enough one day afore she caught you goin out the door. She didn't like it none when I told her I was comin to help but Maggie told her they ain't no need for me to stay since they have Amanda May to help if they need it and all the chores was caught up and ain't nobody ailing who needs our help." She glanced at Emma and Melody, cuddled up on the bed watching her, and lowered her voice. "Don't know what we're gonna do if Sarie gets it in her head to come up here. You know how she is. Ain't no tellin what she'll say if she sees them."

"I guess we'll just have to cross that bridge when we come to it." I took her coat and scarf and placed them on a hook by the door then gestured toward a rocking chair close to the fire. "I'm fixing to get dinner started, why don't you relax?"

Abbie nodded but before going to the fire crossed over to the bed to check on Emma and Melody. I listened to their low voices as I finished the potatoes and began on the apples. After a bit, Abbie joined me and began to help. I wanted to delay talking to her about the cabin but had become excited at the prospect of having my own place, so after dinner, while we cleaned the dishes and Emma and Melody sat in the rocking chair in front of the fireplace, I said, "Abbie, I think I might want to live here."

She put down the wooden plate in her hand and studied me a long moment. "You reckon so?"

I nodded. "I'd love it if you'd live here with me."

Abbie looked around at the cabin and I found myself praying she'd say yes. "Well, it ain't a bad cabin. Seems snug enough with the fire goin and ain't too crude. Got some right nice woodwork." She shrugged. "I'll talk to Sarie about it. Might be nice to live away from her for awhile." She glanced at me and we both smiled.

"It would be wonderful," I whispered.

She giggled. "Just think, Lizzie, we could stay up as late as we want, sleep past dawn, do our own chores without having to do ever'body else's. And we could go out searchin for your light without havin to sneak so we won't be caught."

I nodded excitedly. Since Abbie and I shared a fondness for books, I added, "And read all day if we want."

"Oh, Lordy, Lizzie, I can't think of anything I'd rather do."

"And we're close enough they could fetch us in a hurry if they needed us," I said.

She opened her mouth to respond, but before she could do so, the door opened once more, blowing in frigid air. We turned to see who had come inside, both relaxing when we recognized Josh, bundled up against the night air. He quickly closed the door behind him, nodding toward Emma and Melody, then joining Abbie and me in the kitchen. "Miss Abbie, Lizzie."

After we greeted him, Abbie said, "What in tarnation are you doin here, Mr. Josh? It's freezin cold out there."

"I wanted to make sure everything is all right," he said, looking at me. "Make sure no one's found you out yet."

"Not yet," I said, "although Sarie and Maggie know we're here."

Alarm tracked across his face.

"Just Abbie and me," I revised.

"Don't worry," Abbie said, "Sarie may be fierce but she cares for people. She won't get too het up over them bein here, not after we tell her what's goin on." Seeing his look, she continued, "But we ain't gonna do that till we have to, don't you worry none about that."

Josh nodded as he looked around. "I made sure I wasn't followed," he said after a bit.

"Why don't you sit down and I'll make some tea?"I asked.

"That'd be welcome, Lizzie." He removed his coat and walked over to the table, Abbie joining him.

After I made the tea, I took the cups over to the table. We made small talk as we sat, drinking. After a bit, Josh looked toward Emma then back to me. "Once she has the baby, how long do you think it will be before she can travel?"

I looked at Abbie. In my time, women were allowed off work for several weeks after having a baby. I wasn't sure what the protocol was here.

Abbie shrugged. "A few days maybe, then she ought to feel up to travelin. It's gonna be hard, Josh. She'll have a baby she'll have to carry in a sling. And if it gets hungry or …" her voice trailed off. "Babies can be loud," she finished.

I nodded.

"We'll have to travel after dark, I reckon. I can get her to the next station in a night once we get going. Everything's set in place for her as soon as she can travel. I just need to let them know when we'll be coming."

"Once she has the baby, I'll get word to you," I said. "But for now, I think it's best if you stay away from here, so no one will see you and wonder what you're doing up here."

"I reckon you're right." He sighed then gave me his crooked smile. "It's just, it's getting harder and harder to stay away from you, Lizzie."

I blushed at the look in his eyes.

Abbie snickered.

Josh looked embarrassed. "I'm sorry, ladies. Sometimes my mouth speaks before my brain tells it to shut up." He stood, saying with reluctance, "I best get going before Papa misses me. I've got my horse outside but it'll still take me a while to get back."

I put my cup of tea down on the table. "I'll walk you out." I didn't miss the knowing look Abbie gave me.

I wrapped a shawl around me while Josh donned his coat and scarf then we went out into the night. The air was frigid, so much so it hurt to draw in a breath, but I didn't notice this for long as Josh pulled me against him and put his mouth on mine. Oh, don't ever stop, I thought as I returned his kiss, perhaps with more ardor than I should have because he pulled back, giving me a confused look.

"What?" I whispered.

"Nothing, it's just, well, I've kissed girls before, Lizzie, but none of them's ever kissed me back like that."

I could feel my face redden. "Oh, I'm so sorry," I said, searching for a way to explain, thinking people who were courting in the 19th century probably exchanged chaste kisses rather than the passionate ones I had shared with other boyfriends in my time.

"No, no, don't be sorry. I love it. I could do nothing but kiss you for the rest of my life and I'd die a happy man, Lizzie Baker," he whispered before putting his lips on mine.

When I returned to the cabin, my lips felt bruised, swollen, but for the first time since I had come to this time and place, I felt true happiness. Abbie, thank goodness, had the good sense not to say anything but I knew from the looks she gave me she had a pretty good idea what was going on in my head and heart.

The next few days settled into a routine as we went about our day, doing chores around the cabin and homeplace, constantly checking Emma, and playing or singing with Melody. I gauged her age around five and found her a delightful little girl with an easy smile and laugh. Using the smooth side of a slab of bark and a piece of charcoal, Abbie and I began to teach her the alphabet. I taught her the ABC song, which Abbie, of course, was not familiar with, and it didn't take Melody long before she knew it by heart. During times when Melody napped or entertained herself by playing with her doll or drawing on the piece of bark, I tried to get to know Emma, who seemed shy and reserved. She told me she had been born into slavery on a plantation near Asheville. I wanted to ask her about Melody's father but refrained since I didn't know if Melody actually knew her father. I was aware that many times, the children women slaves bore were fathered by the plantation's owner or overseer.

One day after lunch while Melody napped and Emma sat in the rocking chair in front of the fire, I asked if she had a particular place she wanted to go once the baby was born.

"Up north to Canada. I hear they ain't got slaves up there."

I nodded, wondering exactly how many miles she would have to travel. And on foot most of the way. It seemed a huge distance, especially carrying an infant and leading a five-year-old. Not to mention the added worry of getting caught as she was transported from place to place along the Underground Railroad system. I glanced at Melody, asleep on the bed, looking angelic and serene. "I wish you could stay here," I found myself saying.

Abbie, piling logs near the fireplace, gave me a sharp look.

"I know that's impossible," I said to her, "but it's such a great distance and I fear for their safety."

"Don't you worry none, Miss Lizzie," Emma said. "I'll take good care of my babies. I'll get them to safety or die tryin."

I gave Abbie a questioning look: would they make it to safety?

She shrugged, sending the message she didn't know, which scared me.

Emma gasped and put her hand on her belly. I reached out to touch her abdomen, which felt as hard as concrete, holding it there until it softened. "Contraction," was all I said but it was enough to get Abbie to her feet and rushing over to us.

"Let's get you on the bed, Emma," Abbie said, helping Emma stand. Melody stirred when Emma lay down on the bed but didn't wake up, instead, turning over and facing the opposite direction.

"Don't you worry none, Emma," Abbie said in a soothing tone. "Lizzie and I have birthed many a baby, we'll take good care of you."

"I had an easy birth with Melody," Emma said. "Wasn't in labor but an hour or two, I reckon."

Abbie and I looked at each other, sharing the same thought; usually the labor during the second pregnancy wasn't as long as the first.

And we were right. It seemed only minutes passed before Emma's contractions grew two minutes apart and it wasn't long before she was straining to push. Our frenetic movements woke Melody, who scooted off the bed and ran over to the rocker, where she climbed up, watching us through the back slats as she hugged her corn shuck doll.

I smiled at her. "Everything's going to be fine, Melody. Mama's having her baby but she's doing really well." I cringed when Emma screamed.

Abbie clamped her hand over her mouth. "Shhh, somebody might hear you," she said in a shrill voice. She looked at me. "Go find something she can bite down on."

I hurried over to the fireplace, searching for a thick stick. I couldn't find one so peeled a chunky piece of bark off one of the logs and returned to the bed. Emma took it from me and put it in her mouth, biting down hard as another contraction ripped through her. Abbie got behind and supported her back while I fetched an old quilt we had found and put it under Emma after folding it several times, hoping to catch fluids.

Time passed quickly after that, and within the hour, a baby boy slid out of Emma's body and into my hands. I breathed a sigh of relief when he let out a loud cry, his face red as a beet. Placing him in Emma's arms, I said, "See if you can soothe him so he'll stop crying," glancing at the door, fearful someone might be passing nearby and hear. Emma held him close to her body, murmuring soothing words, and he calmed enough to begin rooting.

"I reckon he's a good healthy boy." After cutting the cord, Abbie began massaging Emma's stomach in order to help her pass the afterbirth.

I went to the kitchen for a bowl and water to clean the baby but noticed the bucket was empty. Picking it up, I told Abbie we needed water and I'd be right back as I stepped outside, closing the door behind me. I crossed over to the well and drew water up, thinking I needed to wash my hands before I went back inside. I heard movement nearby and looked up expecting Josh, gasping when I saw Constable Jackson.

"What are you doing here?" I said in a loud voice, trying not to glance at the cabin, praying the baby wouldn't begin crying again.

He raised his eyebrows at this. "I heard about ol' Luther dying so figured I'd come on up here and check to make sure nobody's been ransacking his cabin. And look what I find, you with blood on your hands."

I looked at my hands, coated in blood.

"Who'd you kill this time?"

I stepped back, shocked at the accusation. "I've never killed anyone," I said in a defensive tone. I heard the chickens clucking and added, with relief, "I tried to help one of the chickens a coyote got hold of, but I was too late, it lost too much blood."

He stared at me for a long moment before finally saying, "I might ask you what you asked me, what are you doing here?"

"I'm not here illegally if that's what you're thinking. I took care of Luther before he died. He told me he didn't have any family or close friends and in payment for my services he said to take anything of his I wanted." I gestured at the cabin. "I came to clean his cabin and liked it well enough I figured I might stay."

"Well, seems to me you could be lying about that. How am I to know what he told you before he died?"

The cabin door opened and Abbie stepped out. "Good afternoon to you, Constable Jackson," she said as she drew near. "You here for a reason?"

He tilted his head in my direction. "Checking on Luther's cabin. Didn't expect to see either of you here."

Abbie nodded. "Lizzie tended to Luther afore he died and I guess he appreciated it so much he told her she could have anything of his she wanted. We been cleanin his cabin, making sure it don't need no work or repairs. Lizzie here likes it, I reckon, 'cause she's thinkin about stayin." She shrugged. "A-course, I'd rather she lived with us, but it's up to her."

Jackson looked back and forth between us, his brow furrowed. I didn't know what we'd do if he told us to leave. When we heard a short squawk from the cabin, Abbie and I froze, grasping at one another's hands. Jackson narrowed his eyes as he looked that way. "What was that?"

Abbie and I exchanged a quick, panicked glance.

Abbie turned back to Jackson, waving her hand in a dismissive gesture. "Probably that old barn cat that got in the house and don't want to leave. Caterwauling all the time for no reason a'tall. Lizzie here likes cats so I guess he'll be her companion if she lives here. Me, I can't be around em for long else I start sneezin." She rubbed her arms and shivered. "Unless you got business with us, Constable Jackson, I'd like to get back inside where it's warm."

"Maybe I'll take a look inside before I go," he said.

I forced my expression to remain calm, not reflect the panic I felt, as I searched for a reason to give him not to go inside.

Abbie made a face. "Don't know if you want to do that. Luther died of consumption, I reckon you know, which is highly contagious, according to Lizzie. We've been tryin to clean his place of all the ..." She squinted as she turned to me. "What do you call them, Lizzie, them things that float in the air and you can breathe in and they get in your lungs and give you consumption?"

"Germs," I said.

"Germs," she repeated. "So I got to warn you, if you go in there, you're liable to get it if you breathe in."

"You two ain't worried about getting it?" he asked in a suspicious tone.

"Pokni give us an herb to drink, said it might help. 'Sides, I've been around consumption enough, I reckon if I'm gonna get it, I would have by now."

I nodded as if I totally agreed with her.

He backed up a step. "I reckon I can come back later."

"You do that, but give us a bit of time to get all them germs out of this cabin. Lizzie said it'll take at least a week or two."

"I'll be back," he promised as he mounted his horse and left after giving us what I'm sure passed for his intimidating look.

"Whew," I said after he was gone. "That was close."

Abbie turned and looked toward the cabin. "I liked to died when I peeped out the window and seen him out here talkin to you. I told Emma to try to keep her baby as quiet as she could but I was a-feared the whole time he'd start squalling and give us away."

"Same here when I saw Jackson."

Abbie waited as I washed the blood off my hands then drew a fresh bucket of water. When we stepped into the cabin, I knew at once something was amiss when I noticed Melody staring at Emma, a shocked expression on her face. Tears ran down Emma's cheeks as she pressed the baby's face against her chest. His color, which before had a pink, healthy hue, now appeared bluish, almost bruised. Asphyxiation, I thought immediately as I pulled him away, placing my shaking fingers over his heart.

"What happened?"

"He started to cry," Emma sobbed. "I couldn't let him give us away, so I put his face against me, to stop him."

Oh, no. I immediately began CPR using my fingers while alternately blowing into his mouth. "How long?" I asked between breaths.

"I don't know," she wailed. "Oh, I done gone and killed my baby boy."

Melody, catching her mama's angst, began to cry.

Abbie tried to shush them, her voice a hissing contrast to their keening.

I ignored them as I continued to work on the baby, praying Constable Jackson wouldn't return and hear all this ruckus and that God wouldn't let this innocent little being die just to save us. I stopped, placing my fingers over his heart again. Was that a flutter I felt? I licked my finger and put it under his nose and felt a light breath of air against my skin. "He's breathing," I said, with relief.

We watched as his skin began to pinken and all sighed with relief when he moved his little hand and made a soft mewling sound.

"You reckon he gonna be all right?" Emma asked, her eyes wide. "Is he gonna live?"

I shrugged as I continued to watch the shallow rise and fall of his chest. "I hope so, Emma." I glanced at Abbie, wondering if she feared brain damage as I did. She shook her head, indicating she didn't know. I tried smiling at Emma but my mouth wouldn't cooperate. "We'll keep a close eye on him." To change the subject, I asked, "Were you able to get him to nurse?"

"Not yet. I'll try again if you want me to."

"Let's get him cleaned up. He'll let us know when he wants to nurse again. We'll just have to try our best to keep him quiet."

The next few days were spent in a constant state of anxiety, trying to foretell the baby's needs by his expressions and sounds and hurrying to meet them so he would not cry. I spent as much time as possible outdoors in order to waylay anyone who came by for a visit but the frigid, snowy weather kept everyone home, I surmised when no one stopped by. Not even Sarie, who Abbie and I knew would eventually make her way to the cabin if for no other reason than nosiness.

A couple of days after the baby was born, Abbie fetched Jonah from the sisters' place and rode him down the mountain to Josh's plantation to let him know Emma and her children would soon be ready for travel. Although I had wanted them to stay longer, the stress of keeping an eye outside while taking care of matters inside began to wear on me, such that I was relieved when Josh appeared near dusk one night several days later, ready to take them on to the next station. He brought heavier coats for Emma and Melody along with scarves and mittens which would help keep them warm as they traversed the mountain. I bundled Melody in her thick wool coat and wrapped a scarf around her head and neck, concerned that the frigid air would make travel harder.

As if sensing my concern, she placed her little hand on my cheek and whispered, "Don't you worry, Miss Lizzie. Mama says we're goin to a better place, where we can be free and I can go to school and we can always be a family."

I put my hand around hers, kissed the palm. "That is my prayer for you, sweet one." I leaned close and whispered in her ear, "When you learn how to write, I do hope you'll send me a letter and let me know you're safe and happy."

She smiled as she nodded.

I wiped at my eyes. "Now, go tell Miss Abbie bye while I get some things for Mr. Josh to carry."

I crossed over to the table, where I had placed an old saddlebag Abbie found in the barn. I took it to Josh and handed it over. "I've packed food in there, along with some diapers I made out of old sheets Abbie and I found in the cabin."

Josh's expression grew alarmed at the word *diapers* and I couldn't help but smile.

"Emma can take care of that part."

His look of relief was almost comic. "What if he starts crying? We need him quiet."

I glanced at Emma, holding the baby while she watched Melody and Abbie say their goodbyes. "He's a happy baby. As long as he's warm, fed and dry, he'll do well. Emma's a good mama. She knows how to read his signals." I reached out and squeezed his hand. "Be careful, Josh."

He smiled as he squeezed back. "I always am, Lizzie. Although it's frightful cold out there, it works to our advantage. I doubt there will be any hunters out tonight and surely Constable Jackson has the sense to stay inside by a warm fire instead of traipsing all over this mountain trying to catch me at something."

"I pray so."

He glanced at the others and, seeing no one watching us, leaned close and brushed his lips against my cheek. "I'll see you soon."

"Yes."

I kissed the sleeping baby goodbye before tucking him in a sling inside Emma's coat then kissed Emma's cheek.

"I can't thank you enough for what you done for us," she said as she hugged me.

"Getting there safely and leading a happy life is all the thanks I need."

With a nod, she held out her hand for her daughter and they stepped out into the dark night. Abbie and I stood in the doorway watching until the swirling snow hid their dark shapes.

We stepped back inside, hurrying over to the fire to get warm. Our eyes met and I knew mine held the same worries as hers. Abbie finally shrugged. "I don't always see what happens. I guess it'll have to be enough knowin we did what we could," was all she said before reaching for the kettle to make tea.

Chapter Nine

Winter 1860

100 Years Ago

I was delighted Sarie didn't oppose Abbie moving into Luther's cabin with me. I suspect her reasoning was a pragmatic one. Their cabin was a bit crowded now that they had taken on Amanda May and I imagine it must have been a relief to have us gone. I loved living with only Abbie which meant I could speak freely at all times without fear of giving my secret away. Of course, Sarie and Maggie already knew, though I doubted either one of them was entirely convinced my story was true, but Amanda May didn't and it was a strain having to constantly watch what I said around her. The one person I really wished I could tell was also the one person I didn't have the courage to: Josh.

Abbie and I stayed busy fixing up the cabin as best we could when weather allowed. She had learned carpentry from her father and was patiently teaching this to me, and I discovered, much to my surprise, a joy at building things. Many an evening was spent planning what we would do to spruce up the place, such as building a wooden fence and broadening the small front porch, even putting in our own inside privy which I assured her was doable. On mild days, we began to work on the rickety barn, shoring it up and replacing rotting or missing planks, in hopes of bringing Jonah back home in the spring. At least once a week if weather permitted, Josh visited and was more than willing to pitch in and help with whatever project we were working on. Abbie and I would occasionally venture out to visit Pokni or when called upon by Sarie or Maggie to help someone in need. Other than a nasty flu that traveled the mountainside and the run-of-the-mill colds, we didn't have any major outbreaks or accidents. I was thankful Luther hadn't proved contagious as no more episodes of consumption were reported to us.

On days when the weather was foul and we only went outside to visit the outhouse, we spent hours by the fireplace reading books Josh provided from his father's extensive library, sometimes to one another or just to ourselves. Although many were classics, I longed for the more contemporary and popular books of my time, such as *To Kill a Mockingbird, Rosemary's Baby, Slaughterhouse Five, The Godfather, The Andromeda Strain, Up the Down Staircase.* It was during that time that I started playing back in my mind some of the movies and television shows I'd seen or stories from some of my favorite books. I would choose one then silently practice telling it to Abbie, which I usually did while lying in bed waiting for sleep to take us. Judging by her reaction, she enjoyed hearing them almost as much as I did relaying them. True, she sometimes fell asleep listening to my voice, but the next morning or perhaps the next night, she always asked me to tell her the rest of the story.

These were the best days for me, spent with my dear friend without Sarie hanging over us demanding we do this or that.

I'd never experienced cabin fever before, but around the first of February, the temperatures plummeted, leaving us with no choice but to stay in the cabin as much as we could. The hardest part for me was the long, dark evenings when it seemed as if the sun would never shine again and all we could do was sit around the fire and think our thoughts, which for me were all about spring and summer. Abbie had her stitching to occupy her mind and spent most of her time working on a gorgeous quilt top. She assured me this was the coldest part of the year, and once that was over, the weather would slowly start to warm. My mind clung fiercely to that thought as those dreary days and nights crept by.

Warmer weather and longer days, when they finally arrived, were met with a smile and a wonderful sense of awe at the beauty of a late winter or early spring day in the mountains. Wildflowers sprang up everywhere, trees budded with misty green leaves or beautiful, colorful blossoms of soft pink or bright purplish red or, in the case of the dogwoods, brilliant white with greenish-yellow centers. Best of all, I could go back to bathing in the creek and dispense with the whore's baths I was forced to take indoors while the weather had been cold. As always, the water was chilly but I would have braved even a few chips of ice if it meant I could submerge myself to bathe my entire body and wash my hair. That alone was enough to turn my attitude from grim to optimistic. With that tiny seed of hope in my heart, along with the longer days, I began to feel as if I could face anything this challenging life had to throw at me.

It seemed to me by early March Mother Nature had finally gotten over her grumpy winter snit and wanted nothing more than to show off her glorious side and shower us with happiness, especially after we received some wonderful news from Josh.

Abbie and I were in Luther's vegetable garden hoeing the dirt in anticipation of planting some radish and carrot seeds. The day was gloriously warm, almost hot, so my sleeves were shoved as far up my arms as they could go and I had fastened the skirt of my dress to resemble a rather baggy pair of pedal-pushers, a pair of knee-length pants young women wore in the late 1960's.

Abbie laughed every time she looked at my makeshift fashion. "Women actually wear things like that in your time? It's kinda indecent, ain't it? Showin their ankles and legs and all."

I laughed, thinking of the miniskirts and jeans shorts that were my usual spring and summer attire in the future. "Not to me. It might shock you, but this is pretty modest compared to the things I usually wore."

She shook her head. "Why, you'd be arrested if Constable Jackson caught sight of you in a get-up like that."

I smirked. "Then I'd hate to see his reaction if I wore my bikini, slathered myself with baby oil and iodine, then stretched out on a beach towel to lay in the sun."

"Can't say I know what any of them things are, but if they showed more of your legs than that get-up does, you'd be in jail so fast it'd make your head spin. And why in the Sam Hill would you lay in the sun? You'd get burned to a crisp, wouldn't you?"

"A bikini is a type of bathing suit or swimming suit that women wear and a beach towel is just what it sounds like, a towel you take to the beach with you. Here, I'll show you." I knelt down in the dirt and traced with a twig an outline of a woman lying on a beach towel spread out on the ground underneath her. Then I sketched a bikini on her body. "That's what kind of bathing suits we wear in the future. It's a little skimpy but it feels wonderful when you're at the beach or a swimming pool. As for the baby oil, it's a special oil made to use on babies as a moisturizer. The iodine is a reddish medicine used on wounds that, when mixed with baby oil, gives you a better tan."

Abbie shook her head. "People in the future shore do some really strange things. You actually been to a beach and seen the ocean?"

"Lots of times. That's where my family always went on vacation, Marco Island or Clearwater Beach on the Gulf side of Florida."

Abbie squinted at me. "Where's Florida?"

"South of here, the southernmost state in America, actually." I thought a moment. "It's probably 600 miles away or so. It butts up to the Atlantic Ocean on the east side and the Gulf of Mexico on the west. Anyway, when I started college, I went to Daytona Beach on the ocean side of Florida every year with friends." I sighed. "Brings back memories of good times and good friends. Ben and I were hoping to go to Coney Island up in New York on the way back from Woodstock."

She leaned on her hoe. "Vacation? Coney Island? Woodstock? Sounds to me like you're speakin some kinda foreign language."

I smiled. "In the future, a vacation is a period of time you take off from work, usually a week but sometimes two. Coney Island is a well-known beach in New York. They're famous for, among other things, their hot dogs." Seeing her frown, I explained, "Hot dogs are a food made from beef or pork meat stuffed into a sausage casing so it looks like a long, thick cylinder. And Woodstock in upper New York state is where Ben and I were headed when I touched the light and it brought me here."

"What about the tan you say you got from layin in the sun? What does that mean?"

"Oh, in my time most people want to be a darker color in warm weather. You know how your hands get in the summer, browner than they are in the winter? People in my time think a tan makes you more attractive so they go to the beach or simply lie on a towel or blanket in their yard when the sun's out. Women wear bikinis and men wear swimming trunks so they can get a tan over most of their body."

She looked at me with doubt. "A tan over most of their body? Sounds silly to me."

I opened my mouth, but before I could get a word out, she shushed me. "You better make yourself decent." She nodded toward the trees that surrounded our little cabin. "Somebody's comin."

I hastily yanked the skirt of my dress free and let it drop then turned just in time to see Josh emerge from the woods on a beautiful bay mare.

He raised a hand and smiled. "Good day to you, ladies."

Abbie and I responded in unison. "Good day, Mr. Josh."

He ran his forearm across his sweating forehead. "A little hot for this early in spring."

"What brings you out this way, Mr. Josh?" Abbie asked. "Somethin wrong with some-un at your place?"

He grinned as he dismounted. "No, everybody's all right, far as I know. I needed a break so I decided to come share some happy news."

Abbie smiled. "Is that so?"

"Tillie and Samuel are getting married."

She clapped her hands with glee. "They are? Tillie finally said yes?"

"Yep and yep. Viola gave them her blessing—'course she did that a long time ago—and my father approved it."

"When?" Abbie asked as I said, "What do Viola and your father have to do with it? Sam and Tillie are adults. Can't they just get married if they want?"

"Oh, no, Lizzie," Abbie said, "They's certain rules, I guess you might call em."

"Really? Seems to me they're old enough to know their own minds, and from what I've seen, it's pretty obvious they love each other. Why, they can't be in the same room without sending off enough vib—sparks to start a two-alarm fire." I wanted to take that last back as soon as it came out of my mouth. Abbie frowned but Josh simply nodded.

"They are in love and Samuel has been asking, no begging, Tillie to marry him for more than a year now. Fact is, that's the very reason he ran away last year, Tillie's refusal to his latest proposal. I reckon he's asked her going on a thousand times but she always said no because of, well, she didn't want to marry Samuel because ..." He glanced away.

Abbie finished for him. "If there was any chance she could be carrying another man's child."

I thought about that for a minute then nodded. "Oh, you mean Eustus?"

Josh nodded, looking embarrassed.

"But what changed? Eustus is still your overseer, right?"

Josh grimaced. "He's not mine. He's my father's man. If I had my way, he'd have been discharged of his duties a long time ago."

"Then why hasn't he been?"

"It's my father's decision, not mine. Not yet anyway."

"It ain't Mr. Josh's fault, Lizzie," Abbie said. "For some reason, Mr. Hampton wants Eustus as overseer."

"Yes, I've talked to him numerous times about getting rid of Eustus, but my father is adamant he does his job well, so there's no reason to let him go."

"Then why has Tillie agreed to marry Samuel now?" I had a feeling I knew the answer to that question already and Josh's frown confirmed it.

"Eustus has moved on, you might say."

I nodded. "Meaning he's ra ... uh, forcing himself on some other poor girl? Is she a slave?"

Josh winced.

"Of course she is, who else would have that despicable piece of ..." I broke off at Abbie's warning hiss. She'd heard me cuss before and usually only laughed so the warning must have been about Josh. In 1860, proper Southern women would choke on their own tongue before cursing in public, especially in front of a man. I sighed. "Who is it this time, Josh?"

"You've never met her. Papa just bought her last month at an auction in Charleston. She's a house servant, works mainly in the kitchen, helping the cook."

I threw up my hands in disgust then turned on my heel and stomped away. I wanted to scream at Josh and hold him accountable though I knew it wasn't his fault. No, the blame lay entirely at Mr. Hampton's feet and the idiotic racism of this totally screwed up time I was stuck in. Bad enough that anyone who had the money could purchase a human being like they might buy a horse or a pair of shoes but the fact that people like Eustus could do anything he wanted to that person was so much worse in so many ways.

After a few seconds, I turned and looked at Josh. His dismal expression softened my anger a bit. He'd come here hoping to share good news and give us some happiness but my tirade had wiped all that joy away.

I walked back to him and laid my hand on his arm. "I'm sorry, Josh, I really am. I just don't understand how this can happen. I mean I understand it, of course, I just don't like it."

"Neither do I, Lizzie, but it's the way of the world and nothing can be done about it."

I nodded. "Of course. I shouldn't take my anger out on you. I apologize."

He caught my hand in his. "Apology accepted."

I smiled. "So tell us more about Samuel and Tillie. Will there be a ceremony we can all attend? When will it be? And where? Who's going to preside over it? Oh, and will there be a cake? If you ask me, that's the best part of any wedding. You should ask Maggie to bake it. I know from personal experience she can make a truly fantastic cake for the happy couple. Will Tillie have a shower?"

Abbie had been laughing at me but her laughter cut off when I asked about the shower. She frowned at me then tried to cover my mistake by asking Josh if his father was going to marry them.

His puzzled eyes cut to me, but thankfully, he played along with Abbie. In the past, Josh had said a few things about the lights that hinted he thought there was more to them than swamp gas. Several times now I had used language of my time around him which he would look puzzled about but never question. Not for the first time, I wondered if he knew or suspected that some of the lights were portals that opened to another world or another time.

I had no way of knowing, of course, unless I told him the truth, which I was still reluctant to do. I wasn't sure if he would believe me or write me off as a lunatic and stay far, far away from the wigged-out girl. By relaying my secret, I chanced ending my relationship with him so decided I would have to think long and hard about it before doing anything drastic.

Abbie was chattering on about the wedding, asking almost as many questions as I had. I tuned back in to hear Josh say, "Tillie and Samuel are two of my father's favorites so I imagine he will perform the ceremony after Violet questions them about their certainty that marriage is what they want. Then she'll lead the other slaves in a prayer to bless the union."

The prayer sounded nice but I was curious what sort of questions Viola would ask them and why she would have to ask them anything at all. They were both adults and knew what they wanted. It didn't make sense to me, but before I could go off on another tirade, I reminded myself this was a different era, and no matter how much it irritated me, I didn't have the right to be questioning Josh or the traditions of this time.

"You haven't said when or where the wedding will take place, Josh."

He grinned. "I haven't, have I?"

"No, you haven't."

"Well, it ain't been decided yet. Tillie wants it to be in May after the weather warms up sufficiently that they can be married outside. It may be she just wants to wait to make sure she's not ..." A blush crept up his neck.

"Carrying," Abbie said, turning to me. "She shouldn't put it off for that. Maggie has her chewin on Queen Anne's lace seeds to keep her from catchin."

Josh glanced away, looking uncomfortable, as if he wanted nothing to do with this conversation.

I didn't know anything about what they used as birth control in the mid 19th century but had to assume Maggie knew what she was doing. Still, Queen Anne's lace seeds? I guess they were easy to find here on the mountain but I wondered how effective they were.

Answering my unspoken question, Abbie said, "Queen Anne's lace seeds ain't foolproof by any means but they's the best thing we got here on the mountain. They's fields of them ever'where you look so they ain't no trouble to get."

I thought about the little circular container of birth control pills I had left behind, tucked safely inside my duffel bag with the other stuff I packed for our trip to Woodstock. They weren't foolproof either but were better than the other methods that were available at the time. Although the Supreme Court granted married women only this option of birth control in 1965, it had been easy enough to find a doctor willing to bend the rules for those of us who didn't have a husband. I remember the relief I'd felt when I first started taking the pill. After that, I didn't give it much thought, just popped one every day and tucked all my worries about pregnancy away.

"As for where," Josh was saying, "no one has said yet, but I imagine it will be outside Viola's cabin since it sits a little ways away from the others. Or maybe it'll be outside the cabin my father has assigned them."

"Oh, you know where they should have it? Down at that clearin by the creek. In the spring, the fiddlehead ferns with their pretty little coils of green grow heavy right there on the bank. And there'll be lots and lots of spring wildflowers bloomin." Abbie had a dreamy look in her eyes, sort of like the one on Maggie's face when she came home from seeing her secret beau in the woods. It was the first sign I'd ever seen that Abbie hadn't let Sarie's views on men sour her own.

"Is that the one directly behind the cabin where Viola lives?" I asked.

Abbie smiled. "You know it, Lizzie?"

I nodded. That lovely clearing by the creek was where I had gone for privacy after I had given Sarie and Josh the first of the many variolations for smallpox. I'd been sick at the thought I might have just killed them both and had walked out of Viola's cabin and ended up in the clearing. Abbie was right, it was a beautiful spot. "Oh, that would be perfect for a wedding. There's enough open space for the guests to gather around and to set up a table for the cake and other refreshments if they have them."

Josh grinned. "I'll be sure and suggest that to Samuel and Tillie." He glanced up at the sky. "I'm afraid I need to get back to the scraping, ladies. Eustus is there but I don't like to leave him alone with my men for any length of time. He has a heavy hand with that damned whip of his, especially when he thinks they're lazing around when they should be working."

Puzzled, I asked, "Scraping? What's a scraping?" at the same time Abbie sniffed and said, "I thought I smelled pine sap on you."

Josh smiled at her. "Yep, it's a right nice smell, ain't it?" He turned to me. "Scraping is the process of removing the bark and then carving a shallow scoop out of the trunk of a pine tree. It makes it possible to gather the pine sap so it can be sold or made into turpentine." He squatted down, picked up a stick and drew in the dirt. "Like that. After we make the scraping in the trunk, we set a bucket beneath it to catch the sap or resin that seeps out. We sell that to a place down in Morganton that turns it into turpentine. Old man Westcott had a still set up to do the job on his place. Noah and I have been considering doing the same but we're waiting to see if it's worth it to the farm. This is only our second year. Last year was mostly choosing the trees and preparing them. This year we've chosen a good size grove of trees but we have to use the shorter needle pines that grow around here. The best turpentine comes from long needle pines like they grow over near the coast."

"A still? I thought those were used to make whiskey or moonshine."

"They are and it's the same technique but these are solely for making turpentine out of the pine sap." He looked around at the small plot of land Abbie and I had been working on. "It's a hot day for this kind of labor. Why don't you walk into the woods with me and cool off before you get back to it?"

Abbie smiled. "Lizzie can go with you. I'm gonna go inside and get a cool drink of water and maybe get something goin for lunch."

I looked at her sly grin. I knew exactly what she was up to but couldn't be too mad since it was exactly what I wanted to do.

Leading his horse by the reins, we walked a little way into the coolness of the forest before Josh stopped and turned to me, dropping the reins on the ground. He cupped my elbows then ran his hands up to my shoulders and drew me to him. The kiss was brief and innocent but my heart immediately went into overdrive. He started to step back but I banded my arms around him and kissed him again, longer and with more passion. Afterwards, I hugged him as he buried his nose in my hair and nuzzled my neck.

"You appear to be shaking, Miss Lizzie."

I knew I was, couldn't seem to help it where he was concerned, but I snuggled into his chest and tried to quiet my body. After a minute or more, I said, "I think that's you shaking, Mr. Josh."

He kissed my neck. "Maybe it is, Lizzie. That seems to happen every time I'm around you."

"I know the feeling," I mumbled as Ben's face flashed into my mind. Dropping my arms, I moved away. I loved this wonderful man and it sometimes troubled me that I had turned from Ben so quickly. If I could manage to return to my time, I wondered if I would still be interested in him and whether he would still feel the same way about me or if another girl had caught his interest. I sighed. The only way I would ever know is if I did manage to find my light and had the courage to step into it again.

"What's wrong, Lizzie?"

Looking at the ground so he couldn't see my tearing eyes, I said, "I'm fine, Josh, just a little flash of homesickness. Missing my father and friends back in Knoxville."

"Would you like me to take you back? We could take one of our wagons and get there in a few days. Or I could take you into Asheville and you could catch the train."

I looked up, stood on tiptoe and kissed his cheek. "You're a sweet man, Josh, and I appreciate the thought but I don't think so. My father and I had a horrible argument before I left and I'm not yet ready to go back. I haven't really forgiven him and I don't want to see him until I have." It bothered me that the lie came so easily to my lips.

"Maybe you just need some more time, Lizzie."

"Yes, I think I do." I kissed his cheek again. "I'd better get back and help Abbie. Thank you for the walk."

"Think nothing of it, Lizzie." He bent to pick up the reins and vaulted onto the horse's back.

I leaned against a sturdy oak, watching until he was out of sight. Think nothing of it, indeed. He obviously didn't know the power he held over my heart.

Chapter Ten

Spring 1860

Look What You've Done

In April, I realized with a start that we were a year away from the beginning of the Civil War. Would I still be here then, I wondered, and said a quick prayer against that. I wasn't sure if the war had touched this mountain but knew of the brutality soldiers and innocents alike endured. This thought kept running through my mind as I went about the daily chores and it was at this time that I first began to hear talk about the presidency and the first rumblings of the anarchy and chaos that would lead to this horrific conflict.

This all came to a head at, of all things, a church picnic to herald in the warmth of spring and bid farewell to the cold, freezing days of winter.

The day was warm and fair as Abbie and I made our way down to the sisters' cabin, where we would meet Sarie, Maggie and Amanda May and continue on to the church. Abbie and I had spent the prior day trying our fare at baking. We knew we couldn't compete with Maggie but I felt the apple cobbler and apple tarts packed in our basket wouldn't be scoffed at. They were tasty to me, at least. Besides our baked goods, our basket also contained books we were returning to Josh in hopes that he would bring more to replenish our dwindling supply.

The sky was such a brilliant blue, I found I couldn't keep my gaze off it for long. "I've never seen a sky so beautiful, Abbie," I said.

She glanced up and smiled. "Is the sky different from when you came from, Lizzie?"

I nodded. "More hazy, not as clear. Not that pretty. And at night, all the stars in the sky we look at? You can't see a lot of them in my time."

"Why would that be?"

"Pollution, I imagine."

Her forehead furrowed. "Pollution?"

I nodded. "Dirty air. In my time, we have big industrial plants, factories, where things are made, such as the cars and planes I told you about. Furniture for houses, appliances and their parts. Big steam plants where coal is burned to generate electricity. All produce carbon emissions which go into the air and, I don't know, form a haze over everything, I guess. Last year, I went to California with my dad and—"

Her eyes brightened. "Did you fly in one of them airplanes you told me about?"

I smiled. "Sure did. Only took five hours or so. I swear, Abbie, the air was so dirty out there, everything looked brown to me."

She shook her head. "Leave it to man to destroy this earth, along with ever'thing else."

I looked up at the sky again. "Seeing this clear sky, I would have to say I agree."

When I looked down again, I spied Sarie, Maggie and Amanda May waiting on us up ahead. Maggie smiled widely while Sarie gave us her usual disgruntled look. Amanda May simply watched us approach with a slightly apprehensive look on her face.

"We been waitin forever," Sarie said when we reached them.

Maggie stepped behind Sarie and shook her head at us, negating this.

"Well, we're here now," Abbie said happily.

I smiled at Amanda May. "Good morning, Manda. You look awful pretty today."

She blushed and looked away. Amanda May was a shy girl who still wasn't comfortable around us. I knew how she felt and hoped she would soon begin to feel as if she were part of our group, not an outsider.

Without saying a word, Sarie turned and began to lead us down the trail toward the church. Amanda May stayed by her side but Maggie dropped back to walk with us, asking about the food we'd prepared and telling us what she had in her basket.

When we reached our destination, people were milling about the church yard, men huddling in groups telling tall-tales, women busily placing and arranging food on the tables. Abbie and I made our way to an empty one and began unloading our goods, debating with one another whether they would be eaten or left behind.

"Well, any leftovers, we'll just take them home and eat them ourselves," I said, smiling as Josh joined us. I had decided by this time there was no way I could avoid him or my feelings for him. Josh had been so kind to Abbie and me, helping us with the barn and providing us with food and essentials from his plantation's larder when ours began to dwindle. Without him, we wouldn't have had the flour or sugar for the fare we brought today. I looked forward to his visits and even more to his departures, when I would walk him outside for a few stolen kisses.

"Lizzie, Miss Abbie," he said, nodding at us.

"Mr. Josh, it sure is a fine day, ain't it?"

"Sure is, Miss Abbie. Looks like you two ladies have been busy in the kitchen." He reached out and picked up an apple tart, biting into it before I could warn him it was our first attempt.

Abbie and I waited, watching his face for a reaction. Josh grinned as he chewed then paid us the highest compliment by asking if Maggie made it.

Abbie shook her head, beaming. "We did, Mr. Josh."

"Well, I reckon it's the best apple tart I've ever eaten," Josh said.

I smiled at him. "Don't tease, Josh. We know it's not up to Maggie's standards."

"Then I reckon you haven't had a taste yourself," he said, grabbing another one.

Abbie and I laughed as we watched him finish it off.

"We brought your books back," I said.

"And I brought you more. Plus something I think you might like. Come on over to my horse and I'll show you."

As he and I walked away, he turned to Abbie. "You're welcome to come too, Miss Abbie. It's for both of you."

"Why I thank you," Abbie said, falling into pace with us.

Josh had hobbled his horse in the field so he could graze, a well-used saddle and large saddlebag lying on the ground nearby. He picked up the saddlebag and opened it, showing us several books stored inside. "You reckon that will do you for a week or so?" he teased, knowing our love of reading.

I shrugged as I smiled. "Maybe."

Josh unfastened a pocket on the outside of the saddlebag and reached inside, pulling out sheets of paper along with several wooden pencils and what looked to me like a fountain pen with a stoppered bottle of ink. "I remembered y'all teaching Melody to write using bark and a piece of charcoal so figured this nib pen and paper might come in handy in case you ever need it." He held up the pencils, five in all. "These wooden pencils Pa ordered from the Eagle Pencil Company in New York. He used to have to order them from Germany." He leaned closer to us. "Hide them if you see him, he keeps close tabs on his pencils."

"Oh," I breathed. "This is wonderful, Josh." I spontaneously reached out and hugged him, realizing too late other people were around. I quickly stepped away. "Thank you," I said, my face reddening. I ran my hand over the paper, noting it had more of a rough texture than that of my time and was not completely white, with some sort of impurities in the grain. I wondered what it was made of.

"Well, if people didn't know y'all was a-courtin afore, they sure do now," Abbie said with a grin.

Josh packed everything inside the saddlebag, giving me time to gain my composure. "Let me know when you're ready to leave so I can give this to you," he said as he placed it on the ground near the horse.

"We sure do thank you, Mr. Josh," Abbie said. "This will come in handy when we have to write notes to each other." She hesitated then turned to me. "You should start a journal, Lizzie, about all you're learnin and doin here, something to look back at later in your life."

I smiled with delight. "That's a great idea, Abbie." A commotion near the tables drew my attention.

Josh frowned as he looked that way. "You two stay here," he said and quickly walked in that direction.

Abbie sighed. "I reckon we ought to go, Lizzie, in case they's a fight."

"At a church picnic?"

"I'm sure some of the men's liquored up by now so ain't no tellin what's goin on over there."

Abbie and I made our way toward a group of people gathered around two men who were shouting at one another.

"Do you know them, Abbie?" I asked as we drew nearer.

She nodded as she pointed to the one on our right. "That there's Fleming Walker and the other one's his brother Carter." She shook her head. "They can't neither one get along. Always fightin about somethin or other."

As we drew nearer, Fleming shouted, "You call that bastid a rail splitter when he ain't nothing but a country splitter."

Rail splitter. That rang a bell with me.

"It don't make sense to me why you're against him," Carter said. "Hell, we're too poor for slaves." He waved his arm at those gathered around watching the argument. "Most of the people on this mountain can't afford em either."

And I knew the argument was about Abraham Lincoln which Carter confirmed as he continued, "Way I see it, we ain't got no dog in that fight. And if Mr. Lincoln can do half the things I been told he talks about, I say he's the man for the job."

"He ain't even declared he's running, you idjit," Fleming yelled. "And you know well and good if he does get elected, the South won't abide it. There'll be war."

Abbie looked at me with alarm.

"It's starting," I whispered.

A loud gasp from the crowd drew my attention to the two men, who were now locked together in combat, pushing and shoving at one another, pummeling each other with their fists.

"Shouldn't someone stop this?" I asked Abbie.

She shrugged. "We usually let em fight it out. They'll get tired afore long and go their separate ways."

I grabbed Abbie's arm when I saw Fleming pull a knife from a sheath on his belt and go after his brother. Josh and a few other men immediately reacted, stepping into the fray, but not before Fleming stabbed Carter in the back as he turned to get away from him. With a grunt, Carter fell to his knees. Josh wrenched the knife out of Fleming's hand as we all watched Carter collapse onto the ground.

Abbie and I immediately went to him, joined by Sarie and Maggie. I heard someone in the crowd yelling for the doctor.

Blood was everywhere, coating the ground beneath Carter, soaking into my skirt as I knelt beside him. I pulled his shirt up, checking the placement of the wound, and knew immediately he would not be saved. Regardless, I bunched my skirt up and held it against the wound to staunch the flow of blood. "The knife appears to have nicked the kidney," I said to Sarie in a low voice. "He won't survive."

She looked up at the crowd. "Don't let him get away," she said in a loud voice, pointing at Fleming. "He's got to be held accountable for what he's done."

I checked Carter's eyes, noted he was already unconscious.

"How long?" Sarie said.

"Seconds, minutes."

And all we could do was watch as Carter lost his life, there on what I felt should be considered sacred ground. I placed my fingers against his carotid artery, and when I felt no pulse, rose to my feet. "He's dead," I told Josh as I stepped away. I heard several women gasp and it appeared one fainted into the arms of her companion.

Men pushed at one another as they rushed toward Fleming and I feared there would be another death. Josh stepped in front of them, holding out his hands. "He ain't going anywhere. Let's wait for the sheriff and let him take care of this." Josh looked around the crowd. "I saw him earlier. Can someone go fetch him?"

"I seen him down at the cemetery," a young man said. "I'll go fetch him."

Fleming was being restrained by two men, one holding each arm, and he struggled to get away from them. "Let me see him," he yelled, tears gathering in his eyes. "Let me see my brother."

"You done killed him," one of the men said, jerking his arm. "There ain't nothing left to see."

"Oh, God, what did I do?" Fleming yelled, his voice filled with pain. "I didn't mean it, Brother," he said, hanging his head, "I didn't mean it."

As we waited for the sheriff, it was hard not to feel sympathy for the man who had killed his brother and who now seemed crushed by his actions. I knew this was only a small taste of what was to come, brothers fighting against brothers, fathers against sons, and selfishly prayed I would not be here to witness that. Although a bloody, violent war raged during my time, it was half a world away and did not pit families against one another as brutally as the Civil War had done, so I had always felt somewhat removed from it. But here, standing on ground where a life had now been lost over the issue of slavery, knowing hundreds of thousands more were doomed to the same fate, I felt overwhelmed to the point that I wanted to run away, screeching. I looked at Abbie and she must have seen the panic in my face, for she clutched my hand and squeezed hard. I squeezed back, thankful for my sweet friend, wondering what I would have done if I had not found Abbie in this cruel time.

It wasn't until after Sheriff Brittain took possession of Fleming and carted him off to jail that I noticed the drying blood on my skirt. "I guess I need to go home and change," I said to Josh and Abbie, standing next to me.

Freda Hennesy, the preacher's wife, apparently overhearing this, rushed over. "Oh, please, you must stay for the picnic," she said, waving her hands frantically. I looked at her flushed face and wondered if her demeanor was from witnessing a murder or something else. She was a small, frail-looking woman who reminded me of a bird, with her small, sharp eyes and pointed nose. Her body was so narrow, her shoulder blades protruded from her back, akin to a bird's folded wings. "Come with me to the house," she said, taking my elbow. "I have some strong lye soap that should get those stains out." As she steered me away, she said, "You're a hero, after all. You valiantly tried to save that young man's life and I'd just be beside myself if you went home hungry and ..." Her voice trailed off as she waved at my skirt.

"I appreciate your help," I said, seeing her discomfort.

She leaned close to me as we walked, still grasping my elbow. "It seems I never have a chance to visit with you, Lizzie Baker, and perhaps this will give us the opportunity to get to know one another."

I glanced at her, thinking I wasn't sure I wanted her to know me better. Although I wasn't well-acquainted with Freda, I sensed she was something of a busybody and admit to a bias against religious folk. In my time, it seemed the Christians I met were nothing but hypocrites, thinking that paying heed to God on Sunday gave them leave to commit all the sinful atrocities they might want during the other six days of the week while judging and condemning those who did not fit into their little boxes, such as homosexuals and people of color, those of lesser means or intelligence.

She led me to a charming cottage that sat directly behind the church, adorned with a wide wraparound porch and large brick chimney peaking above the roofline. I glanced around when we stepped inside, appreciating the painted walls and natural light pouring in from well-placed windows. Following her to the kitchen at the back of the house, I glanced into two bedrooms as we passed by. Both had high iron beds adorned with colorful quilts and lacy white curtains at the windows waving in the spring breeze. The kitchen was modern compared to most I'd seen with the exception of plantations, with a sink set into a long wooden countertop and a large wood-burning stove with warmer. What I'd give for that, I thought to myself.

Freda pulled out a chair from a round wooden table and lightly pushed me down into it. She immediately set to work filling a bowl with water and finding rags and a bar of lye soap. Her movements were jerky and hurried as she began to work at the large stain on the bottom of my skirt, and I began to wonder if she wasn't going to hyperventilate. I finally put my hand on her arm. "I can do this. I think you need to sit down, Freda, you seem awfully agitated."

She placed her hand on her chest, below her throat.

"Just breathe deep and let it out slowly," I said.

She sat in the chair next to me, making an effort to calm herself. "It was just so frightful." She bit her lip, tears springing to her eyes.

I nodded.

"I've never seen anyone die before." She wrung her hands. "I imagine as a healer, you have witnessed it."

"Not often," I admitted.

"That poor boy," she said more to herself than me. "We've all seen those brothers fight but always assumed it would pass. I never imagined one would kill the other." Her eyes met mine and she shook her head. "And all over something most of us don't even care about." She seemed to shudder. "Well, nothing to do about it now," she said, in a low voice. "Let's see if we can save your dress."

I let her work on the stains, thinking busywork might help her. I imagined a lot of men and women were feeling the same way Freda was, and Abbie, Maggie and Sarie were probably staying busy helping those women who were in a state, as Sarie called it. I hoped one of them would remember Amanda May, as to me she appeared to be skittish and could very well suffer from witnessing the murder of a man.

Freda calmed down after a bit and seemed pleased she was, indeed, able to remove the blood stains from my skirt. She smiled at me when she finished. "I think I could use a cup of tea. Would you like one, Lizzie?" I glanced outside, wondering if the picnic had started. "It will only be a minute or two."

I smiled at her. "I'd love one, thank you."

As she filled the kettle, she said, "Tell me about yourself, Lizzie. I understand you're from Knoxville."

"Yes."

"And your family, are they still there?"

"My father is."

"I understand he's a doctor, is that right?"

"Yes."

"And the sisters are your cousins?"

"Yes, on my mother's side."

"Where is your mother, if I might ask?"

"She died several years ago."

"Oh, I'm so sorry." She turned and faced me, a curious look on her face. "I find it interesting you have stayed here on Brown Mountain as long as you have. I'm sure if your father is a doctor, your family is one of, well ..." She waved her arm around. I didn't know if she was searching for the word or wanted me to fill it in. I refused to do so. She finally said, "Some means." It was all I could do not to look around at her bright, sunny kitchen and comment her husband apparently had means of his own. "And the sisters," she continued, "although they are truly gifted healers and essential to the mountain people, aren't as well off as your own family must be. So why do you stay?"

I shrugged. "I'm learning from them. I'd love to be a doctor—"

"Oh child, I've never heard of such a thing, a woman being a doctor." She made a face as if she found this ridiculous.

I almost said in my time there were plenty of women doctors but caught myself before I did. Although women had come a long way by 1969, there were still barriers to be conquered, and I couldn't help wondering if I would ever be a part of that as I said, "Well, if I can't be a doctor, I want to be the best healer I can be. And who better to learn from than the sisters?" I smiled at her to take the edge off my voice.

She studied me for a long moment and I sensed she didn't believe me.

"Once I've learned all I can from them, I'll return home where I hope to be able to help my father in his practice."

Her smile was insipid at best. "Well, I'm sure you'll be of much help to him, dear, once you return home."

A knock on the door drew our attention and we both looked up when the door opened and Josh stepped in. "Picnic's about to start, Lizzie. I was hoping you'd be done by now."

Freda smiled widely at Josh. Of course she would, I thought, looking at him. He's so handsome and a truly good man. How can I leave him, my inner voice whispered, but I ignored it as I rose to my feet, shaking out my damp skirt. "Freda got the stains out so I believe I'll stay and eat." I walked toward him, smiling.

Josh smiled back. "I've asked Miss Abbie to save me a couple more of those apple tarts of yours. I figured that'll make a mighty fine ending to what looks to be a glorious meal."

Freda fluttered about us, asking about the tarts, engaging Josh in conversation. As we walked toward the field, she put her arm through his and leaned into him and I couldn't help but smile to myself, wondering how many other women on this mountain had a crush on Josh. He winked when he caught my smile, as if acknowledging my thought.

I noticed as we walked to the tables that someone had placed a horse blanket over the bloodied ground, but as we ate, my eyes kept going to that spot and I noticed several others doing the same thing. Constable Jackson had made an appearance by then and was walking around, talking to people about what had happened. He kept shooting dark glances my way and I knew it would only be a matter of time before he made his way to me and would in all likelihood accuse me of helping that poor boy die.

Josh tried to keep my attention averted, but my thoughts had gone back to the brutality of the Civil War and at times I had to force myself to keep from telling him that whatever he did, to not engage in that war. I feared for his life to the point that I became quite anxious about it. I finally stood abruptly and said, "I need to leave, Josh. I'm sorry but, well ..." My eyes wandered back to that spot.

Josh rose to his feet. "I know, Lizzie. I think it's affecting all of us. Why don't I saddle my horse and I'll take you home?"

I shook my head. "I came with Abbie. I guess I should go home with her. I wouldn't want her walking by herself."

He glanced at the sky, which was beginning to darken. "Why don't I walk with both of you?"

I wanted to put my arms around him and hold him close or, truth be told, have him hold me close, but refrained. It had become apparent to me that Josh's father didn't approve of his friendship with me. The times he looked our way, his demeanor was one of displeasure and condemnation. I wondered what he said to Josh when they were alone. I imagined he felt I wasn't a proper fit for a young genteel man like Josh. I was looked upon as a mountaineer whereas Josh was the son of a plantation owner and a certified attorney. My life did not coincide in any way with theirs. I was curious what Mr. Hampton would think if he knew where I had actually come from and the life I led before this one. But he would never know because I could never tell him.

The walk home was mostly in silence other than occasional soft nickering by Josh's horse, trailing along behind us. I think all our thoughts were on the death of young Carter and what would happen to his brother. I prayed I wouldn't be called to testify at the trial although feared I might be since I had tended to him. We stopped to rest on the mountain at an area that looked down into Linville Gorge. We were all, for some unknown reason, staring down into the valley as we caught our breath and gasped synchronistically when we saw a row of white lights seem to rise from beneath the ground.

"What in the world?" Abbie said.

"It's the lights," I said.

We watched, fascinated, as they hovered above the ground for several long moments then as one rose up and quickly separated, darting here and there into the sky, until they were out of sight.

I looked at Abbie. "Have you ever seen that?"

She shook her head. "Pa claimed he seen somethin like this once, a row of lights, all different colors, hangin in the air, but they disappeared by the time he reached em. 'Course nobody believed him, we all thought he was drunk. Most of the lights I've seen are white like that, but I ain't never seen so many at once. Have you, Mr. Josh?"

"Can't say I have," he said, wonder in his voice. "Fact is, the only light I've ever seen is the one that shocked the constable." He stared at the sky. "Although I've heard about them all my life. Some folks claim the lights are nothing but marsh gas, but we all know better, don't we?" He looked at me, then Abbie.

We both nodded.

"Let's just hope we don't encounter one on our way up the mountain," he said.

Abbie and I glanced at one another but said nothing.

Once home, Abbie took the saddlebag from Josh. "I thank you for these fine things, Mr. Josh. I'll just take them on inside now." She gave me a knowing look.

After she closed the door behind her, I threw myself in Josh's arms, kissing him long and breathlessly, delighting in the feel of his body against mine, his mouth warm and insistent. After a bit, we parted, smiling at one another.

He took my hands in his and leaned close. "I've never known a woman like you, Lizzie. You're smart, smarter than anyone I know, caring, brave, and the best kisser I've ever met."

I snorted. "That's a big compliment, coming from you," I teased.

His face remained grave. "There's something you're not telling me about yourself, Lizzie, and I respect that." His lips touched my ears. "But I want you to know that you can tell me anything, anything at all, and it will never change the way I feel about you or my admiration and respect for you."

I drew back, looking at him, wondering if I should say anything. I finally said, "There is something, Josh, something you might not believe and I'd love to tell you but not yet."

He cocked his head at me.

"Soon," I promised, kissing him again, using him to take my mind off what was coming.

Chapter Eleven

Spring 1860

I've Been Loving You Too Long

The spring days drifted by, as mercurial as a crotchety old woman with a bad case of indigestion. The shifting weather with its sudden thunderstorms, unpredictable temperatures and winds that often blew so hard Abbie and I had to hold on to each other just to walk out to the outhouse, proved to be a challenge. But I welcomed it, secure in the knowledge that a constant deluge of warmer days was not too far ahead. Besides, on the coldest days, we stayed inside next to the fire reading or taking care of various chores like mixing up Abbie's spring tonic which consisted of ginseng root, hawthorn berries, rose petals and a myriad of other plants and herbs.

Other than people coming by for a dose—Abbie's tonic was a well-known spring pick-me-up on the mountain—we didn't see much of anyone at all. Josh dropped by occasionally to check on us and ask if we needed anything and Maggie often stopped by on what she claimed was a gathering trip but I suspect was one of her romantic meetings with her secret man. We didn't see hide nor hair of Sarie, which I considered a blessing. Maggie told us Sarie had taken Amanda May under her wing, teaching her the proper time and process for gathering plants and describing them so she could recognize the many varieties that grew on the mountain, how to prepare the different concoctions and what illness or condition they were used to treat. She said Amanda May was a quick learner and probably wouldn't be with them for the usual time most bound children stayed with a family.

About the only excitement we had was when Thomas and Zeke showed up one morning in early May. It was one of the beautiful days with warm temperatures, no wind and not a cloud in the sky. Abbie and I were sitting on the front porch steps, taking a break from hoeing the garden. I thought I would hate this chore but it turned out I loved the smell of newly overturned dirt and the sight of the neat, straight rows we made in the soil in preparation for planting the summer seeds.

We both jumped when Thomas and Zeke appeared, riding helter-skelter on their horses, yelling for Abbie. They pulled back on the reins so hard, I fully expected to see blood pouring from the corners of their poor horses' mouths.

Abbie and I stood up, saying in unison, "What's wrong?"

Thomas answered as Zeke looked to be too distressed to speak. "We need you to come quick, Miss Abbie. Zeke and I was scything my lower field and Zeke's boy Simon wandered a bit too close." He rubbed his hand over his face. "We thought he was inside with Bethie and Ginny but he must've got away from them. He's bleedin real bad. We couldn't get it to stop. I think he needs a Bloodstopper."

Abbie stepped off the porch, saying, "Lizzie, get my saddlebag from inside and make sure my Bible's in there."

As I ran into the cabin, leaving the door open, I heard her say, "You doin all right, Zeke?"

When Zeke answered, his voice was low and strained with desperation. "Please, Miss Abbie, please. It's my boy. You got to come help him."

As I walked back out on the porch, I saw Abbie swing up behind Zeke on his horse. She settled herself then patted his arm as he scrubbed his hand over his face, trying to dry the tears. "It'll be all right, Zeke. I promise I'll do what I can." She glanced at me. "Lizzie, get up behind Thomas. I may need you." She turned to Thomas. "Where's the cut, Thomas?"

"On his arm, Miss Abbie."

I was barely on the horse before Thomas clicked his tongue and sent the horse off in a fast trot, Abbie and Zeke right beside us.

"Lower arm or upper?" Abbie asked, her voice quavering from being jostled.

Thomas frowned. "Inside of his wrist, Miss Abbie."

Abbie looked at me, her concern obvious.

"We left him with my Bethie and his ma in the house. Bethie wrapped his arm and said she'd do her darnedest to stop the blood until we got back with you. Ginny's right het up."

Abbie nodded. "I'm sure she is. It's good that Bethie's there. But we need to get to Zeke's boy quick as we can."

As the trail ahead cleared and opened up, both Zeke and Thomas dug their heels into the horses' sides, sending them both into a gallop. I hung onto Thomas, holding Abbie's saddlebag between us, wedged against his back.

I was worried about the boy, of course, but in truth, I was more excited at the thought of watching Abbie's skill as a Bloodstopper. I'd only seen her do it once before when a young slave cut his leg with an axe as he cut some kindling. I had thought for sure the boy was dead but Abbie, after checking his wound, rose to her feet and walked away from him, reading a passage from the Bible as she did. The procedure intrigued me so much I'd taken the time to find it and memorize it: "And when I passed by thee, and saw thee polluted in thine own blood, I said unto thee when thou wast in thy blood, live; yea, I said unto thee when thou wast in thy blood, live." For the bleeding to stop, this passage from Ezekiel had to be repeated three times by the Bloodstopper as they walked in an easterly direction, followed by the full name of the person who was bleeding. Abbie had explained to me after we left the plantation that once a person became a Bloodstopper, the secret of the power could only be passed to three other members of the opposite sex. If Abbie chose to share it with me, a female like her, or four men rather than three, she would lose the ability.

It wasn't long before we arrived at a small cabin set in the middle of a clearing. The front door was propped open and a woman stood in the doorway, anxiously wringing her hands in her apron. Abbie jumped down as soon as the horse stopped and I followed suit. We both ran up the steps as the woman rushed past us, sobbing and calling for Zeke. Abbie and I hurried inside only to stop when we saw the boy slumped in another woman's lap. She held one of his arms above his head, gripping the blood-drenched towel wrapped around his wrist. A large jar of honey and a small round tin sat on the table beside her.

"Is he still alive, Bethie?" Abbie asked.

"I ain't checked in a few minutes. I was a-feared to," the woman holding him said.

I shoved the saddlebag into Abbie's hands then walked over and took the boy's other wrist in my hand, checking for a pulse. After a few seconds, I looked up at Abbie. "It's weak but it's there."

She pulled the worn Bible out then let the saddlebag drop to the floor as she hurried over to us.

"How long has he been unconscious?" I asked Bethie.

"Not long, maybe five, ten minutes or so."

I nodded, still holding the boy's thin wrist in my hand. "He could've passed out from fear, Abbie."

"Coulda but it's more likely he passed out from losing blood."

Zeke helped the other woman, who I assumed was Ginny, his wife and the mother of the boy, into the cabin. His arms were wrapped around her and my guess was if he hadn't had hold of her she would be flat on the floor. It surprised me when she spoke from behind hands clasped tightly over her mouth, her voice wavering. "Is he dead, Miss Abbie? Bethie wouldn't tell me nothin."

"I didn't want to scare you any more than you already was, Ginny." Bethie's breath hitched as she looked at Abbie. "Kin you fix it, Miss Abbie?"

"I'm goin to do my best."

"You did right, holding his arm up above his head. That may have just saved his life," I said.

Abbie took the boy's raised hand in hers. "Let go the towel now, Bethie and let me get a look-see." When Bethie did as she asked, Abbie gently unwound the towel, holding it close so she could put it back on the wound if it was still bleeding. She breathed in and let it out slowly. "Come have a look, Lizzie."

I moved over to stand beside her, smiling when she revealed the injury under the bandage. Where I had expected to see blood flowing from the cut, if not actually gushing, there was only a long gash covered in some sort of dried leaf and flower, I thought must be yarrow, barely oozing blood.

"What did you put on it?"

Bethie answered, her voice anxious. "Did I make it worse?"

I smiled. "No, like I said before, you may have saved his life." I gently prodded around the wound. My finger came away with part of a limp flower covered in some sort of sticky, syrupy liquid. I raised my finger to my nose and sniffed. "Is that honey?"

"Yes'm," Bethie answered. "I remember my granny treated all kinds of things with honey."

Though I already knew, I wanted to keep her talking as it seemed to settle her a bit. "And what is the plant?"

"Jist some dried yarrow leaves and flowers. Learned that'un from my Granny too."

"Your granny sounds like a smart woman," Abbie said. "What do you think, Lizzie?"

"Yes, very smart. The honey's a good antiseptic and will help ward off infection. I've seen Abbie and her sisters use yarrow lots of times before to curtail bleeding. It must be a common plant around here."

Bethie nodded. "Oh, yes'm, it's all over the mountain. I can show you where to find it if'n you want."

I smiled. "I'm sure Abbie can show me." It never failed to amaze me the many ways the sisters and apparently the other mountain folk used the plants and herbs around them to heal whatever might turn up. "That cut looks to me like it needs a few stitches and he'll ... what's his name, Simon?" I asked.

"Yep," Zeke said.

"Simon's going to need a few stitches but he should be all right." I picked up the saddlebag then turned to Abbie. "I'll stitch him up while you tell Ginny and Zeke what else they'll need to do to build his blood back up."

Abbie nodded. "Ginny, looks like your boy's lost some blood, but Miss Lizzie is right, he oughta be fine. He just needs to rest until he builds it back up again. One of the best ways to do that is to have him drink as much dandelion tea as you can get down him. If he don't like the dandelion, you can give him red raspberry leaf or hawthorn berry tea. Any of those oughta help get his strength back." She stopped and laid her hand on Simon's head. "He's gonna have a nice scar to show off to his friends after the stitches come out and I reckon he'll make up a good bloody story to go along with it."

Ginny, instead of smiling or laughing as I expected, burst into tears then rushed over to grab Bethie in a tight hug.

"Here now, Ginny, don't take on so. Your baby boy's gonna be fine."

Simon stirred and moaned. I immediately stopped stitching until I was sure he wouldn't tug his arm away and hurt himself.

"And lookie there, he's wakin up," Bethie said. "Dry your eyes, woman, so you don't scare the boy. He's gonna be scared enough as it is."

Ginny quickly scrubbed her face with her apron before kneeling beside Simon and placing her cheek gently on his. She whispered something in his ear. I couldn't hear her words but the effect on her son was instant. He stilled for a moment but whimpered before I could go on with my stitching.

I looked at Abbie. "He's in pain. What do we have?"

Abbie dug into her saddle bag. "Wild lettuce is the best but I don't know if we have any left." She muttered to herself as she continued searching.

"Anything else we can try?"

"Oh, lots of things but wild lettuce sap is the best. Ah, here it is." She pulled out a jar and shook it, causing the milky white substance inside to break apart. Opening the jar, she pulled out a minuscule piece and handed it to Ginny. "Put it in his mouth and have him chew it up, if he can. It's a bitter taste but it works pretty fast." She bent down and looked into Simon's tear-filled eyes. "Can you be brave for your mama, Simon?"

He wiped his eyes and sniffed. "I'll try."

"Good boy." She patted him on the head then said to Ginny, "It might make his mouth go numb. If he can get this one down, we'll give him another piece."

We all watched anxiously as Simon took the piece and chewed. Other than scrunching up his face as if he had just bitten into a lemon, he got it down. After his second piece, he was sitting up in his mama's arms, snuggled into her as his eyes drooped.

Abbie smiled. "I reckon I forgot to mention it might make him sleepy."

I breathed a sigh of relief and went back to stitching Simon's wound while Abbie gave Ginny the rest of the wild lettuce along with a tin of calendula salve to prevent infection.

By the time we were done, Simon was sound asleep. When Abbie and I left a few minutes later, we both had contented smiles on our faces.

Thomas helped us mount Zeke's horse for the ride home. Abbie chatted about the weather and other things with Thomas as I rode in silence behind her, thinking about how in my time most people had given up on natural remedies and cures and stuck with pharmacological medicines prescribed by their physicians. And about how I could use the knowledge I was learning from the sisters to treat people if I ever got back there. I didn't know if I'd be seen as some sort of witch or possibly a crazy woman or merely a doctor who used outdated procedures to cure my patients but hoped if I ever was lucky enough to find my light and return to my life and became a doctor, I would use any and all methods, not just the ones I learned in medical school.

Thomas's hooting laughter brought me out of my thoughts and I focused on the conversation he was having with Abbie.

"His granny always told him to cover yer eyes and run fast as you can in t'other direction if you see one. That's 'xactly what Sheldon did." His laughter rang out again. "Only problem was, he forgot to uncover his eyes so he could see where he was goin." He continued to laugh as he slapped his hand against his thigh. "Ran across his cornfield and trampled a good bit of it to the ground but he didn't stop there, he kept on a-runnin until he run straight into a bramble patch and come home all covered in blood and a good bit of blackberry juice."

He laughed harder, trying his best to wipe the tears running down his cheeks on his shirtsleeve. He finally withdrew a red bandanna from his back pocket and swiped it across his face before blowing his nose with a loud honking sound. I was surprised it didn't spook his horse.

Puzzled, I asked Abbie, "What in the world is he carrying on about, Abbie?"

She giggled. "I don't reckon you've ever met Sheldon Carter, have you, Lizzie?"

"No, I haven't. Who is he?"

"Sheldon's a ... well, I can't really call him a farmer 'cause he don't grow nothin but corn since his wife left him a few years ago. She run off with a blacksmith from Morganton. Don't know where they got to but nobody's seen her or him since.

"Sheldon plants a small crop of corn ever year, enough to keep his still runnin so he can fill up a bunch of old mason jars with moonshine. He's been known to sell some of the corn liquor to friends if they catch him in a good frame of mind, but he keeps most of it for hisself.

"He's a rough'un. I don't think he washes but once a month, if then, and his clothes all look to be hand-me-downs from his pa who died a long time ago. They hang off him since he's skinny as a rail and his pa was a good-size man.

He don't usually come to church but Thomas was telling me he'll probably be there this Sunday."

"Why's that?"

She turned and smiled at Thomas. "This is your story, Thomas, so I'll let you tell it."

"All right, Miss Abbie. Well, Miss Lizzie, seems Sheldon was out picking elder berries t'other day when he heard a rustlin from behind him. When he turned to look, he didn't see nothin so he went back to fillin his bucket with berries."

"'Scuse me, Thomas. I should've told you, Lizzie, Sheldon has a nice stand of elderberry bushes on the far edge of his cornfield. He picks the berries and uses em to make elderberry wine for when his stash of corn liquor runs out."

Thomas picked the story back up. "Well, it was gettin near about sundown and he heard the noise again, only this time it come from in front of him as if somethin was in the elderberry bushes. Then he says he heared it from all around him but he couldn't see nothin t'all. The noise kept getting louder and louder till 'stead of pickin all he was doin was turnin in circles tryin to find the critter that was makin the noise.

"Accordin to Sheldon, he finally saw something out of the corner of his eyes, and he swears on his very soul it was a wampus cat."

"A what?"

"A wampus cat or a catty-wampus as some people call it."

"I always thought catty-wampus meant someone that was crazy or something that was messed up so bad it couldn't be fixed."

Thomas nodded. "That's what a lot of people think. But people from round 'bout these parts know it's a critter."

"What kind of critter?"

Thomas's laughter ended with a loud snort. "Beg pardon, Miss Lizzie. Some people say it comes from an old Indian legend. See, the Cherokee believe it's a evil demon called Ew-ah or the Spirit of Madness that was terrorizing their village a long time ago. The shamans sent out their fiercest warrior, name of Standing Bear, to get rid of it. He was gone a long time, and when he finally come back, he was crazy as a Bessie bug, screamin and clawin out his own eyes.

"Standing Bear's wife, Running Deer, knew her husband wouldn't be any good to her in that condition, and by Cherokee law, he was dead. So she decided to go after the Ew-ah her own self. When she told the shamans, they give her a booger mask what looked like a bobcat's face to wear while she hunted for the critter and told her she had to be the one to surprise the demon in order to win. The war chiefs also give her a black paste and told her to rub it all over her body to disguise her scent and make her invisible. She tracked the critter through the woods for many days, finally catching it unawares as it took a drink at the creek. When that evil demon turned and saw the Cat Spirit Mask, it began to tear at itself 'cause the spirit of the mountain cat turned the magic back on it. It thrashed around somethin terrible until it fell into the creek. Running Deer immediately turned and ran away. And that was the end of the wicked critter.

"Now the way I heared it from my grampa and the way most of the mountain folk around here believe, it's a howling devil critter, half-cat, half-dog, that can run upright or on all fours. It has yeller eyes that can pierce the heart and soul of anybody who sees it and can drive a man crazy with one look.

"My grampa told me the same thing Sheldon's ma told him: If'n you see a wampus cat, cover your eyes and run as fast as you can in t'other direction. Which is what ol' Sheldon did, 'ceptin he forgot to open his eyes the least little bit to see where he was goin. He trampled most all the corn and then he got tangled up in some blackberry bushes. When he finally got free, he stumbled into town all bloody and stained with red juice 'cause them blackberries weren't ripe yet. I tell ya, he was red from his head all the way down to his toes and was carryin on about how he just saw a wampus cat. Preacher Hennesy was there and put the fear of God into him and that's why he'll probably be at Sunday meetin this week."

By this time, Abbie and I were both laughing so hard tears ran from our eyes. When I finally got my breath back so I could talk, we were at the front of our cabin. I slid down off Zeke's horse, waited for Abbie to do the same. As Abbie handed Thomas the reins, I said, "Thank you for telling us that, Thomas. I really enjoyed it and think I'll be looking forward to meeting Mr. Sheldon Carter this Sunday."

Thomas grinned as he tipped his hat to us. "Why, you're welcome, Miss Lizzie. I'll see you ladies at church."

Tillie's and Samuel's wedding was set for the first of June on a gorgeous day that was warm and sunny with a slight breeze that kept us cool even in the full sun. Josh sent Noah to pick Abbie and me up in a buggy. While Abbie chatted with Noah, I admired the scenery as we rode, noticing more wildflowers than a week ago and the way the sunlight bounced off the water of the creek.

When we arrived at the small clearing beside the creek where the wedding was to take place, I couldn't help but smile at the sight of Josh in a formal suit and hat. Samuel stood beside him looking more than a little bit anxious as he wrung his hands. Mr. Hampton stood a few feet away, chatting with one of his daughters.

When Josh caught sight of us, he patted Samuel on the shoulder, said something that made Samuel smile, then started walking in our direction. I swear, my heart rate increased with every step he took. Judging by his self-satisfied grin, I think he knew exactly what was going on with my heart. I had no doubt it was clearly written all over my face. I could only hope his was doing the same thing.

When he got to us, he took off his hat and bowed dashingly, sweeping the arm that held the hat across his abdomen. It took my breath away.

"Miss Lizzie, how are you this fine day?"

I smiled. "I'm just fine, Mr. Josh. Thank you for asking. May I say, you look mighty debonair."

He reached up and helped me down from the buggy. It surprised me that my knees didn't buckle when he set me on my feet. Then he turned and helped Abbie, saying something I have no doubt was charming and sweet. I couldn't hear over the sound of the blood rushing through my veins and my heartbeat thrumming in my ears but Abbie giggled.

When I caught sight of Eustus standing beside Mr. Hampton with his thumbs hooked in the waistband of his pants, the smile dropped from my mouth. He looked around with a smug grin on his face as if he was responsible for the event or was the proud papa of the bride. I really wished I could go up to him and slap that look off his despicable face. After all, if it wasn't for him, Samuel and Tillie would have been married a long time ago.

"Lizzie?" Josh said, drawing my attention back to him. "Is something wrong?"

I forced my lips to smile. "No, no, everything's fine." He held out his arm and I took it, vowing to ignore Eustus for the rest of the day and not let him spoil my happiness.

After Abbie took Josh's other arm, he led us over to Viola who stood on the bank of the creek. Like Samuel, she looked anxious and I hoped it was only because she would be expected to lead the group in prayer, not because something had happened.

"Is Viola all right?" I asked Josh. "She looks a bit nervous."

"I'm sure she is but maybe it would help if you talk to her for a little while. I know she likes you."

I smiled. "Of course. I always enjoy talking to Viola."

Unfortunately, that was one of the few moments of joy I knew all day. When we got to her, Viola greeted us but other than that didn't have much to say. Abbie wandered away to speak to Sarie, Maggie and Amanda May when she saw them emerge from the woods. I would have gone with her but I couldn't shake the feeling that something was wrong with Viola. It was so unlike her not to talk and laugh about some silly bit of nonsense or some mischief one of the children had gotten into.

But today, she was silent, and when I saw a tear slide down her cheek, I knew for sure something was bothering her. Given the steely stares she shot in Eustus's direction, I felt sure he was the culprit.

When I laid my hand on her arm, she turned to look at me. "Viola, what is it? Has something happened?"

Her mouth formed a straight, hard line which I thought signaled her unwillingness to confide in me. I debated what I could do to get her to talk when she nodded toward Eustus and said, "That Mr. Eustus over there, he a bad man."

My heart sank. "I agree. What has he done now?"

She sniffed and wiped her cheek. "He says he caught one of the young'uns sneaking around the house, peeking into the parlor window. Said the boy was lookin to steal somethin, food or some such thing."

"Oh no, what did he do? Did he whip him?"

She didn't answer for a few minutes, and when she did, my heart stopped. "No'm not yet, but he plans on it. He put him in my cabin and told him he'd be back after the wedding and Jonas better be there if'n he knew what was good for him. Then he set a couple of other men to guard the door." She turned to me and gripped my hands. "He's gonna whup him, Miss Lizzie, or worse."

"Worse? What could be worse than being whipped? Why, he almost killed Samuel and Samuel's a grown man ... a healthy grown man. I can't imagine what that kind of treatment would do to a young child."

She lowered her voice so that I had to strain to hear her. "He could claim he caught him stealin and cut off one of his hands if'n he wants to. Mr. Hampton'd take his word for it."

I stepped back, shocked. "Why would he do that, Viola?"

"Mr. Eustus has got a lot worse over the last few months. Some say it's 'cause he's scared of us."

"Scared? Of you? Do you mean of the slaves? But what can you do to him? What can anyone do? According to Josh, he's a favorite of his father's so his position is secure. I'd say that gives him all the power."

"Yep, it do. Don't know what kind of sickness is ridin him. Alls I knows is I don't trust him no more than I trust a rabid polecat." She punctuated this by looking down at the ground and spitting.

"Viola, look at me." Her eyes met mine and I could see what I'd taken for nerves was actually rage. "What are you thinking of doing?"

When she didn't answer, I gripped her arms tightly. "You have to be careful, Viola. I can see the fury in your eyes, and if I can see it, others can, too. You need to keep your cool … uh, I mean, remain calm and stay away from Eustus. Please, tell me you'll do that."

"I knows how to hide my feelings from white folk, Miss Lizzie. I been doing it practic'ly my whole life. Don't you worry about ol' Viola."

"Of course I'll worry about you. You're my friend and I love you. Promise me you won't do anything. Please."

Her eyes softened a bit. "Ain't never had no white lady say she my friend. But you're different from most white folk. I can promise you I'll be careful but I jist don't know if I can keep that promise. He messin with my people, Miss Lizzie. Messin with one of my chillin. I can't stand by and let him do that. I can't—" She shook her head violently. "No, no, what I mean is, I won't.

"Viola, you have to, you don't really have a choice right now. Don't interfere with him and get yourself in trouble, please don't. You don't know what he'll do to you."

Her lips curved upward but stopped short of an actual smile. "Don't you worry, Miss Lizzie. If I do somethin, I have ways to hide it so that black-hearted devil will never know."

"What ways?"

She shook her head. "I ain't sayin no more about it." She looked over my shoulder and once again her lips curved but this time they made it into a full-blown smile. "Look at that. If that ain't a pretty sight, I don't know what is."

I turned and saw Tillie walking toward Samuel and had to smile too. Her dress, while not the traditional white of most brides, was a soft creamy yellow with tiny flowers sprinkled all over it. Her dark eyes stayed on Samuel as if he was the only person or thing worth looking at. "Oh, my, doesn't she look lovely?"

"She shore do. Mz Hampton give her the dress. Said it didn't fit her no more and Tillie needed to be dressed up on her weddin day. Mz Hampton's always been partial to Tillie."

"Is she here? I've only seen her a few times at church but we've never been introduced."

"Nope, she down with one of her blindin headaches this mornin. Wish I knew what to give her to make her feel better. She gets em a couple of times a month, sometimes more, and they so bad all she can do is take to her bed and wait for em to pass. Real shame the way she suffers."

"Can't the sisters help her?"

"Don't rightly know. Miz Hampton's a might 'ticular when it comes to her health. Won't let nobody treat her but the doctor in town and most of the time she refuses even that. Says all he does is give her medicine that makes her sleepy and she don't like that. You'd best git over yonder to your people, Miss Lizzie. Mr. Eustus been watching you ever since you come over. Can't say what he thinkin but he don't look like he likes it. 'Sides, it don't look right you spendin all your time over here talkin with me but I do appreciate it." Her grin widened. "Go on, now. It's time."

Before I could object to her comment about it being "right" for me to be with her or ask what time it was, she raised her arms and called out, "Let's us say a prayer for Samuel and Tillie."

As requested, I went over to stand with Abbie and the others, telling myself I'd talk to Viola again after the wedding was over.

The ceremony was beautiful in its simplicity. First Viola asked Samuel and Tillie if they were sure they wanted to get married then she led the slaves in a prayer for the union of the couple. After that, Mr. Hampton read a short passage from the Bible, from the book of Ruth, I think. Then he took Tillie and Samuel through a shortened version of the customary vows. It surprised me when he ended with "Until death or distance do we part."

I'd never heard that and whispered to Abbie, "Death or distance?"

She frowned. "They say that 'cause there ain't no guarantee they'll be together till death. Slaves are sometimes sold to another plantation. I think it's sad it has to be that way but ain't nothin we can do about it."

After Mr. Hampton pronounced them husband and wife, Samuel kissed Tillie, a chaste peck on the cheek, as everybody cheered. Then Viola led the group in a hymn. And that was it.

"Oh, I was hopin they'd do the broom thing," Abbie said after it was over.

Josh chuckled as he joined us. "Samuel ruled that out. He said it took Tillie long enough to agree to marry him and he wasn't giving her a way out of it. Said she had to stay with him for life no matter what."

"What do you mean, the broom thing?" I asked Abbie.

"Some of the slaves believe all they have to do to be married is jump over a broomstick. It's usually placed in the doorway of where they're goin to live. They jump over it once and that makes em married."

"That's right and some of them believe they have to jump over it three times to make it official," Josh added. "And if they ever want to break up the marriage, all they have to do is jump backwards over the same broom."

I couldn't imagine sealing or ending my marriage to a man with a single jump over a broom but then I couldn't imagine marrying someone who could be taken away from me simply by his owner's whim. It gave me another reason to hate this time. "I've never heard of that."

"It's believed to be an old custom from their homeland. I've heard it depends on the plantation too."

"Do they ever have a preacher or a justice of the peace perform the ceremony? I mean, that's how it's done where I come from."

"Yes, but that's the decision of the plantation owner. I've heard tell some of them have a minister present but most of them don't. Outside of that, the slaves have their own beliefs. Samuel and Tillie and the others here believe in a matriarchal society. Viola is the elder of their family and the whole group looks to her for leadership." Josh shrugged.

"Anyway, what you saw today was at their request. That's the way they wanted to get married."

"You mean your father lets them choose how they want to be married?"

"Yes, he does. Samuel and Tillie are two of his favorites and my mother is particularly fond of Tillie so he agreed to the ceremony. He even allowed them to choose the Bible verse."

"I see," was all I could think to say about that. How in the world did these people profess to have favorites among people they owned, who stayed with them only because they couldn't leave, and who would be severely punished if they stepped so much as a foot off the property without permission. I doubted I would ever understand this place and time.

I caught sight of Viola walking in the direction of the woods. Eustus was watching her too, but I wanted to speak to her a bit more. "Abbie, I need to see Viola before we leave. Can you give me a few minutes?"

"A-course, take your time. I want to spend a little more time with Sarie and Maggie anyway."

Josh took my hand. "I'll go with you, Lizzie, if you don't mind."

"All right," I agreed reluctantly. I had planned on talking to Viola with no one around but maybe it would be best to have Josh there to back me up.

We walked in the direction I'd seen Viola going. I noticed Eustus had started heading the same way which made me glad I had Josh with me. Maybe Eustus wouldn't bother us if Josh was there.

We beat him to the path in the woods, and as soon as we got under the trees, I shivered. It was a lot cooler in the shade than it had been out in the full sun plus I could almost feel Eustus's ugly glare boring a hole between my shoulder blades.

"You all right, Lizzie?"

"I'm fine. Is Eustus still behind us, Josh?"

He turned his head to look over his shoulder. "No, he's standing at the edge of the woods talking to a few of the slaves about something but he keeps glancing our way."

I huffed out an irritated breath. "Of course he does. I have to tell you, Josh, I don't like that man. He always makes me feel like he's watching me or judging me for something."

"Well, he isn't today. In fact, he's looking in the other direction now. What is it you need to talk to Viola about, Lizzie?"

"I'm worried about what Viola might do when Eustus decides how to punish the young slave boy."

"What young slave boy?"

"Eustus has a boy in Viola's cabin. Said he caught him sneaking around the main house, looking in some windows. Eustus said that means the boy was looking to steal something and he has to be punished. Whipping is bad enough but Viola is afraid he might do something worse like claim he caught the boy stealing and cut off his hand."

He stopped and turned me to face him. "Wait, let me get this straight. Eustus says he caught the boy lurking around the main house and is threatening to punish him because he might have been thinking about stealing something?"

"Yes. And Viola says if he does that, she's going to do something in retaliation. She wouldn't tell me what but I'm afraid what Eustus will do if she does and he catches her. He spent most of today watching her, and from the look on his face, he isn't happy."

"I know there's bad blood between them. Eustus has never trusted her, says she has too much influence over the slaves. But I can't imagine my father letting him do anything to her. She's the elder of the group and Papa trusts her to keep the slaves calm." He rubbed a hand over his face. "Did Eustus actually say he was going to cut off the boy's hand?"

"Well, no, but Viola said he could claim the boy was stealing and use that as an excuse to cut off his hand, and she says she's not going to let him. I'm scared for her, Josh. And for the boy too."

He put his hands on my shoulders. "All right, here's what we're going to do. You're going to go back to Abbie. Noah will take the two of you home, he'll take Sarie and Maggie, too if they want. And the little girl Sarie's training, what's her name, Amanda?"

"Yes, Amanda May. But, Josh, I want—"

"I think it best for you to go on home and let me handle this. I'll go to Viola's cabin and talk to the boy and I'll come up with some way to prove to Eustus the boy wasn't doing anything he needs to be punished for." He grinned. "Shoot, I'll get my mother involved if I have to. Eustus has always been afraid of her and I guarantee my father will listen to her before he listens to Eustus."

"And you'll warn Viola against doing anything to Eustus?" I loathed the man and would love to see him suffer for scaring the poor boy but I loved Viola more, enough to let Josh handle it his way.

"I promise I'll talk to Viola and see that she doesn't do anything that will get her in trouble. All right?"

I nodded. "All right. I'll stay out of it for Viola's sake, but please, will you come to see me and tell me how it all works out?"

He kissed me on the cheek. "I promise. I've got some things going on right now so don't panic if I don't come in the next few days. It'll probably be mid-week at least before I can get to you."

Since the kiss on the cheek wasn't enough for me, I put my arms around his neck and laid my lips softly on his. "All right, Josh. I'll wait for you to come to me."

In my head, I added, I'll wait for you forever. But I couldn't say that, even though it was the way I felt.

Chapter Twelve

Summer 1860

That's How Strong My Love Is

My second summer on Brown Mountain in the year 1860 proved to be a mild one with temperate weather during the day and cool nights. As one who had grown accustomed to air conditioning, this was a great relief to me. It was bad enough I only owned two dresses—and those borrowed at that—but to have to wash one every day was time consuming, involving drawing water from the well, pouring it into a large tin tub sitting over the fire, rubbing lye soap into the garment and scrubbing stains away—as more times than not there would be blood from treating an injured person—pouring out the water, adding more, rinsing, rinsing, rinsing, then hanging it to dry over a bush. Until I bartered for rope and hung a clothesline, which Abbie came to love as much as I did. So if the day was relatively cool and I didn't spend it working in the garden or treating the ill or injured, and hadn't sweated a lot or gotten body fluids on it, I found I could wear the dress a day or two longer without washing. Oh, how I longed for washing machines of my time, where you could just throw dirty clothes into the washer, add detergent, turn a dial and let the machine do all the work. Abbie, for some reason, could not grasp the concept of this, and I wished I had the ability to invent one just to show her.

It also seemed to be a time of good health on the mountain as we weren't called out too often which gave us more time to work on our little homestead and on Sundays to attend church. I had come to look forward to this because I would see Josh there and more times than not he would offer to walk me home. It was one such Sunday in late summer as we were walking up the mountain, hand in hand, when he told me his father was having a dinner party the following Saturday for some journalist from up north and asked me to attend as his guest.

"Oh, Josh, I'm honored you asked me, but I don't have anything to wear," I said, thinking of the way the wives and daughters of the wealthy plantation owners dressed, with great hooped skirts, bodices embellished with lace and embroidery, and wide pagoda sleeves with undersleeves.

"Lizzie, you're the most beautiful woman in North Carolina," he said with such sincerity I wondered if he truly believed that. "I don't care about any of that and neither should you."

"Yes, but your family probably does," I said. "I wouldn't want to embarrass you," I added, thinking in my life, in my time, I had never really thought about class distinctions. Although they existed and were perhaps more of an issue in certain parts of the country, in this time, they seemed much more prominent and prevalent.

"You would never embarrass me. Never." When I didn't respond, he sighed. "Lizzie, my family has been trying to push me to court other young ladies. I think they've decided I'm of an age I need to be married and settled down." He squeezed my hand. "But I don't want to even look at those women, can't bear the thought of being with them. It's you I want to be with."

"Josh, I'm sure your father would never approve."

"It's not their decision," he said, his mouth a firm line. He watched me for a moment then resumed walking. "At least think about it, Lizzie."

"I will, Josh." I said this more to appease him than anything.

At this point Abbie caught up with us. I smiled at her. "I thought you were going to your sisters' cabin for lunch."

She shook her head. "Sarie's in a tiff about something or t'other and I shore didn't want to sit there all afternoon listenin to her fuss and fume when I could be at home doin something useful." She grinned. "Or mayhap not useful but somethin that makes me happy, like readin."

I smiled when she referred to our cabin as home. I'd begun thinking the same thing. "Well, if you're not going, I'm not." Sarie was a bit scary when she got in a tiff.

She squinted her eyes. "Looked to me like you two was discussin something awful important. Hope I'm not interferin with that."

I glanced at Josh. "Not at all."

"Well, to be honest, we're having a bit of a disagreement," Josh said. I squeezed his hand as warning but he ignored me. "I've asked Lizzie to be my guest at a dinner party my parents are having and she doesn't seem disposed to come."

Abbie looked at me. "Why not?"

"Because I don't have anything to wear to such a thing, Abbie." I gestured toward my dress, the better of the two I wore. Formerly owned by her mother, it was a pretty but simple affair made out of cotton with a flowery print flowing over it. The long skirt wasn't puffed out by a cage crinoline or multiple petticoats and there was no sort of embellishment on the bodice or sleeves. "You see the way the women from the plantations and in town dress. I don't have anything that comes near that."

Abbie cocked her head as she thought then turned to Josh. "She'll be there, Mr. Josh."

"Abbie."

She frowned at me. "I got an idea, Lizzie, trust me."

Josh grinned. "It's settled then." He kissed me on the cheek. "I'll come by to fetch you at five." With a wave, he hurried off, disappearing before I could work up an argument against going.

I turned to Abbie. "Why did you say that, Abbie?"

She gave me an impish smile. "I remembered we have Mama's wedding dress stored away. It's awful pretty, and I figure with a bit of work, we can make it right fittin for a fancy dinner party." She grabbed my hand. "Come on, let's go to the cabin and I'll show you."

So we ended up at the sisters' cabin for lunch anyway. Maggie outdid herself, and Abbie and I gorged as if we hadn't eaten for days. It wasn't due to hunger but to lack of an abundance of good food. We had gotten better at cooking, but more times than not, Abbie and I would make do with fresh vegetables out of the garden and whatever fruits Josh would bring as gifts. We were simply too busy to spend hours in the kitchen.

After lunch, Abbie pulled me into the downstairs bedroom and over to the trunk where I had formerly kept the few items that came through the light with me, the watch my father gave me, a small pot of lip gloss, and a crumpled up pack of Virginia Slims cigarettes. I now kept those at the cabin Abbie and I shared, along with the maxi dress, panties and ballet flats I had been wearing. Abbie had been fascinated by the watch and at times when we were alone would wear it on her wrist, admiring the way it looked. The pack of Teaberry gum was gone, having been chewed by Abbie. We both used the gloss until the little ceramic pot was empty. Abbie wanted to keep the pot because she liked the way it looked, so we made our own lip gloss using mashed rose hips and lard Josh provided, tinted with crushed wild strawberries.

I watched as Abbie opened the lid and began removing quilts and clothing until she reached the very bottom, where something wrapped in soft linen rested. Abbie stared at it a moment then carefully took the package out of the trunk and placed it on the bed. She opened the linen with great care and I made a small sound of admiration as I stared at the dress she revealed. It was beautiful, an ivory color made of lace and silk, with a scooped neckline and tight-fitting sleeves ending at a V over the back of the hands. Abbie held it up against me. "Good thing Ma was tall like you, Lizzie, or we'd have to do a lot of work to get it long enough." She sighed as she studied it. "I reckon I can embroider a pattern on the skirt, something in a dark green, I think. Put a pretty dark green ribbon in your hair, maybe one around your neck. Oh, Lizzie, you'll be beautiful."

Sarie stepped into the room, glaring at us. "What are you two goin on about?"

Abbie smiled at her temperamental sister. "Mr. Josh has invited Lizzie to a dinner party this Saturday but she said she ain't got nothin to wear, so I thought Mama's wedding dress would be right proper for that, with some changes, a-course."

Sarie's face softened as she looked at the dress.

"Sarie, I won't wear it if you don't think it's appropriate," I said. "Besides, you're as tall as me and this could be your wedding dress or even Maggie's and Abbie's one day."

Sarie made a face at that. "I ain't got no use for men, why would I want to marry one? They're useless to me."

Maybe if you meet a kind man you can trust to treat you properly, you'll change your mind, I thought but pressed my lips together before I said it out loud. Trying to appeal to Sarie's soft side would only make her angry and that was the last thing I wanted to do right then.

She crossed over to us and touched the material, as if in awe. "Our mama was a beautiful woman, Lizzie. She come from a well-to-do family and it's always been a mystery to us why she married our pa. He weren't worthy of her and her family disowned her because of it. She was an angel and he was the devil and all he did was wear her down till she couldn't take it no more and just died." She shook her head. "I hope he's rotting in hell."

"Sarie," Abbie said, shocked.

"Well, I do." She surprised me when she said, "You wear the dress, Lizzie. It's just been stuffed away in that trunk all these years, servin no purpose."

"Are you sure?"

She nodded.

I hugged her hard. "Thank you, Sarie. Thanks so much."

She pushed me away, looking embarrassed. "Just make sure you don't rip it or get nothin on it," she said before turning on her heel and leaving.

"I won't," I called after her. "And I'll bring it back so you all can wear it for something or other." I lowered my voice to a whisper so she wouldn't hear. "Maybe your own wedding."

Beside me, Abbie snickered.

Sarie only ignored me as she continued on her way.

Maggie poked her head in. "I was waitin for her to leave. She's a bear today." She smiled at the dress as she crossed over to us, touching it with reverence. "I heard what y'all were talking about. It's such a beautiful dress, Lizzie, why, I reckon you'll outshine everyone there."

"Thank you, Maggie."

"Go on now, try it on, let's see if it fits," Abbie said.

I pulled off my dress, smiling when Maggie's eyes bugged at my underwear.

"What in tarnation are you wearing?" she asked.

I had shown Abbie the bikini panties I wore when I crossed over, explaining how comfortable they were. I hated the stiff drawers the sisters wore, which were baggy and came to the knees and were made from burlap or old flour sacks. As Abbie explained, it was that or wear nothing, as some women did, so I chose the uncomfortable drawers since I wanted to save the panties as a remembrance in case I never made it back. Until Abbie, who was a talented seamstress, came up with a close facsimile, using soft material from old dresses and drawstring ribbons at the leg and waist openings instead of elastic. They were actually quite pretty. "They're panties," I said.

Maggie examined them closely. "Why there's nothin to em."

"I wear em too," Abbie said. "They're a whole lot more comfortable than those old drawers we wore. If'n you want, Maggie, I'll make you some."

"Would you?" Maggie's eyes lit with interest. "This looks like somethin those women over in Europe would wear."

Not for a few more decades, I thought to myself.

"Just make me one, Abbie, and I'll use it as a pattern for more."

I slipped the dress over my head as Maggie and Abbie discussed the panties. I shook out my hair and stepped away from them, wishing I had a full-length mirror.

Abbie made a sound in her throat and I turned around. "Oh, Lizzie, that dress fits you perfect."

I smiled at her.

"It fits her right well, and she's so thin, she won't need to wear a corset," Maggie said.

"A corset?" I asked with alarm. This contraption had been developed by man, of course, to force a woman's body into the fantasized hourglass figure. They were heavy garments, made from separate-shaped pieces of fabric that were reinforced with strips of whalebone, cording, or leather and tightly laced at the back. I remembered with horror that scene in *Gone with the Wind* with Scarlett clinging to the bedpost while her slave Mammy tugged on the laces until she could barely breathe.

"A-course, she'll need a chemise," Maggie said.

"Do I really need that?" I asked. "The dress is lined." Chemises were sleeveless shirts that usually hung to the knee. I imagined women wore them to protect their dresses and possibly for more covering over their nipples. The wealthier women added corsets on top of that for more protection. I found chemises particularly uncomfortable and hot during the summer months so had talked Abbie into making me a bibbed apron which I wore over my dress for protection against dirt and body fluids and to cover my breasts. Abbie liked it so much, she made several for both of us.

"And don't tell me I have to wear one of those god-awful hoops," I said, looking at the long skirt which flowed so elegantly. "I see women with those huge hooped skirts and wonder how in the world they go to the bathroom."

Abbie and Maggie giggled.

"Their drawers ain't got no crotch in em," Abbie said.

"What?" I asked, shocked.

Maggie raised an eyebrow. "Sounds like you ain't never worn one."

"I've never worn a hoop," I said.

She gave me a puzzled look but Abbie distracted her by saying, "Well, you can't pull one of them hoops up. They're too heavy for one and so cumbersome you're liable to topple over. So the drawers are open at the crotch so you don't have to get to em."

"Hell, no. As awkward as I am, I'd probably take a tumble and turn upside down."

They laughed.

Maggie studied me for a moment. "Old Mrs. Pendelton's got the gout and I been seeing to her ever week or so over at their plantation. She gets these what she calls fashion magazines from New York and shows em to me while I treat her. There's a new fashion that she claims is all the rage called the artistic dress. It looks a lot like this one, real simple without hoops or a large skirt. You might just start what's known as a fashion trend, Lizzie."

I nodded. "That'll do."

After Abbie rewrapped the dress, we headed home, discussing the embellishments she planned to do to it. I found myself excited about the dinner party. Maybe I would make a better impression on Josh's father. Although he had thanked me for the role I played during their smallpox outbreak, he had never warmed to me and treated me distantly, as if I were an employee. I meant to show him I was not.

The Saturday of the dinner party, I bathed then washed my hair using the shampoo I had learned to make from Pokni. I even shaved my legs and under my arms, something that had become a luxury to me now. Then slathered on lotion made from mashed rose hips and scented with lavender. My hair, which fell just below my shoulders when I came through the light, now touched below my shoulder blades. I usually wore it tied back or in a bun when I attended church but Abbie had plans for it this evening. She combed it out for me then began to weave dried wildflowers through my hair. She had made a choker out of dark-green ribbon and fastened that around my neck. Then she helped me don the dress, which took some time due to the many tiny buttons in the back and down the sleeves. Finished, she stepped back and regarded me, a smile coming to her face.

"Oh, Lizzie, you look like an angel," she breathed.

I laughed, running my hands over the skirt. Abbie had embroidered a dark-green vine pattern over the dress which was just beautiful. I reached out and hugged her. "Abbie, I've never seen a dress so pretty. I feel like a princess."

"I reckon Mr. Josh is gonna go bug-eyed when he sees you."

I sighed. "I wish I could see what I look like."

"Let's go to the crik. You can stand on that big rock that juts out over the water and see your reflection."

As I stood on the rock looking down into the water, I barely recognized myself. To me, I looked like a fairy from a distant land. As I stared at my reflection, I felt transformed, as if I actually were part of this time, had always been here. It was a strange, discomforting feeling to me.

And then I remembered something we had overlooked. "Abbie, we didn't think of shoes."

She looked shocked then smiled. "What about them slippers you was wearin when we first met? They're the same color as the dress. I reckon they'll do."

My ballet flats. Of course. We rushed back to the house where we searched frantically for the shoes. I finally found them under the bed, put them on and walked around. The dress fell to the floor so the shoes wouldn't be noticeable other than the toe.

Abbie watched me move this way and that, staring at my feet. "I reckon them shoes look like they go with that dress."

"I hope so. I don't want to have to answer any questions about why they're so different from the slippers those other ladies will be wearing." I glanced at the calendar hanging on the wall as I walked past and with a shock realized what day it was. I stopped, stunned.

"What's wrong?" Abbie said, noticing this.

"It's August 11th." I looked at her. "One year ago today, I came through the light."

"Oh, Lizzie."

We glanced at the door when we heard footsteps on the porch. I was glad for the interruption. I quickly swiped at my eyes, telling myself I could get upset later, while Abbie opened the door. When she saw it was Josh, she swung it wide, stepping back so he could see me, standing in the center of the room.

He stepped inside, his eyes widening. A smile crossed his lips. "I reckon I'm seeing a vision," he said in a soft voice.

"Oh, Josh, don't tease."

"I'm not, Lizzie." He crossed over to me and leaned down to kiss my check. "I reckon you're the most beautiful thing I've ever seen. I'm afraid I'll break you if I touch you."

Abbie laughed.

"It's just me, dressed up like this thanks to our sweet friend Abbie." I smiled at her. "No one is as skilled as you, Abbie. I can't thank you enough for all you've done for me."

She waved her hand dismissively, looking embarrassed at my words. "You'd-a done the same for me, Lizzie."

"I would have tried but I could never accomplish what you did."

Josh bent down and kissed her on the cheek. "You're a wonder, Miss Abbie."

"Oh, go on, get on out of here," she said, pushing him toward the door.

He laughed as he turned and held out his hand to me. "I'll have her home before midnight."

"You better, else I'm liable to turn into a pumpkin."

Abbie smiled. "She shore does look like Cinderella." She turned to me. "I'll be waitin on you, Lizzie. I want to hear all about it."

I blew her a kiss goodbye.

Josh helped me into the small buggy he'd brought up the mountain. After he settled in his seat, he looked at me again. "A vision," he repeated.

I leaned against his arm. "Stop."

"I hope you don't get upset with me tonight, Lizzie, I don't think I'll be able to take my eyes off of you."

I smiled at him, thinking how handsome he looked. "Or me you."

He leaned closer and we shared a kiss before he clicked to the horse and we were off.

I could see the plantation from at least a mile away. It glowed with lights in each room downstairs and up, and along the drive leading to the house. By this time, I was beginning to feel anxious about the night. I would know a lot of the people from treating their slaves, but I knew they looked upon me as lower class and I wondered how I would be received.

The circular drive in front of the house was lined with horses and buggies. Samuel met us when we stopped in front of the steps leading up to the wide veranda. I figured he was the valet for the night but wasn't sure what his official title would be during that time. He smiled at me as he helped me down.

"How are you, Samuel?" I asked.

"Oh, I reckon I'm right as rain," he said, darting a smile in Josh's direction when he joined us before turning back to me. "You shore do look awful pretty, Miss Lizzie." An approaching buggy caught his attention. "Y'all have a nice evening," he said, before heading off to help another woman down.

"You ready?" Josh asked.

"I suppose so."

Josh tucked my hand in the crook of his arm and we went up the steps. When we crossed the threshold, we were met by his mother and father. Mrs. Hampton eyed my dress while his father stared.

Josh's oldest sister Charlotte appeared at her parents' side. "Oh, Mama," she said to Mrs. Hampton. "Lizzie is wearing an artistic dress. Isn't it just beautiful?" She took my hands. "You look absolutely stunning, Lizzie. I love your hair. Did you do it yourself? Where on earth did you get your dress? Did you order it from New York? I must have one."

"Thank you, Charlotte. Actually, Abbie made the dress and did my hair."

She cocked her head. "Abbie? Your cousin Abbie?"

"Yes."

She smiled at me then Josh. "Well, perhaps we can convince Abbie to add dressmaker and hairstylist to her list of duties." She waved at a friend behind us and rushed off to say hello.

I chose to ignore that, thinking Abbie's "duties" as healer were much more important to the people she tended. After we said a rather uncomfortable hello to his parents, neither of whom seemed impressed with Josh's choice of dinner companion, Josh steered me toward the drawing room where the other guests were gathered. I couldn't help but stare at the accoutrements of each part of the house we passed through as we made our way. Up to this point, I had only seen the kitchen which was functional but not particularly attractive. But the main house must have cost a fortune, with its marble floors and dark wood paneling and crystal chandeliers. The furniture was ornately plush although elegant in style. The velvet draperies covering the many windows looked like they could be made into hundreds of dresses, I imagined, smiling to myself as I pictured the scene in *Gone with the Wind* where Scarlett pulls down the velvet drapes to use as material for a suitable dress.

I glanced at Josh, seeing him in a different light. I hadn't realized they were this wealthy. As the oldest son, he was slated to inherit this place and all its opulence. I couldn't see myself living in such luxury and doubted I would want to, I thought, as I looked around at all the slaves dressed in black and white, rushing here and there, serving drinks and appetizers. But then, if Josh owned this plantation, there would be no slaves.

There were a good many guests gathered, talking in small groups, and Josh took me around the room, introducing me to those I didn't know and chatting with those I did. Many of the women commented on my dress, asking if I had purchased it in New York, seeming surprised that a mountain woman like Abbie had the skill to make such a thing. I made a mental note to be sure to tell Abbie her dress and skill as a hairstylist were a smash. Many of the younger women watched Josh and me closely, whispering to one another behind their hands. I am sure they did not like the most eligible bachelor in Morganton squiring around someone whom they did not consider one of their own.

The guest of honor was a political journalist with the "New York Tribune" named Ezra Hall. He seemed likeable enough although had an inflated sense of worth and liked to brag about events he had covered. We listened to his exploits in Washington DC until the bell rang for dinner, then all proceeded into a large dining hall. I tried hard not to stare at the table, loaded with burning candles in silver candlesticks lighting dinnerware made of luminous china, sparkling crystal glassware and gleaming sterling silver flatware, with fresh flower arrangements artfully placed here and there. I had never seen such extravagance in my life. I made sure to thank each servant who served me, noting with irritation that most of the others simply ignored them unless making demands.

I found myself three seats down from the journalist. I didn't know the man on either side of me so was glad that the vociferous Mr. Hall dominated most of the conversation, relaying his recent trip to Chicago for the Republican National Convention. I listened closely to this, thrilled at the chance to hear history firsthand.

"Although the convention was a political gathering, it was so popular that the city's population was doubled by the delegates and candidates' supporters," he said, looking around the table as he talked. "There were 450 delegates and their gathering place, of all things, was a Wigwam built just for the convention."

"Wigwam?" I asked.

He nodded. "Exactly. An enormous, round, barn-like structure made of rough timber with the capacity of holding, I'd say, ten or twelve thousand people. It was decorated so completely with flags, banners and bunting that when filled it looked to be a stunning pavilion aflame with color. The first of its kind and something of a wonder." He smiled at me and I found myself returning the smile.

"The stage was large enough to hold all the delegates, who were seated on either side of an elevated dais occupied by the presiding officer. The secretaries were just in front, and beyond them, my kind, representatives of the press." A quick smile at this. "The parquet below was for the alternates and holders of special tickets from the delegates. The galleries were reserved for ladies accompanied by gentlemen, and the public, four or five thousand strong, I'd say, stood in the aisles and all the unoccupied space. This went against past conventions, as the delegates could be seen and heard from all parts of the auditorium.

"Now, Abraham Lincoln, or the Rail-Splitter as some call him, had the advantage as well as the disadvantage. He was less well-known than the other candidates, but this actually worked in his favor as he had not acquired their enemies. Of major importance is that the convention took place in Chicago, and with Mr. Lincoln being from Illinois, this definitely was to his advantage."

"It surprised me Lincoln was able to win that nomination," Mr. Hampton observed. "Why, he's nothing more than a backwoods lawyer."

Mr. Hall nodded in agreement. "Although William H. Seward was considered a front-runner, several things worked against him."

"Such as?" a man who looked to be too young to shave asked, leaning forward with interest.

"Well, part of the Seward plan was to carry the convention by outside pressure but his hard-driving, hard-drinking contingent from New York actually hurt his image because many thought the corrupting influences of men such as these would transfer to Washington. This wasn't helped by the fact that they offered money to influence votes for Seward.

"Lincoln's plan was to convince wavering delegates that Seward couldn't win the key battleground states in the North such as Indiana, New Jersey and Pennsylvania, and that without those states, he couldn't win the presidency. Last but not least, Seward was undermined by my own editor, Horace Greely, who was a former top ally of his. Mr. Greeley, serving as a delegate from Oregon, supported Edward Bates, the most conservative of the Republican candidates, and badmouthed Seward's chances although he actually thought he would win the nomination.

"On May 9th, the day of voting, Lincoln's supporters planned to pack the hall by printing and distributing counterfeit tickets to his supporters, doing this while Seward supporters drank heavily and attended parties the night before. The Stop Seward movement by Lincoln's allies convinced enough delegates Seward was not electable while they made bargains and did everything possible to make sure Lincoln won. Although Seward led the first ballot, Lincoln closed in on the second and on the third ballot he had overtaken Seward and was 1-1/2 votes shy of victory which was accomplished when the Ohio delegation chairman was convinced to shift four of his state's votes to Lincoln. And the celebration when he was nominated ..." He shook his head. "I've never seen or heard anything like it."

The table had grown quiet while he talked. I looked around at all these plantation owners, wondering if they had any idea what was in store for them.

"Do you think he has any chance at all of winning the presidency?" an elderly woman queried.

Mr. Hampton harrumphed. "Highly unlikely. Southerners have been president of the United States two-thirds of the time since 1789 and none of the Northern presidents has ever won reelection. Besides, he's a former Whig turned Republican. They're a young party, don't have much influence."

"But it could happen," I said. He glared at me and I could have kicked myself for speaking out loud but I couldn't let it go. "The Southerners have how many candidates? Stephen Douglas by the northern Democrats and Vice President John C. Breckinridge for the South. Not to mention the Constitutional Union Party who nominated John Bell." I sat back, relaying what I knew to be true. "It would seem to me all these other candidates could split the vote enough that Lincoln could easily win."

Several women, including Mrs. Hampton, murmured disapprovingly while the men glowered.

Mr. Hall smiled at me. "A politically savvy woman. What a delight."

I wasn't sure whether he was teasing me or not.

"Lizzie's the smartest woman I know," Josh interjected. "She's a healer, Mr. Hall, cured our plantation of a smallpox outbreak last year."

I smiled at him while thinking, oh, Josh, you just made things worse for us.

Mr. Hall looked at me as if studying a bug under a microscope. "How interesting. I'd love to sit down and talk with you further, Miss Baker."

Mr. Hampton cleared his throat, placing the focus back on him. "Well, if Lincoln does manage to win the election, war won't be far behind."

Most of the men raised their voices in agreement at this.

Mr. Hall turned his attention to Mr. Hampton. "I've heard rumors that South Carolina is already talking about seceding. Will North Carolina follow suit?"

"I would imagine so." Mr. Hampton looked around the room then back to Mr. Hall. "Our political colleagues in Raleigh may call those of us in the mountain districts Southern Yankees but they'll listen to us about secession. Slaves make up 25 percent of the population of Burke County and we have to protect what's ours."

"That many?" Mr. Hall said. He shrugged. "This is mountainous terrain. I didn't realize there were so many slaves here."

"Well, we have quite a few plantations that use slaves for farming and such, plus a plug tobacco factory in Morganton staffed entirely by slaves. Since the Western Carolina Railroad ends just east of here, we have need of them to help drive livestock down to South Carolina and other parts."

Mr. Hall looked as if he wanted to ask a question but Mrs. Hampton interrupted by giving a polite cough. "Enough talk about politics. Let's retire to the drawing room for coffee and dessert. I'm sure Mr. Hall has more entertaining stories for us although I hope ..." Mrs. Hampton mock-frowned at him "... to hear no more about the election."

Mr. Hall gave her a stiff smile in return.

I looked at Josh, who was staring at me but smiled when our eyes met.

The rest of the evening passed uneventfully. Josh and I stayed close together, listening as Mr. Hall held forth on stories his newspaper had covered and gossip from the capitol. We left early, our excuse being that it would take Josh awhile to take me home then he would have to make the return trip.

Once in the buggy, Josh's horse picking his way up the mountain, I leaned against him. "I'm afraid I wasn't able to win your parents over to my side, especially your mother. I should have kept my mouth shut about the election."

"I imagine you gave them all something to think about." He glanced at me. "I want Mr. Lincoln to win, but if he does, I'm afraid there's going to be a war, Lizzie."

"There will be."

He nodded as if he knew I was right. I wondered then if he suspected where, no *when*, I actually came from. I opened my mouth, deciding it was time to tell him, but he interrupted. "No matter what comes, I hope we'll be together."

Would he go back with me if I asked him, I wondered.

"My father will expect me to enlist," he went on. "For the South."

"And will you?"

"Not willingly. I won't fight in a war I have no belief in. I've been thinking about what I can do, what role I can play, but I'll tell you this, Lizzie, it won't be as a soldier fighting for the right to own slaves."

"What will your father do if you refuse?"

He shrugged. "Probably disown me." He darted a smile my way. "He may anyway."

"Because of me?"

His non-response was answer enough for me.

"Oh, Josh, I'm sorry I've caused you such trouble with your parents."

"It's not you, Lizzie, so much as it's me wanting what I want, not what they want for me. I won't marry a woman I don't love, don't want to be with." He turned to me. "I don't think I'll ever love another woman the way I love you, Lizzie. I see you and nothing else matters but you and me and being together. I don't know if you feel the same way about me, but whatever comes, whatever happens, I want us to be together."

"Me too, Josh. Whatever happens." I have to tell him about me, I thought, convince him to go back with me. My thoughts were interrupted when he put his lips on mine.

"Forever," he murmured against my mouth.

Chapter Thirteen

Fall 1860 - Spring 1861

Tell Me

As summer morphed into fall, the sisters and I stayed so busy, I had very little time to mourn the fact that I had been on the mountain over a year now. We were often called out to treat men injured from physical altercations over the issue of slavery and the Presidential campaign. There was much discussion and debate among the Burke County residents about the upcoming election, and it seemed wherever we went, we heard our fair share of news as this was the only thing being talked about. I listened intently, knowing the outcome, but curious as to how it came about. The Lincoln-Douglas debates of 1858 were often cited, pointing out that then Senatorial candidate Abraham Lincoln had argued against the spread of slavery while Stephen Douglas held that each territory should have the right to decide whether it would be a free or slave state. In the Presidential election, Lincoln found himself once more pitted against Douglas, who represented the border states and Northern faction of the heavily divided Democratic party, as well as Southern Democratic candidate John C. Breckinridge, who was the current Vice-President, and the Constitutional Union candidate John Bell, representing those loyal to the former

Whig party. From what we heard, the campaign was a particularly nasty one, with Republicans trying to convince Western homesteaders their farms would be carved into plantations if Breckinridge won the election. They also sought to minimize the differences between Douglas and Breckinridge, arguing that the only way to reject Bell was to vote for Lincoln.

Democrats, fearing a Republican victory, attempted to forge fusion tickets among the Douglas, Breckinridge and Bell groups but were unsuccessful. Senator Jefferson Davis of Mississippi tried to broker a withdrawal of both Breckinridge and Douglas in favor of a candidate who would be acceptable to both factions of the party, but his efforts were for naught because Douglas, feeling betrayed by the Southern Democrats, believed that only he was acceptable to the Northern Democrats.

Lincoln wasn't even on the ballot in ten Southern States, turning the election into a sectional contest with Lincoln against Douglas in the North and Breckinridge against Bell in the South.

And when on Tuesday, November 6, 1860, Abraham Lincoln won the presidency of the United States, Southerners howled in protest, claiming the combined vote for Bell and Douglas was almost one hundred thousand more than that for Lincoln, with Lincoln receiving only 40% of the popular vote, while neglecting to admit they lost in the electoral college due to Lincoln's win in the North. My "prediction" at the dinner party came true: if the Democratic Party had remained united, it would have won.

South Carolina initiated secession proceedings the following day which were formalized on December 20th, 1860, followed in January, 1861 by Mississippi, Florida, Alabama, Georgia and Louisiana with Texas following suit in February. The Civil War began just months after when Confederates opened fire on Union-held Fort Sumpter, South Carolina on April 12, 1861. That same month, Virginia seceded, followed by Arkansas, Tennessee and North Carolina in May. The remaining four slaveholding states, Delaware, Kentucky, Maryland and Missouri, chose not to secede. I feared it wouldn't be long before we would all be drawn into this bloody war and warned the sisters we needed to find places to hide our animals and valuables in case Union or Confederate soldiers decided to raid our mountain. So we stayed busy searching out caves nearby for this very purpose.

At first, Burke County didn't seem particularly vested in the war. Although it was deeply divided, with some supporting the Union and others the Confederacy, peace, for the most part, held for the time being. Several young men immediately signed up, those favoring the South marching off to Asheville, where companies were being mustered, to be armed and placed in a regiment by the State Adjutant General's office. Some, I think, enlisted more for the sense of adventure than any deep-seated feeling of loyalty toward either cause, and I suspected many of these young men would never be heard from again. I feared Josh would enlist but his father's health began to deteriorate, and as the eldest son, he was required to take over the running of the plantation under his father's supervision. He seemed to become busier than ever with the Underground Railroad, his way of contributing to the war effort, but I sensed in him an eagerness to be away and doing more. I knew his father expected Josh to support the Confederacy but Josh claimed he would never do this. As winter marched toward spring, we discussed this often. When he began to talk of finding a more covert way to help the Union, this frightened me even more.

This fear came to fruition one mild late spring day when Josh was walking me home after church services. I knew from his quiet demeanor he had something to tell me and silently prayed it wouldn't be that he was going off to war. Unable to stand not knowing any longer, I squeezed his hand. "You have something to say, Josh, so maybe it's best if you just went ahead."

He raised his eyebrows at me. I tried to smile at him but my lips seemed frozen.

"Lizzie, I know you fear for me being involved in this war effort but I need to do something more and, well, I've been offered the chance."

I stopped walking and turned to him. "You're enlisting?"

"Not yet, not now. You remember the journalist Ezra Hall, our guest at the dinner party last year?"

"Yes, of course."

"Well, we talked a bit then and he became aware of my sympathies for the North. We recently met in secret and he's offered me a proposition I can't refuse."

Alarm skittered up my back at this. "What is it?" I asked, my mouth dry.

I could see Josh struggle to contain his excitement but he wasn't able to as he smiled broadly. "He wants me to spy on the Confederacy. Pass on information about what they're doing in Burke County and Western North Carolina."

"I put my hand to my mouth as I stepped away from him. "They'll look upon that as treason, Josh."

"If I get caught."

"They'll hang you, take you to the Demon Tree and put a rope around your neck." My voice had risen to a screech.

Josh glanced around us before putting his hands on my arms. "It's all right, Lizzie. It will all be very covert. Anything I pass on will be in code."

I couldn't get out of my mind the picture Abbie had painted of Frankie Silver's hanging at the Demon Tree, supplanting Josh's body for hers as the sheriff put a noose around his neck and the deputy drove the cart right out from under his feet and left him dangling. Tears sprang to my eyes.

"Lizzie," Josh said, pulling me into a hug. "You yourself don't believe in slavery, have told me often you want to do more to help. It's harder for you because you're a woman, but I can do more and I will."

"You'll be branded a traitor, your father will disinherit you. Are you willing to suffer that?"

"Of course." He looked intently at me. "And so would you, Lizzie, don't deny it."

I couldn't, but my fear for him was so great, I felt faint. "Josh, listen to me. This war, it will be brutal, hundreds of thousands are going to die. Innocent and soldier alike. Families will fight against one another, homes and plantations will be raided and burned."

He stared at me for a long moment, and when he spoke, his voice was very quiet. "Lizzie, for as long as I've known you, I've felt something was different about you. You told me once you had a secret." He paused, searching my eyes. "I've heard rumors and speculations about the lights all my life and I have my own opinion on what they are. Did you come through the lights, Lizzie, from a different place, maybe a future place?"

Here it is, I thought, the moment I've wanted and dreaded for so long. I could only answer, "Yes."

He nodded. "I've thought so for awhile now. Where did you come from and when?"

So I told him everything, from the moment we hiked up Brown Mountain to see the lights in August 1969 and how I came to be in this time and place, how much I hated it, wanted to go back to my time, but could not come to terms with losing him.

He surprised me when he said, "I don't want to lose you either, Lizzie. I'll go back with you."

I threw my arms around him. "Oh, Josh, that's wonderful, but we have to go back through the light I came through, the same one Jackson touched. Abbie and I have been looking for the light for over a year now and have only seen it that one time." A horrifying thought flashed into my mind. What if my light rejected Josh and only took me? What would I do then? My arms tightened around him.

Before I could say anything, he drew back. "You have to promise me, if you see the light and I'm not with you, go through. Don't wait for me. I remember it well enough, I should be able to find it. And when I do, I'll join you."

"I doubt it will work that way, Josh, because Constable Jackson touched it and it didn't take him. I think we need to be together, holding hands so we're connected to one another. Oh, I pray we find it and leave this place before the war comes to the mountain. We need to go as soon as we can."

"We will, but in the meantime, I plan to do what I can to help the North win."

"I need to tell—"

He shook his head. "I know there's a lot you can tell me about the war and I want to hear it, but, Lizzie, maybe in some small way I can contribute, help end it. Do you want to interfere with that?"

"You don't know that, Josh."

"Neither do you."

"Listen to me. In April, 1862, the Confederacy will pass the Conscription Act requiring all males between the ages of 18 and 35 be drafted into the Confederacy. We have to be gone before then or you'll be forced to fight for the South or flee to the North. Either way will be dangerous and I can't bear the thought of something happening to you."

He took my hand and began walking. "We have plenty of time to talk about that, Lizzie. For now, tell me about your time and how much better it is. Because I know if it produced such an amazing woman as you, it has to be better than this."

Oh, the relief I felt as words poured out of me, painting a picture for him of what the future held, of all the beautiful changes he would see.

We stayed on the mountain late that night, talking and searching, but never saw the light. My greatest concern as I said goodnight to Josh was that I would find it first, without him. Would I go ahead, hoping he followed at some point? But if Constable Jackson hadn't gone through the light when he touched it, I suspected Josh wouldn't be able to as well. However, if I waited until we were together, I chanced never finding the light and never going back. I feared when the time came, if it did, I would have to make a split-second decision and could only pray it would be the right one.

Chapter Fourteen

Late Spring 1861

Get Off of My Cloud

Before my time on Brown Mountain, I had never particularly thought about where the food I ate came from. Hadn't really cared, to be honest. But in this time, without food factories or manufacturers or farmers' markets, refrigerators or freezers, knowing how to raise your own food was essential. So Abbie and I planted a garden in late spring and since we were the only two living in Luther's cabin, all the tending and harvesting fell to us. I didn't mind the harvesting so much—there's nothing tastier than a tomato you've grown yourself plucked fresh off the vine--but tending it was a devil of a chore I came to dread. It seemed for every weed I pulled from the ground, several more sprang up, and more times a week than not, I found myself in the garden, chopping at those dratted weeds with Luther's old hoe.

I was doing this very thing, cursing like a sailor and sweating like one too, when a voice spoke from behind me. I startled, throwing the hoe into the air and squeaking in fright.

"It's just me, Miss Lizzie," Tillie said, looking at me with concern.

I smiled at her, feeling my face redden from embarrassment at my language and the fact that I was so jumpy.

"I'm sorry, Tillie," I said, hoping the apology covered both.

"I reckon I should have hailed you as soon as I stepped into the garden."

"No, it's quite all right." I wiped the perspiration from my forehead with my apron. "Let's go sit on the porch where it's cooler and we can talk."

As we walked that way, I said over my shoulder, "Is there a problem at the plantation? Anyone sick? Abbie's gone off to help Sarie today but I can come if you need me to."

Tillie didn't answer as we stepped onto the porch and I waved her into an old rocker Luther left behind.

I took the rocker next to her, waiting for her answer. She looked uncomfortable, her eyes darting this way and that.

I leaned toward her. "Tillie? Is everything all right?"

When she looked at me, I noticed tears forming in her eyes.

"Oh, hey." I reached out and patted her forearm. "Whatever it is, I'm sure we can make it better."

Tillie dabbed at her eyes with her sleeve, shaking her head. "It's Viola, Miss Lizzie."

Viola. I hadn't seen her since Tillie's and Samuel's wedding but Josh had assured me he had taken care of the young slave Viola was worried about without involving her. But I knew Viola hated Eustus, the Hampton's overseer, and my stomach roiled in fresh worry for her. "Is she all right? Let me get my medicine bag and we'll go right now." I started to rise but Tillie shook her head.

"It ain't that." She looked around again. "Miss Lizzie, you got to promise me you won't tell nobody where you heard this."

"Of course I won't, Tillie. You have my word."

She glanced around once more before speaking. "I was in the kitchen this mornin and heard Mr. Hampton and Mr. Eustus talkin outside the door. Mr. Eustus was tellin Mr.

Hampton that Viola ain't no real use to the plantation, she too old to do much of anything anymore. He said she gots too much power over the other slaves and he fears she gonna rile em up now with the war goin on."

I put my hand to my mouth, shocked by this. "No real use? She helps in the house, doesn't she? She also tends to the sick and I know is loved and respected by the other slaves. And what in the world is he talking about her having too much power?"

"Mr. Eustus ain't never liked Viola 'cause she don't kowtow to him like most of us do. She ain't afraid of him and he knows it. She ain't no fool, though. She knows enough to stay out of his way 'cause if she don't, he'll find a way to hurt her, but she don't let him scare her either."

"What is he proposing they do with her?" I asked, still in shock.

"He wants to sell her to a plantation down in South Carolina. Said they was lookin for a woman who could tend to the young'uns and the sick." She chewed her bottom lip for a moment. "But Samuel knows a slave who come from that plantation and he told Samuel they treat they slaves somethin awful, give em only one meal a day and make em sleep on the hard ground, out in the open during the summer and inside tents when it's cold. Viola's old, she's frail, she won't last long there, not livin like that."

"No, she won't." I shook my head, trying to wrap my mind around the type of people so willing to get rid of a person simply because they didn't find them of use anymore. "We can't let that happen to her."

"What are we gonna do, Miss Lizzie?"

I sat back and thought. "Where's Mr. Josh?"

His pa sent him to Asheville to see about some supplies. He won't be back for a few days."

I nodded, a bit relieved. I had wondered why I hadn't seen or heard from Josh and had begun to worry maybe he had decided he didn't want to go back through the lights with me or his parents had finally convinced him I wasn't good enough for him. I looked at Tillie. "There's only one thing we can do, Tillie. Help her escape."

"But Mr. Josh ain't here."

"No, but I am. I can bring her here until he gets back and then he can take her to the next station. She can stay here in our cabin."

"Will Miss Abbie go along with it, do you think?"

"I know she will. She loves Viola as much as I do."

Tillie nodded as she considered this.

"Did Eustus say when he plans to sell her?"

"He said he could get it done in a day or two."

"Then she needs to leave tonight."

Tillie's eyes widened. "So quick?"

"Yes, before he takes her away." I reached out, took her hand. "Go back and tell Viola I'll come for her tonight. I'll ride Jonah and be waiting for her right outside the gate to the plantation. Can you help her get that far?"

Tillie nodded. "Samuel and I'll help her. Samuel will carry her if he has to."

"Good. Let's plan on meeting at midnight. She can ride behind me and I'll bring her back to the cabin until Josh gets back. Hardly anyone visits us here unless they're looking for us to come tend to one of their sick so we can keep her tucked away inside, out of sight."

Tillie grasped my hand. "Oh, Miss Lizzie, you reckon we can do this? You reckon you can get her to safety?"

"Yes, I'm sure. That is, if she's willing to do it. Do you think she will be?"

"Oh, yes, ma'am. She's so old and Mrs. Hampton works her so hard, she can barely stand when the day is through. I reckon it'll do her good to have a good, long rest."

I smiled at her. "And that's exactly what we'll give her, Tillie."

After Tillie left, I went back to hoeing, in a much better frame of mind than when I started. I was excited at the prospect of helping Viola escape. I found myself wishing I could help all of the slaves escape before realizing how naïve that thought was. Well, I could start with one, I told myself, and go from there. Abbie appeared just as I began lunch preparations, and while we worked, I filled her in on Tillie's visit and what we had planned.

Abbie shook her head. "It shore is a shame the way them plantation owners treat their slaves, like nothing but animals to be sent away when they get too old to be useful. Viola's been with the Hamptons as long as I can remember. Can't believe they don't have some sort of feelings for her, want her to stay with them. Especially Mrs. Hampton since Viola takes care of her when she's ailin." She glanced at me. "They's a few plantation owners who keep their slaves when they get too old and let em live long, peaceful lives. Some even give em their freedom. I thought that was the way Mr. Hampton is. I ain't never knowed him to sell off any of the slaves afore this."

"Then why's he doing it now? Viola's still able to help tend the sick, look after the small children. Does Eustus have that much influence with him?"

Abbie smiled a sad smile. "I reckon he does. Mr. Hampton always did care more about the almighty dollar than he does his slaves and he's gotten an awful lot worse since he hired Mr. Eustus. I shore am glad Mr. Josh ain't nothing like his pa."

"Me too, Abbie."

Abbie wanted to accompany me to fetch Viola but I pointed out all three of us wouldn't fit on Jonah so she stayed behind, making up a cot for Viola to sleep on and getting the cabin ready for our visitor.

I arrived at the gate to the Hampton plantation a little early. After I dismounted, I led Jonah into a copse of trees and waited there, deep in the shadows. Jonah contentedly grazed while I kept vigilance, searching for anyone passing nearby. There was a full moon tonight and I worried we might be seen. About half an hour later, I heard movement nearby and peeked out. I saw two figures hurrying toward the gate, one of whom I surmised had to be Samuel due to the broad build. The other must be Tillie, I thought, knowing Viola was not that fast and lithe. After they passed through the gate, I stepped into view, whispering, "Over here."

When Samuel moved closer, I noticed he was carrying Viola on his back, piggy-back style. Samuel smiled at me in the dark, his white teeth glistening. "I shore do thank you for doin this, Miss Lizzie," he said, setting Viola on her feet.

Viola lightly touched me on the arm. "Are you sure you don't mind havin me, Miss Lizzie?"

"We'll love it, Viola. In fact, I wish there was a way we could have you live with us forever."

"Oh, child, that's a lovely thought," she said.

Tillie handed over a small bundle wrapped in a purple shawl. "Here's her things. You sure she's gonna be safe there? If Mr. Eustus finds her, he's liable to kill her." She stopped, looking shocked. "Oh, Miss Viola, I'm sorry I said that."

Viola patted her on the arm. "Don't you fret, child, you're only speakin the truth."

"Tillie, I promise you, he's going to have to go through Abbie and me before he gets to her. We won't let that happen."

Tillie nodded but didn't look convinced.

Viola turned to me. "Well, I guess we best be on our way, Miss Lizzie, afore the night gets away from us."

"Yes, you're right. Samuel, after I'm up, can you put Miss Viola behind me?"

"I shore will," he said.

I mounted Jonah and waited, watching as Samuel and Tillie, both obviously tearful, said their goodbyes. "I'll take good care of her," I said as Samuel easily lifted Viola, as if she were as light as a small child, and placed her behind me. "You two be extra careful going back. It wouldn't do for anyone to catch you."

"We shore will, Miss Lizzie," Samuel said as Tillie grasped my hand and whispered, "Thank you."

With a wave, I turned Jonah and headed for home.

We rode mostly in silence, in case anyone might have been hunting on the mountain and could hear our voices. Jonah, who was usually quite vociferous, for some reason, remained quiet as well. I once more acknowledged to myself the intelligence of this animal. I had come to love Jonah as I loved Buck and considered us blessed to have such fine animals.

When we reached the cabin, Abbie had a comfortable pallet made up for Viola near the fireplace and had heated water for tea. We sat at the table, talking quietly among ourselves, discussing with Viola how we could keep her hidden.

Abbie had made curtains for the small cabin's window which we had so far neglected to hang but I noticed that she had done that while I was gone. "Abbie the curtains are beautiful," I said, going to them and admiring the colorful embroidered border.

"I figured we could keep em closed all the time, that way nobody passing by could see in."

"That's a great idea. Viola, at night, it should be all right for you to use the outhouse but during the day maybe you should use a bucket inside."

"Oh, child, that just won't do, what with the hot weather and all."

I looked at Abbie as I returned to the table. "You and Abbie are about the same size. We could put a scarf over your head and maybe that will hide who you really are."

Abbie smiled. "We'll make it work, Miss Viola, don't you worry none about that."

Viola took both of our hands in hers. "I can't thank you two young ladies enough for what you're doin for me. Why, if they sold me off to that plantation down in South Car'liney, I reckon I wouldn't be long for this world. Maybe now I'll have the chance to live my own life, have time to myself, not spend it all on someone who don't appreciate who I am."

I squeezed her hand. "You deserve that and more, Viola, and I mean to see you get it."

The next few days passed by slowly. Abbie and I were on edge, rushing to the window at the slightest noise or looking around us when we went outside, hoping to waylay anyone who came near before they could go into the cabin. Viola, however, seemed at ease or perhaps she had decided to accept come what may. She proved a blessing to us, preparing delicious meals, something we had missed since we left the sisters' cabin and Maggie's cooking. When we were called out to tend to the sick, we always made sure to warn Viola to lock the door after us and hide under the bed if anyone came. I felt awful asking her to do such a thing but feared what would happen to her if Eustus got his hands on her.

The third day, Abbie and I were outside, mending the small fence we had put around the garden to try to keep critters out but that, truth be told, didn't seem to be doing much good, when Constable Jackson rode that fine steed of his onto our small front yard.

"Oh, shit," I said in a low voice.

Abbie glanced at me in shock then followed my gaze to the constable, dismounting from his horse.

She planted a smile on her face and walked toward him, saying, "Mornin to you, Constable Jackson. Is there anything we can do for you today?"

With a sigh, I hefted my hammer, grasping it tightly in my hand, before joining them, thinking I'd knock him out good if he caught sight of Viola.

Jackson nodded at Abbie then waited for me to join them. His eyes darted to the hammer I held but he didn't say anything about that as he gave me a challenging look. "Eustus sent word they've got an escaped slave on the loose so naturally you two are the first people I thought of."

I rolled my eyes and knew I had accomplished my purpose when his own narrowed and his mouth pinched in irritation. "I know it was you two and Joshua Hampton helping that slave escape. I know I seen that with my own eyes. That light might have knocked me unconscious but not before I saw that."

"Or maybe you hallucinated it or dreamed it while unconscious," I said, "and it's implanted itself in your brain as a real event, which you can't seem to convince yourself isn't."

He looked at me as if he didn't understand what I said.

"As you can see, we're busy," I gestured with the hammer to the broken fence, "so if you would just tell us what you want, we'll address it so you can get out of here and leave us alone."

"I come here to search this place."

"And who exactly are you looking for?" I asked, trying hard not to glance at the house and give us away.

"I reckon you know."

"No, actually, we don't. We haven't been to the Hampton plantation in a while."

He glanced at Abbie who had the sweetest, most innocent expression on her face, then looked back to me. "An old woman goes by the name of Viola."

I acted like I was thinking hard. "Oh, I remember her. She helped us when we dealt with the smallpox outbreak."

Abbie nodded. "She shore did. Don't know what we would have done without her."

I shrugged. "She's elderly, Mr. Jackson. How in the world could she escape that place and not be found nearby?"

"I reckon 'cause she had help." He looked from one of us to the other. "From you two. Josh is lucky he was in Asheville when she disappeared or I'd be talking to him too."

"I think you're mistaken," I said in a haughty tone. I turned to Abbie. "She was awful old, Abbie. Maybe she got lost going to the privy or walking from one place to the other and something happened to her. She was so little, do you think a coyote or a bear could have gotten her and dragged her somewhere?"

"That's not what happened and you know it," Jackson roared.

We both drew back, startled.

"I've had enough of your lollygagging around." He began walking toward the cabin. "I come here to do a job and I mean to do it."

Abbie and I grasped each other's hands. I leaned into her and said, "If he finds her, I'm hitting him on the head, Abbie, I'll knock him out."

"Oh, Lord help us," she moaned.

I let go of her and ran to catch up with the constable, stepping in front of him just before he mounted the small porch step. I drew myself up, staring at him. "We need to see a warrant before we let you inside our house."

He glared at me. "I don't need no warrant to search your cabin," he snarled. "I'm the law and that gives me—"

"Nothing without a warrant," I hissed.

He shoved me hard and I fell onto the porch. "That's my warrant."

He pushed through the door before I could stop him. As Abbie helped me to my feet, we exchanged frantic glances then followed him in. And watched as he searched the small cabin, even lifting the mattress and peering underneath, throwing aside anything that got in his way. I was thankful each morning we unmade Viola's pallet and stored it in a trunk, had hidden her things in the barn beneath a bale of hay. When we realized Viola wasn't there, we gave each other questioning looks. Where was she? The only other place would be the outhouse, and I prayed he wouldn't think to look there.

He turned and stared at us.

"I told you so," I said.

"We'll see about that."

We followed him to the barn and watched as he looked in the two small stalls, then back outside where he cast his gaze around, searching for a hiding place. His eyes landed on the outhouse. Oh, no, I thought. I followed him closely as he made his way up the path, holding onto that hammer, determined to use it on him before he could get his hands on Viola. He yanked the door open and we all peered inside but it was empty. I figured she must have been in the privy, heard all the commotion, and gone into the woods. I prayed she was well away, because if I knew the constable, he wouldn't give up easily.

He turned around, his eyes filled with rage, his fists clenched. "Where is she?" he yelled.

"You tell me," I said.

Abbie stepped up beside me, put her hand on my arm and squeezed hard. "Constable Jackson, as you can see, she ain't here." Her voice was low and soothing. "I reckon maybe what Lizzie said might be true. She could be hurt somewhere, waitin for somebody to come help her." She looked at me. "I reckon we ought to go on down to the plantation and see if we can get together a search party, try to find her. What do you think, Lizzie?"

"I think that's a plan," I said.

Jackson pointed his finger at us. "You two ain't going nowhere. I know you had something to do with it and I aim to prove it." He walked toward his horse, jerking the reins hard when he reached him. Oh, how I wanted to hurt him for the brutal way he treated that beautiful animal. After he mounted, he looked at us. "I reckon you got her hid so I ain't going far. I mean to keep an eye on you 'cause I know you're involved with this, just like that other slave, and I aim to prove it. You might have sweet talked the sheriff out of that first one but you won't this one." He dug his heels into the horse's side and rode off, glaring at us as he went by.

I resisted the urge to blow him a kiss, just to irritate the devil out of him.

"Oh, sweet Jesus," Abbie said when he was gone. "What are we gonna do, Lizzie?"

I smiled at her. "Find Viola, of course." I trounced into the woods in search of our visitor. Abbie caught up with me, a basket in hand. "What's that for?"

"So in case he comes back, we can tell him we're gatherin herbs."

"Smart girl."

As we walked along, she said, "You got any idea where she might have gone, Lizzie?"

I nodded. "I was talking to her about Pokni the other day and told her if things ever got hairy around here, to go to Pokni. I told her to take the shortcut we found. It isn't far and I figured she could travel it without any hardship. So we'll go look there." We followed the shortcut, as well, a well-hidden trail most people on the mountain weren't aware of which took us to the clearing surrounding Pokni's small hut in a short time.

We looked for Pokni outside, where she spent most of her time during temperate weather, but didn't see her anywhere. As we drew nearer, we were met by a small wolf pup Pokni had found that had either been orphaned or abandoned by its mother. It was a beautiful dog with light blond fur intermixed with dark gray and large ears that stuck straight up. Its paws were a testament that this would be a huge dog. Pokni had named him Nashoba.

I picked up the pup, laughing when he licked my face. "Nashoba is never far away from her so she must be inside," I said, heading for the small hut. Sure enough, we found Pokni and Viola sitting on the ground inside, smoking Pokni's hand-rolled cigarettes.

"I hope you've got one for me," I said, sitting beside Pokni. Nashoba squirmed out of my hands and began to sniff around, as if he had picked up a trail.

She smiled, reaching into her pocket and drawing out a cigarette and handing it to me. "Abbie, do you want one?" I asked, leaning toward the small fire and lighting it.

Abbie waved a hand in front of her face. "Shoot, no. Never could stand the smell of them things. Pa smoked em all the time. Wherever he is, I'm sure he's got one in his mouth, puffing away."

I glanced at Pokni, wondering if she suspected, as I did, that Sarie had killed their father. She looked away, but not before I saw the look in her eyes. She either suspected or knew.

"Come, child, sit with us," she said to Abbie, gesturing to a place beside Viola.

"Viola, how in the world did you get gone before the constable saw you?" I asked as Abbie settled in beside her.

She grinned at me. "Lucky thing I was in the outhouse when he come else he would have found me inside. When I seen him go into the cabin, I took off and headed this way, prayin the whole way he wouldn't catch sight of me."

Abbie shook her head. "I tell you what, I liked to died when he went inside that cabin but Lizzie was right on his heels with a hammer in her hands, said she was gonna knock him out cold if he found you."

"And I would have," I said.

"What are we gonna do now?" Abbie looked at me. "Mr. Jackson said he was gonna keep an eye on us. I'm scared he'll see us when we take Viola back."

"Leave her here with me," Pokni said. "She'll be safe."

"Are you sure, Pokni?" I asked. "What if Jackson comes here?"

"That man does not come here. He knows better."

We all looked at her.

"He thinks I practice bad medicine, that I have the power to hurt him, so we have come to an agreement. He leaves me alone and I leave him alone."

I smiled. "And how did he come to think that, I wonder?"

She shrugged. "I may have caused him some pain at one time." Her eyes met mine. "To make a point."

"Oh, I love you so, Pokni." I leaned into her to kiss her cheek.

She smiled at me. We sat smoking contentedly, all eyes watching as Nashoba poked his nose at a grasshopper who had come inside the hut and was hopping around among us.

"Did I tell you the story of Eskeilay, the grasshopper goddess?" Pokni said, her eyes following the insect who seemed as curious about the dog as he was of him.

"No, but I'd love to hear it," I said, thrilled to listen to another Choctaw legend from Pokni. I had begun to record these stories on the paper Josh provided me and intended to take them with me when I returned. If I returned.

"Eskeilay was the goddess who ruled the underworld, or Earth-womb."

"Earth-womb," I said, liking the sound of that.

"The Earth-womb is where the Choctaw lived before emerging from the Earth at Nanih Waiya. It was a place where spirits came from to be born. Eskeilay means mother of the unliving. She was human in form but had antennae and sat with her arms and legs in the position of the grasshopper. The Choctaw lived in the world below with Eskeilay, her grasshopper subjects and the other life forms. When that world became too crowded, the life forms began emerging at Nanih Waiya. In the rush to evacuate, humans accidentally trampled and crushed many of the grasshoppers, including Eskeilay's own mother. Eskeilay became enraged and called out to our god Nanishta, who blocked the opening at Nanih Waiya to stop the people from evacuating. Many of the people were trapped in the underground world and Eskeilay, still infuriated at her mother's death, transformed them into ants, which is why ants emerge from holes in the ground."

I smiled. Humans as ants. It kind of made sense, the way some humans acted.

"The Crawfish were also inhabitants of Eskeilay's Earth-womb. They started out living on the surface of the world and were a people crawfish. The Chocktaw removed their shells and hair and taught them to walk upright. They tried to teach them the Chocktaw way but the Crawfish rebelled against this. Longing to go back to their life as it was before, they returned to the underground, where the grasshopper goddess permitted them to live as they wished."

Abbie and I smiled at each other when Pokni finished. I looked at Viola. "Do you know anything about your people, Viola? Do you have any stories to tell?"

Viola gave me a sad look. "I wish I did, child, but I was taken from my people when I was just a young'un. I don't know nothin about em or what they believed in." She sighed, a sad look in her eyes. "Sometimes I dream about my mama singin me to sleep at night. I can't remember what she looked like, or my daddy, but I remember her sweet voice. Don't even know if I have brothers and sisters. My only family was the other slaves at the plantation and that awful Eustus and Mr. Hampton wanted to take me away from that." Tears glistened in her eyes and I realized this must be terribly hard for her.

"Do you want to leave, Viola?" I asked.

"I ain't got no choice. If I stay, I might as well be dead. If I go, mayhap I'll have a chance to live."

"Oh, I pray you live a long and happy life," I said.

"Me too," Abbie said.

I looked at her, wondering if she saw anything about what the future held for Viola but Abbie didn't seem to want to meet my gaze and I took that as an ominous portent.

We stayed until shadows began to fall across the yard then bade our goodbyes in order to get home before dark. Before leaving, I told Pokni that Josh should be by within the week to take Viola onto the next station. She assured me

Viola was welcome as long as she wanted to stay. I imagined Pokni would keep Viola entertained with stories of her people.

As we walked down the trail, I said, "Abbie, do you think she's going to make it up north to safety?"

Abbie was quiet for a long time. When she looked at me, there was sadness in her eyes. "No," she said quietly. "She'll die afore she makes it."

I gasped. "Will Eustus get her? Have you seen that?"

Abbie shook her head. "All I know is she ain't gonna make it, Lizzie. I don't see Eustus gettin his hands on her. She's old and ain't in good health and the Lord might take her afore she even gets away. All I know is she ain't long for this world, but when she does die, she'll be free or at least on her way to freedom. It ain't much but to her I reckon it's everything."

"I won't let Eustus get her, Abbie. I won't let that happen," I said with determination.

She didn't answer.

Josh came by a couple of days later and was relieved when we told him we had taken Viola to Pokni. I told him about Jackson's visit and his threat that he would be watching us. "He probably knows you're here, Josh. He still isn't convinced we weren't helping Zebediah that night he touched the light."

Josh nodded. "My father isn't as upset as I thought he would be. In fact, he told Eustus just to let her go, she was old and he wouldn't have gotten much for her anyway." He gave me a pained look. "He doesn't see them like we do, Lizzie. They're nothing but chattel to him. I don't know if it's the way he was raised or just the man he is, but it's not a good way to be, let me tell you."

I put my hand on his arm. "I'm just thankful you're not that way, Josh, that you're nothing like him."

He was silent a moment. "Eustus won't let it go, though. Every day, he's out looking for her, has Constable Jackson all riled up over it." He shook his head. "Eustus expects the slaves to be afraid of him, to bow down to him. Viola is old and well-respected by the other slaves and never let Eustus intimidate her. I reckon she knew due to her age and the way my mother felt about her, there wasn't much he could do to her, or maybe the fact that she had been with my family for so long. Eustus took it as an affront that she wouldn't show the respect he thought he deserved in front of the other slaves. I was afraid one day he'd find a way to force her to show him respect but now I fear he'll kill her if he finds her."

"We tried to convince Constable Jackson that maybe she wandered off and got lost or hurt," Abbie said. "But he wouldn't hear of it."

"My father told Eustus the same thing. He had Samuel lead some of the others out to search for her around the plantation but, of course, they didn't find her." He gave me a sad smile. "I'll wait till it gets dark then go to Pokni's. If she's up to it, I'll go ahead and take her tonight. Looks like Eustus or Constable Jackson aren't going to give up looking for her anytime soon."

Josh helped us work on the barn that afternoon. We found planks Luther had stored behind the barn and were using those to make it a safer, more secure place for Jonah. I had hopes of talking Sarie out of Buck as well although doubted she'd part with him. As we worked, I would feel tingling on the back of my neck, as if someone were watching me, but put it down to anxiety over Viola and Josh leaving.

At dusk, we went inside and made a quick supper, and by the time we ate, it was full dark. I walked Josh outside, where we spent several long minutes saying goodbye. It was getting harder and harder to hold back with him. My body felt afire when he kissed me and I would literally find myself shaking.

Josh finally drew away, smiling at me. "Lord help me, Lizzie, I'm gonna burst out in flames if you don't stop kissing me that way."

I laughed. "It's the same for me, you know."

He looked at me as if he wasn't sure whether or not to believe me.

"The same," I repeated.

"I'm mighty glad to hear that." He gave me a chaste kiss on the lips. "I'd better get going. It's going to be a long night. Viola's old and she won't be moving very fast."

"Take Jonah, Josh. He can get you there faster."

He shook his head. "The terrain we cover is pretty rough. I don't know if he could get through it." He smiled, tracing a finger down my cheek. "Don't worry, we'll be fine. I'll see you tomorrow."

I grasped his hand and squeezed it before watching as he slipped away into the night.

When I returned to the cabin, I remembered Viola's things were still in the barn, wrapped in an old shawl. I had meant to give these to Josh so she could have it for her trip. I turned to Abbie. "We forgot to give Josh Viola's things. I'll get them and try to catch up with him. I'll be right back."

"You be careful. I got a funny feeling about tonight. Something's wrong but I can't see what it is."

"I will be." I hurried out the door and over to the barn. After I uncovered the shawl-wrapped parcel, I headed into the woods, nearly at a run.

And ran practically into the arms of Constable Jackson.

I screeched, placing my hands on my mouth as I backed away from him. "You scared me."

"Where you think you're going to?" he said.

"Nowhere. Just out for a walk."

He eyed the shawl. "What you got in your hands there?"

I held it closer to my body. "My shawl. The night air is cool."

He yanked it out of my hands, peered at it closely. "Looks an awful lot like the one Eustus said Viola wore."

"All shawls look alike, Mr. Jackson," I said with irritation in my voice.

"This one's different, some purple color, just like Eustus described." He shook it out and we both watched as a ragged dress and comb fell to the forest floor. He glared at me. "Where is she?"

"Who?"

"You know who," he yelled, reaching for me. "You got her hid somewhere, gonna help her get up north like you were trying to do with that other slave."

I backed away from him. "I don't know what you're talking about."

He advanced on me, his fists clenched. "You don't tell me where she is, I'll make you. I got ways, ways that won't show so nobody'll believe you if you tell em what I did to you."

"Stay away from me," I said, walking backwards, praying I didn't trip.

He smirked at me, the smile of a demented soul, and I turned to run. But he grabbed me before I could and spun me around toward him, yanking me against him in one smooth motion. "I been wanting to do this to you since the day I met you," he said in a low voice.

I squirmed against him, trying to get away, but he was too powerful. He had me in an iron grip and I could barely move. I opened my mouth to scream but he clamped a hand across it.

"Think you're so high and mighty, can talk to me any way you want," he breathed, placing his face close to mine. "We'll see how you talk to me when I'm through with you." He drew back a fist and punched me in the stomach. The air went out of my lungs as I collapsed with a grunt. He pulled me upright, smiling as he watched me struggle to breathe. "It'll come back," he said, "just give it time." He waited until I got my breath then punched me again. Tears sprang to my eyes and I hung limply in his arms, telling myself not to panic as I fought to take small little gasps. I kept my head down, tried not to let him see when I could breathe again, and when he pulled me closer, drew my leg up and kneed him in the groin. He grunted and let go of me.

And I fled. I must have misjudged the hit because it wasn't long before I heard him right behind me. Oh, please, God, I prayed as I pushed myself harder, lifting my skirt and trying for longer strides. But those two punches to the stomach had taken its toll. I was tiring too quickly. I saw a bright light up ahead, coming right at me. Is that it? I wondered. Was that the light I came through or was someone coming?

I tried to yell for help but had only air for breathing as I sprinted away from him. I felt his fingers brushing my back and this motivated me to run faster. But that only bought me seconds. Those fingers were back, this time entwining in my hair and yanking me off the ground and back toward him. I screamed shrilly, clawing at his fingers with my hands, feeling hair come loose from my scalp. "Let go of me," I screeched, tears running down my face. I heard a man shout in the distance. "Josh, help me!" I yelled.

As he pulled me up against him, I saw the light, much closer now. I had to get free. If I could get to that light, I could go through it, away from this place, away from him. But what about Josh, my inner voice whispered as I thrashed about, trying to free myself. The agony that tore through me at that was almost unbearable. I'll learn to live without him if he doesn't follow me, I thought wildly, frantic to be free of the pain from Jackson's fingers tangled in my hair, screaming once more when he yanked at me again, shaking me like a dog might a kitten.

The light was practically at us now and I began to fear we would both be pulled into it. Panicking, I fought hard to get away from Jackson, thinking God help me if I went through that light with him. Luck was with me when I jabbed my elbow back, catching him in the throat and causing him to loosen his grip. I pulled myself free, feeling more hair come loose, and started to run. But he was right at me, his hand closing on my arm, and there was the light, hanging there, as if a spectator, watching us struggle, waiting to see who would win. With all the effort I could muster, I tried to wrench myself out of his grasp and in so doing caused him to stumble backward, watching in horror as he went into the light, pulling me along behind him. And right before that light began to suck me in, I realized with terror that the center wasn't black.

It was the wrong light.

Coming Next:

Did Lizzie go into the light with her nemesis Constable Jackson or does she stay behind to face the hardships of the Civil War on Brown Mountain? Book 3 of CC Tillery's ongoing *Brown Mountain Lights series*, *Into the Brown Mountain Lights,* will unveil the fate of Lizzie and Constable Jackson as well as all of Lizzie's friends on Brown Mountain.

Books by CC Tillery

Brown Mountain Lights series:

Through the Brown Mountain Lights, Book 1

Seeking the Brown Mountain Lights, Book 2

Into the Brown Mountain Lights, Book 3

Chasing the Brown Mountain Lights, Book 4

Award-winning, internationally published, best-selling *Appalachian Journey* series:

Whistling Woman, Book 1

Moonfixer, Book 2

Beloved Woman, Book 3

Wise Woman, Book 4

Acknowledgements

A big thank you to professional airline pilot and Civil War history buff Dudley Hancock for loaning us books from his personal library about the Civil War.

We used several print and online sources for the historical aspects of this book.

Burke: The History of a North Carolina County by Edward W. Phifer Jr.

The Civil War in the Smokies by Noel Fisher

Bushwhackers: The Civil War in North Carolina The Mountains by William R.Trotter

Civil War Letters and Memories from the Great Smoky Mountains by Hattie Caldwell Davis

The Practical Herbal Medicine Handbook by Althea Press

Appalachian History Collection, © 2006-2017 by Dave Tabler, www.appalachianhistory.net

Slave Marriage and Family Relations by Brenda E. Stevenson, www.afrigeneas.com

Tragic Ends: Frankie and Charlie Silver - BlueRidgeCountry.com

https://blueridgecountry.com/archive/favorites/frankie-and-charlie-silver

Frankie Silver Murder Case of 1833, North Carolina History Project.

Once again, we want to thank our husbands, Mike and Steve, for handling the grunt work at the many festivals, events, and presentations we attend. We love you guys and couldn't do it without you!

And as always, thanks to all our readers who encourage and inspire us as well as make us laugh and/or smile on a daily basis. We say it all the time, but it bears repeating, we have the most awesome readers in the world!

About the Authors

CC Tillery is the pseudonym of two sisters, both authors, who came together to write the story of their great-aunt Bessie in the *Appalachian Journey* series. Tillery is their maiden name and the two C's stand for their first initials.

One C is for Cyndi Tillery Hodges, a multi-published romance/fantasy author who writes under the name of Caitlyn Hunter.

The other C is for Christy Tillery French, a multi-published, award-winning author whose books cross several genres.

To find out more about their work or for more information on their joint writings, please visit their website at cctillery.com or contact them at cctillery@yahoo.com.

Made in the USA
Columbia, SC
20 March 2024

33391677R00122